Also by Maxine Chernoff

FICTION

BOP

POETRY

LEAP YEAR DAY:
New and Selected Poems

NEW FACES OF 1952

JAPAN

UTOPIA TV STORE

Maxine Chernoff

PLAIN
GRIEF

SUMMIT BOOKS

New York   London
Toronto Sydney Tokyo Singapore

SUMMIT BOOKS
Simon & Schuster Building
Rockefeller Center
1230 Avenue of the Americas
New York, New York 10020

SUMMIT BOOKS and colophon are trademarks
of Simon & Schuster Inc.

Designed by Laurie Jewell
Manufactured in the United States of America

1   3   5   7   9   10   8   6   4   2

Library of Congress Cataloging in Publication Data

Chernoff, Maxine, date.
Plain grief / Maxine Chernoff.
p.   cm.
I. Title.
PS3553.H356P5   1991
813'.54—dc20   91-15897
                                                 CIP

ISBN 0-671-72463-0

*For my mother
and sister*

Thanks to Paul and to Laura Yorke

THANKSGIVING

SARAH PLEADED with her eyes for Larry to be civil. He'd promised that last night's scene wouldn't be re-enacted in front of her mother or the children. But even as he dusted the thick-stemmed pewter wine glasses, Sarah could see him register unhappiness, pressing his upper lip toward his nose and making his eyes small and mean. Larry's officially annoyed glance made him look like a fox. On his good days, he used to look like Gregory Peck, but there hadn't been too many good days lately. Their distance, enforced by Larry for years, had provided Sarah with welcome camouflage since she had met Jeremy Bone Shoulder. "As soon as someone else screws you, Sarah, you think it's love," Larry had said last night. "You're a primitive. You and that Indian deserve each other."

Sarah was startled by her mother's voice. "The girls in my building say you have such a pretty, long neck." Sarah smiled as Ivy maneuvered the relish tray onto the crowded Thanksgiving table, making room for it next to a figurine of a mother rabbit holding butter in her flowing porcelain apron.

"Just like a swan, Mom." Sarah blinked to signify agreement. She would have preferred to wink, but the involuntary spasm was beyond her control. Her other nervous habits included hair-smoothing and cheek-massaging. As Sarah saw Larry getting ready to speak, she smoothed her hair twice and forced her eyes to remain wide open.

"What do they say about Sarah's lectures, Ivy?"

"Not much, Larry. What do seventy-year-old women need to know about grammar? Let's see," Ivy recited, patting her tight gray curls into place with each word. "Last week Sarah's show covered joining words: *however, moreover,* and was it *thus?* Most of my friends don't have memories like mine anymore, but they all like to watch her on TV, and they think the little cartoon grammar man is real cute. Ada Kramer thinks he looks like Frank Sinatra."

"If Frank Sinatra looked like Bing Crosby," Larry corrected.

Ivy pressed her frizzy bangs between her fingers, a familiar gesture that made Sarah feel a little more at ease. Sarah responded with a taut smile. "See, you listen, Mom. You should take my course for credit."

"Sarah's the Queen of Cable Grammar, Ivy. She's Leda . . ."

Hoping that Ivy wouldn't understand, Sarah interrupted Larry's obscene allusion in mid-sentence. "Nobody can explain a dangling modifier like me." If only to steer the conversation to safety, she'd be hysterically agreeable. She twisted a leaning rust-colored candle into the centerpiece and blinked twice.

"You two make grammar sound X-rated," Ivy chuckled, lighting her fifth cigarette in a row. Sarah thought maybe she should take up smoking. Then she'd have something to do with her hands, which were kneading her skirt into fan folds.

"Porno-grammar. Copulative conjunctions."

"What are those, Larry?"

"Just another name for . . ." Sarah began to explain.

"Just ask your daughter," Larry sneered.

Sarah winced in the direction of the chrysanthemums in their lacquered willow basket. She remembered the holiday bazaar Ivy's Senior League had sponsored a few years ago. Amid macaroni-bedecked pencil holders spray-painted silver and woven pot holders in seasonal colors, the basket had been one of the few items that looked desirable. "You've always had good taste, Sarah. Mrs. Echols, the hoity-toity one, donated the basket. She bought it at the Rosary Hospital gift shop in Palm Springs."

Sarah felt sorry for the grief she was about to cause her mother. A fanatic on one subject alone, marriage, Ivy had narrated epics of miserable relations, all ending with the same cautionary injunction: *They decided to stay together for the sake of the kids.* She'd told Sarah repeatedly that someday she would come to her senses about Jeremy, whom Ivy still called "that man." But Ivy would have been better off at a diner with chipped coffee cups and pressed turkey loaf than at Sarah and Larry's last Thanksgiving. Never had a holiday seemed more ominous. It was easier to imagine their lace-draped table in a shambles, to conjure up an emotional hurricane moving toward their island with unpredictable speed and fury, than to adjust to this slow dissolution. Almost with relief Sarah pictured their tiny haven being swept away.

The steaming turkey waited on the sideboard, but where were Deenie and Carrie? The girls had promised to be back by four. At ten minutes after the hour, Sarah had already begun to feel uneasy. One Thanksgiving when Sarah's father was still alive, Larry's long-widowed mother had flirted with him out of boredom or perversity. Nothing could restore the celebratory mood after Ivy's little chin began to quiver in outrage. Maybe Larry's relentless infidelity was genetic. Or was monogamy caused by an aberrant chromosome?

Sarah looked at the table set for six. "I'm beginning to worry about the girls, Larry. Did they tell you anything?"

"Just that they were going for a walk. Besides," he added pointedly, "who tells me anything around here?"

Despite Larry's recent anger, Sarah imagined that their marriage would end quietly, both of them agreeing that it was for the general good. *Like a change of administration,* she thought, picturing a faceless Supreme Court justice administering the oath of office. The image of solemn inauguration was comforting and remote. She wouldn't remind herself of what she didn't control in their lives, including the long list of her husband's lovers. His specialty over the years was graduate students in the early-European concentration of the art-history program. Their limited stay at the college provided a natural closure to his affairs. Lately, however, there was a psychologist at the kids' school whose solicitousness made her suspect. There was also a visiting librarian who had blushed deeply when Sarah brought her composition class on a tour of the microfilm section. No longer feeling the betrayal that used to accompany her suspicions, she reasoned that these women were either simply helpful or guilty in general. *Just another bad marriage,* as her friend Rachel had called it long ago, but it was her bad marriage all the same.

Of course, they could begin eating without the girls. On the second day of Deenie's visit from California, she had already informed Aunt Sarah that she didn't like holidays. Sarah knew her niece would just push her food around and drum her dirty fingernails on the plate. But she hated to leave Carrie out of one of her favorite holidays, the one when sweet potatoes and mashed potatoes were served together, when butter was spread liberally as housepaint, when thanks were given for the idea of families. It would be the last Thanksgiving they'd spend together. Then there would be decisions to make. Who would the kids see on holidays? Who would be the lonely parent eating at a fine restaurant with an unimportant date, drinking too much champagne? She wanted Carrie to be here for this final, albeit blurry, snapshot of family resilience.

"We'll start without them," Larry announced suddenly. He stormed over to the television and turned off the Bears–Lions game in mid-play.

"Dad," Scotty protested, "they're going for it on fourth and one!" His voice was a siren of indignation.

"Tough turkey, Scott," Larry replied.

So Larry carved the bird, and Ivy and Sarah apportioned the chestnut stuffing, the potatoes, the cranberries in orange sauce, the creamed peas, the corn muffins, the giblet gravy, and butter, butter, butter. Sarah watched the three attack their food. Staring at the two empty seats facing each other, she picked strips of orange rind and slivers of almond out of the cranberry relish. She didn't feel hungry for much else.

It wasn't like Carrie to be late. Full of accomplishments, she was still such a child who wanted to please people. Why wasn't she home demonstrating the mildly obscene routine of lunges and pelvic thrusts she'd learned in Jazz III? Why wasn't she giving her grandmother, whom she rarely saw lately, demure, withholding embraces?

Sarah excused herself and climbed the staircase to Carrie's room, a place she rarely visited. Long ago they'd reached a truce. If Carrie promised to clean once a month, Sarah would ignore what happened in between. On the desk she saw Carrie's vocabulary-improvement calendar, a stack of books for her report on Eastern religions, and a heart drawn with her initials and R.B., whoever that was. On the pillow next to the sleeping cat she saw an envelope that said Mom.

Then she remembered how Carrie had wanted to talk the other morning when Sarah was rushing to leave for work. She could see herself gesturing impatience as Carrie's forehead furrowed with disappointment. It was her own fault, whatever the letter contained. She felt her own lightness, saw objects waver and break into angles as tears brimmed over. She tore the paper open with such force and ineptitude, her hands might have been stone implements.

> Mom,
> *When you read this, Deenie and I will be gone. Don't ask me where we're going, but we've decided that you (and Mae) can do without us. We know it for a fact. You two have your own lives, especially now that there's Jeremy. If things work out, I'll call you later. Don't worry too much about me. I have my babysitting money, a warm coat, and my retainer. Please feed Lizzy. Don't ask Scotty about it either. All he knows is that everyone's unhappy. He said that the only happily married people he knows are your officemate Russell what's his name and his friend John! Happy Thanksgiving to you and Dad.*
>
> > *Love,*
> > *Carrie*

She sat on Carrie's unmade bed rereading words that thudded at her temples.

"Larry," she called weakly. "Larry?"

His head finally appeared in the door, but without making eye contact, she handed him the note.

"Why in the fuck does everyone but me know about you and Jeremy?"

"Larry, I didn't think the kids . . ." She stopped and watched mutely as his eyes filled with tears. She couldn't remember the last time they had cried over the same thing.

Her impulse was to comfort him. When she placed her hand on the shoulder of his gray sweater, she felt his body stiffen.

"Larry," she whispered, hearing her breath fill the suffocating space between them, "I'm so sorry."

Then he wound back. She saw his small fist clench against all the stupidity of their lives and, with a force she'd never experienced, strike her eye. There wasn't time to avoid it, and strangely she felt herself not trying.

Now she was prone on the floor, uncertain of how she had arrived there. "Larry," she groaned into the carpet, "how could you hit me?" but she saw in the corner of her eye that Larry had already turned on his heel and left the room.

Afraid to touch her own face, she could feel the throbbing of blood toward the bruise. Kneeling, she rocked back and forth and stared with her one good eye at the tiny cornflowers on Carrie's new rug. At her distance she could imagine Larry angrily rattling dishes in the dining room, Ivy's muffled "What's the matter, Larry?" Would he tell her? Retrieving the note from the floor, she folded it into her dress pocket and smoothed over the gaping cloth. She knew she couldn't see Scotty's or Ivy's face in the dining room now that her marriage was over and a fantastic bruise was closing her eye. Grabbing her spring trenchcoat from its hanger in the guest closet, she raced down the stairs and through the hallway, with its well-intentioned ferns in wicker planters and family photographs lopsided with color. She slipped out the back door, ran up the long passageway from her backyard to the front, and, without looking back at the house, made a beeline for the 7-Eleven at the corner. She wouldn't look back at the undecorated windows, which seemed to offer the world full disclosure, or think of the numbing silence at the table.

She didn't notice how cold she felt until she was inside dialing the phone with red, aching hands. "I want to call 555-2240 collect."

"Thank you for using AT&T, and Happy Thanksgiving."

"You're welcome," Sarah mumbled.

"I have a collect call for anyone from Sarah."

Sarah's voice broke in. "Jeremy, thank God you're home." She imagined his large, kindly face, his blue-black hair, and his long torso slumped over the oak phone stand in his hallway. He'd be standing under a poster of a furry cup and saucer that said *Meret Oppenheim* and his dates of birth and death in wavy blue letters. She'd been in Jeremy's apartment so many times in the last six months that it was easy to picture him there.

"Aren't you eating now?"

"Carrie's run away. She knows about us. So does Larry." Her voice cracked.

There was a deep sigh and a silence.

"I'm at the 7-Eleven, Jeremy. Larry punched me."

"Just stand inside, Sarah. If Larry comes near you again, call the police. I'll be there in seven minutes."

"He hurt me, Jeremy."

"That asshole. I'll be right there."

She stood near the magazines watching a young couple buying last-minute accessories for the holiday—canned giblet gravy, jellied cranberry sauce, Pillsbury Parker House rolls in a shiny foil tube. Both wore aviator jackets, tight jeans, and black boots. Their angular bodies were nearly identical. She glanced at foolish headlines in the *Enquirer* and peered outside. The window steamed over with her breath as she hoped that Jeremy could get his wreck of a car to start on such a cold afternoon.

She remembered laughing when Jeremy explained why he still owned a 1977 Ford Fairlane. "It's a shrine to my miserable Indian past," he'd said proudly, patting the greenish-gray dashboard. He had demonstrated how the turn signal could be removed from its shaft and left dangling on a single gray cord.

The bored Korean clerk didn't seem to notice her. Pulling on his chin, he was more interested in his radio-sized TV propped behind the counter. It was the Bears game, a muddle of static and enthusiasm.

Sarah's right cheek felt better against the cold glass window of Jeremy's Ford. She watched the first snow of November fall in discrete flakes and wondered if snow was falling on Carrie and Deenie too. Had Carrie taken a hat or gloves? Children refused to acknowledge the weather. Carrie never wore boots even if the snow was knee-high. She imagined them huddled together in Grand Rapids. Of course, it would be easy for two girls to go nowhere, to hide out in the city's sleazy transient hotels or anonymous street-corner bus shelters heated by amber-yellow lights. Jeremy promised to take Sarah wherever she thought they should look. His first idea had been to stop at the police station to provide a description of the girls, but Sarah couldn't bring herself to admit that men who searched for bodies in dumpsters would be needed. She and Jeremy would look first. Even after she finished talking, she felt her head throb with each word of her plea that Carrie be found. It reminded her of the thudding of blood in her ears when she was little and couldn't sleep. Lying in the dark, she'd think of buffalo stampeding in a cloud of dust. But if she complained about sleeplessness, her mother would give her half of her own sleeping pill, the color of the sky. *Take one,* she'd soothe, and obediently Sarah would swallow.

They decided to take Sheridan Road up to Evanston following the path that Carrie rode with her ten-speed in summer. It wound into parks, past high-rises, and along beaches, where artificial light fell eerily on empty parking lots and unseemly bright snow. When they reached the last beach in the city, at Juneway Terrace, she asked Jeremy to pull over. The beach was adjacent to some large gray rocks that Carrie would hide her bike in, then climb when the lifeguard wasn't looking. She'd sunbathed there all summer, packing some peaches and yogurt, her Walkman, and *Jane Eyre.* Sarah thought of Carrie's broad shoulders, how the sun had baked her a pinkish tan, the color of noon sand.

Sarah asked Jeremy to wait in the car. She'd be back as soon as she checked the beach. Panic filled her body, but her mind kept betraying her, holding ironies up to the light, where they swarmed like translucent moths. She hadn't wanted to run away until she was thirty-nine. Now she was looking for a daughter who'd never threatened to leave.

She stood on the rocks watching the snow beat down into the lake and dissolve. It was getting colder. Soon hellish mist would rise from the freezing water. She looked into the black lake that extended to Michigan and pressed her palms together, wishing she could contract space. Then she was distracted by a bolt of light at the periphery of her vision. Something was stirring on the rocks, alive and moving in a hurry. Following it warily toward the edge of the embankment, knowing the rocks would be slippery with ice, she saw an albino rat, the kind used in experiments. As soon as it noticed her, it squirmed under a rock and disappeared. Thinking of the small, listless face suddenly registering surprise, she felt a shiver ignite her spine and a warmth in her chest that pressed like new life beginning here. *Maybe I'm dying,* she said to herself, and ran back to Jeremy's car.

She sat in the car simply breathing, watching her tortoiseshell coat buttons heave up and down.

"Well, what now?" Jeremy asked, warming her hands in his.

Thinking of the rat's pink, close-set eyes allowed room for her fear to grow. Her cold knuckles felt good pressed against her eye. What do you call damage you don't know how to name? "I saw a white rat. A big white rat was on the rocks. He looked at me. I looked at him, and he ran away. Maybe it's an omen."

"Albinos are good luck, especially in the snow." Jeremy had spoken so evenly that she had to look into his eyes to know if he was serious.

"C'mon," she said. "I can't take it, Jeremy."

"I know, Sarah, but the rat's not related to it, as long as you don't see it that way. In certain myths, it does mean good luck."

"I'm so afraid." With the tips of her fingers, she dabbed at the bruise, where Larry, the bastard, had hit her. Jeremy folded her into his arms and patted her on the back. She closed her eyes and experienced a startling warmth, an obscene closeness. It was like being drunk. Everything was spinning too fast, and she pictured how Carrie had looked when she was born—pale, wide-eyed, and moon-faced. She had a natural calm. Sarah had taken it from her and offered her something bitter and ugly to replace it.

"Maybe I'm the rat," she confessed.

"Nonsense. Don't think about it, Sarah." He kissed her good cheek and touched her eye lightly where it had been struck.

He suggested they try bus stations, O'Hare Airport, and maybe a few more restaurants before they called it a night. Carrie and Deenie, with a three-hour jump on them, could be a thousand miles away by now. The car tires made a loud sucking sound in the snow. Now and then a CTA bus passed them, leaving a wake of gray sleet that covered the windows. Jeremy's ancient wipers made arrhythmic, haphazard swipes at the windshield. He was able to drive only by peering out of a two-inch strip of glass. Even the weather was conspiring to take Carrie away.

As they drove to the bus station, Sarah couldn't help testing, as you do with a sore tooth, the limit of her pain. Unfolding the note, she read it to Jeremy and wept.

"We'll find her," Jeremy assured in his most soothing voice, but Sarah could read the worry on his face.

The Greyhound station was deserted. A few army recruits leaned sleepily on a wooden pew smoking Lucky Strikes and talking in low drawls. Sarah approached them and described Carrie and Deenie.

"Hell, we'd liked to have seen some girls, but it's a ghost town here. We're the only fools with nothing to do on Thanksgiving," a boy with a red crewcut and a bridge of freckles and acne over his nose complained.

"I know a shelter where they'll still be serving Thanksgiving dinner," Jeremy offered, scribbling the address out for them.

A boy of perhaps nineteen, whose cap was ill-fitting and whose broad shaved head seemed more muscular than normal, said, "We don't want to eat next to bums," and turned his back. He pronounced the word as if it were spelled b-u-m-b-s.

"Thank you," Sarah said weakly, and slumped onto the next pew. She picked up a bus schedule and circled all the buses that had left between two and now, seven o'clock.

The young black ticket agent told Sarah that she didn't remember two young girls, one with sticks for legs and wild hair, but if they had already purchased tickets, they could be on a bus anyway.

"Don't you have passenger lists?"

"Only if they used Visa or MasterCard." She left her booth for a minute and returned with a stack of computer print-outs piled on a metal clipboard. Sarah searched the lists futilely for *Drucker* and *Holm*.

"We have a bus for Pittsburgh at ten and a New York express at midnight. The last bus west left one and a half hours ago. The first rest stop, if the snow hasn't slowed it down too much, would be Davenport, at the Regents Hotel. Have you ever seen the Regents?"

"No, I've never been there."

"Are they heading east or west, ma'am?"

"I don't know."

The woman looked at her watch, took a deep breath, regarded a schedule, shook her head, and told Sarah that the stop after that wasn't till morning. At 6:12 A.M. the bus would be laying over for a few hours in Omaha.

"Sometimes parents send a wire ahead or call the juvenile authorities, but if you don't know where they are . . ." Her voice trailed off in bored disapproval of Sarah's vagueness. When Sarah replied with silence, the woman added, "Greyhound gets a lot of runaways. That's one of our big markets." Then she lowered her voice to confide something. "But if I was running anywhere," she said, raising her voice at the end as if formulating a question, "I'd take an airplane. They're much safer, really, and you're able to disappear much faster, you know?"

Thanking the woman, Sarah looked at the ceiling of the terminal, where noisy pigeons perched and rattled around amid strings of dust hanging like old tinsel.

"Why don't you get the car?" she asked Jeremy, sighing with pity for herself and everyone unlucky enough to be in the bus station.

"No luck?"

"Not really. The ticket agent told me she'd take an airplane if she were running away."

While Jeremy went to pull the car around, Sarah walked into the washroom to soak her cheek. She had been careful to resist the earlier temptation of seeing Larry's imprint in the reflection of Jeremy's car window. She turned the only water spout, *cold,* and held a thick brown paper towel up to her smarting eye, remembering a shiner she'd received three decades ago. Dabbing at the purpling mound, she pictured the weedy empty lot on her block where she and Mae used to play in the high sun of summer. She had been spinning into its blinding glare when her face met Mae's swinging bat. Now, in the poor reflection of the cheap metal mirror, she imagined Carrie's features emerging from her own.

HAVING ESCAPED CHICAGO without a hitch, Deenie should have been feeling happier. It amused her to picture all the food she would have refused to eat lined up single file on Aunt Sarah's Thanksgiving table like a dejected army brigade. Why was she so annoyed as she watched Carrie's sleeping mouth suck air and heard a sound coming out of her nose like a cat scratching a basket? Carrie even slept like a baby. All she needed was a little pink bunting. Deenie studied her unconscious face, trying to decide whether it displayed stupidity or nothing. Then again, the big blue Greyhound seats were pretty comfortable, especially for sixty-nine dollars. Everywhere Deenie looked, heads were pressed back and lights out. Just across from them an elderly woman, collapsed in sleep like a lawn chair, was snoring. Next to her was the handsome guy she'd seen in the bus terminal. He was older than her boyfriend, Branch, but that didn't matter. When they'd gotten on the bus, he'd looked at her sideways and grinned like someone who'd selected the right channel. Maybe at the rest stop in Davenport she'd talk to him. It didn't hurt to have interesting travel stories to tell.

Branch always talked about places he'd been, but Deenie had been places only with her family. Deenie could have told Branch how the backs of her parents' heads bobbed in anger as they traveled and argued. She could tell him how, in the middle of an Easter vacation in Bermuda, her father had left abruptly, and her mother had broken a champagne glass and unraveled the entire arm of a rattan patio chair between oaths of vengeance and breathy, self-pitying sobs that had terrified Deenie into silence. All the following year her dad had been seeing someone named Anita Lowns. "This is Anita Lowns," a hopeful voice would announce on the phone to Deenie, as if her existence would be welcome news to her lover's daughter.

Deenie thought mostly about her own legs, how they'd looked after she'd shaven them. Maroon-and-brown blood had covered the long, irregular scratches. She'd left them that way for Branch to see and he'd admired them. If she were with him right now, they'd be on his platform bed with the sea-green sheets. He'd be kissing her all over, or maybe they'd decide to shave more places, her pubic hair this time or that spot on his back where a tuft of blond hair sprouted. Instead, she had come to a place she couldn't even remember. The last time she'd visited Aunt Sarah in Chicago, Deenie had looked plump and round, like a nine-year-old cherub.

"What a fantastic mutilation!" Branch had pronounced over her scratched raw legs. Of course, she wouldn't have shown her mom or dad, who were taking a renewed interest in her, charting the peaks and valleys of her behavior and reporting them to Dr. Weber, the stupid Yuppie psychiatrist who always wore silk paisley ties with knots about as big as his head. He was director of the Eating Disorder Clinic, the Scarf and Barf Center, as Branch called it. Deenie loved Branch because things weren't serious with him like they were at home. He thought her hipbones beautiful. "You look like an antelope," he'd told her, stroking her delicate, sunken flanks in bed the first time.

Three years older than her at nineteen, he understood that her problems were temporary. It didn't take a psychologist to see that her mother was forcing the issue. For all her talk of being aware, Mae could have been Nancy Reagan, with her sucked-in cheeks and pooling, guilty eyes. Deenie figured her mom was simply hysterical about her own life. Really, what had it gotten her? Or maybe she was jealous that Aunt Sarah suddenly had someone named Jeremy while all she had was Tony, who never was hers anyway, and Deenie, who wasn't hers anymore. Of course, Mae would never admit that anything was wrong. Deenie had to practically disappear for Mae to even see her. Maybe there was something in her mother's childhood, forgotten incest or abuse, that made her want to appear so normal to the world.

For the flight to Chicago Deenie had chosen black pegged pants and a man's oversized shirt covered in caricatured bluebirds that reminded her of a song she'd liked in first grade, "Blue Bird, Blue Bird, Through My Window." It had been impossible for Aunt Sarah to tell how thin she was in this outfit. Sarah had never gotten to see that her thighs made perilous angles to her hips or that her shoulder joints appeared rickety and swollen. Branch had told her she had Texas cheekbones, which really meant Indian blood somewhere. Indian blood would have been a dark secret in her family, where Catholicism was viewed as sinister. True, her dad had once been Catholic, but his religion was every bit as mysterious as his affairs. It used to strike her as funny that she knew all her parents' secrets, but now it just seemed sad. She remembered how her mom and dad would stop talking just like that whenever she came into a room. It was like a scene was always closing just when she entered it.

Aunt Sarah was different. She had noticed things from the start, like the big turquoise-studded crucifix Deenie wore, the one that Branch had bought from the Indians in Taos. Branch had been dating Helen then, who'd taken him there to sell her work, lacquered tree bark in stormy swirls of earth-toned enamel colors. Deenie was proud that Branch had slept with a woman as old as her mother before he'd slept with her, but she didn't tell Sarah. Aunt Sarah would have reported Deenie, and without even mentioning it to her, her mom would have recorded it on their chart. Deenie had never known what her parents thought about her until they'd sent her to Dr. Weber.

Sometimes she wondered if they'd known she was there at all. She remembered discovering tickets once for a trip to Brazil. She'd torn through the envelope frantically hoping she'd been included, but Tony and Mae had gone to Carnival alone. They'd never taken Deenie anywhere, if she didn't count the Bermuda disaster and the hundred times she'd been to Las Vegas, where she'd stay in the hotel room dipping strawberries in flat leftover champagne while her mom and dad lost at blackjack.

Deenie checked the hammered-copper flask she always carried in her purse. She hadn't wanted to faint in front of Aunt Sarah, but when the plane was about to land in Chicago, she had gone to the bathroom and taken three quick swigs. The hits of Jim Beam had established the proper expectations. Aunt Sarah had certainly smelled it on Deenie's breath, and the aroma set a tone: it prepared her for the calculated mutilation of Deenie's legs, for the green fringe on her ink-black hair, for the intentional dirt under her short, blunt finger-nails.

All the time she had anticipated the visit, she barely thought of her two cousins or Uncle Larry. They were probably pretty regular. It was strange to think that she had actually looked forward to seeing her aunt, who hadn't been normal at all a few months ago. Deenie could tell from her voice on the phone that she was probably wearing a stained bathrobe all day. Sometimes Aunt Sarah would call Mae and talk for an hour, and on Mae's end Deenie would hear exclamations and expletives about Larry and soothing conclusions that seemed detached from the rest of the conversation. Not that two people could be odd in the same way, but it was comforting to think that strangeness could be shared.

As the plane descended, Deenie had seen neutral-toned buildings and blurry lights everywhere. She had seen what looked like a man-made swamp filled with chartreuse sewage and swirling, shiny oil, and a border of red lights outlining the runway. She had watched her fingers gripping the armrest and thought of her mother's long fingers wrapped around a double shot of afternoon tequila in their kitchen. Sometimes she'd give Deenie the liquor-soaked lime if Tony wasn't home. He disapproved of offering liquor to Deenie in any form. In fact, he treated her like an infant. The few times he'd bought her presents they'd been for little girls: a French porcelain baby doll on her twelfth birthday, a pair of lacy anklets and a diary when she turned fourteen. Mae had jokingly offered Deenie birth-control pills for that birthday, unaware that no boy had ever kissed her.

When her plane landed at the gate, Sarah and Carrie had been waiting. Sarah had looked better than Deenie had imagined. Her eyes seemed clear and warm, and she had on a regular dress, not a bath-robe. Carrie had resembled most of the girls Deenie knew: clad in denim, well-groomed, serious about their lives to the point that their manicured fingernails and kinked hair exuded good intentions. She had studied Carrie's face for a reaction to her. It first seemed that Carrie didn't recognize her at all.

"Deenie!" Sarah waved.

Then there had been a surprised look on Carrie's face before she had smiled a hesitant welcome to her cousin. When Sarah had embraced her, Deenie had wondered if Sarah could feel how small and perfect she'd become inside her clothes. Carrie had nodded a conditional hello, then hung back shyly.

"You probably don't remember each other," Sarah had soothed. "Weren't you both about six the last time?"

"She was nine and I was seven," Carrie had murmured.

"Well, it'll be fun to get to know each other again. You'll be using the trundle bed in Carrie's room if that's okay with you."

Was she supposed to protest? Should she have insisted that

Carrie move out or say that she'd planned to sleep with Uncle Larry? From Sarah's conversations with her mom, it had seemed that everyone else in the world had.

"Your mom says you have a new boyfriend. You'll have to tell me all about him." Sarah draped a heavy arm over Deenie's shoulder.

Her mom had probably told Sarah everything she didn't like about Branch. He's too old, he uses drugs, he doesn't go to school had been her litany for a month. What had Sarah been fishing for? Maybe Deenie would plant some false information just so it would get back to Mae. And there'd be no reason to tell Carrie anything either. The idea that age is a bond is so fucking foolish, Deenie had thought, as she watched Carrie's plump ass precede her out of the terminal. They passed souvenir stands hawking knitted Bears caps, espresso beans dipped in chocolate, Dove bars. Carrie was such a child. She was disgusting. She wanted everything she saw.

"Hungry?" Sarah had asked Deenie.

"How about a soft pretzel?" Carrie had asked without waiting her turn.

Deenie's stomach clenched. She hadn't imagined herself having to refuse food so soon.

"Want one, Deenie?"

"I had a big meal on the plane, thanks." It had been her first outright lie, and Sarah had swallowed it without any trouble. Deenie knew it was going to be easy to cover herself and get out of town around Thanksgiving.

Sometimes it was impossible to think about Branch without considering Helen, who had taken him to New Mexico and Costa Rica. She lived in Costa Rica now, which was where they'd go after they met in Los Angeles. Branch had told Deenie not to feel jealous, that Helen was just a friend now and so busy with her art that she didn't have time for him in a personal way. But she would pay him good money to deliver the rest of her things from storage in Los Angeles and to take some art back to a dealer. Branch would earn twenty-five hundred dollars. Deenie suspected it had something to do with drugs, and she hoped she could change his mind about visiting Helen, but even if she had to swallow bags of cocaine or stuff heroin up her, it was better than riding in her parents' backseat anywhere.

"Wake up!" Deenie shook Carrie's shoulders.

"Huh?" Carrie said, and brought her knees up toward her waist. Now Deenie could see Carrie's little pink socks with tartan-plaid cuffs and brand-new deck shoes. She dressed like the Sears catalog. The cheek closest to Deenie was red from leaning on the seat, and Carrie's blue eyes looked like they hadn't seen anything the whole time she'd lived. Deenie hoped Branch wouldn't be mad that she'd brought Carrie along, but she hadn't known how to get out of Chicago without her. Besides, who wanted to sit next to a stranger whose cranky baby smelled of sour milk or an old woman eating sweet rolls? Carrie was stupid, but at least she was clean and stupid. Deenie could tell her anything and she'd believe her.

"Wake up and enjoy the ride. Here." Deenie gave Carrie the flask.

"What's in here?"

"Chocolate milk."

Opening it carefully, Carrie smelled its contents, then pulled her face back and wiggled her nose like a rabbit. "Yuck! I don't think I can drink this."

The handsome guy was watching them. Flashing him a smile, she rolled her eyes in the direction of her cousin.

"Do you think they know we're gone yet?"

"Why don't you shout it?"

Carrie repeated the question in a whisper.

"Of course they do."

"And they're probably looking for us, right? Do you think they'll find us?"

"Not unless you told Scotty how we're *really* going."

Carrie pouted out the window at the dark road. "I promised I wouldn't, Deenie. Do you think I'm dumb?"

"I plead the Fifth."

"What?"

"Go back to sleep. We'll be in Iowa soon."

"And then what?"

"And then we'll be in Iowa. That's what."

"I'm hungry," Carrie said.

Carrie's bottom lip was fuller than her top one. Deenie hated that too. Not that lips are anyone's fault, but why did hers have to be annoying? Maybe in Davenport she could arrange to switch seats with the folded-over woman. The guy had interesting, heavy-lidded eyes. Maybe he was French. She knew Europeans liked to travel by train and bus.

"I said I'm hungry."

"You can eat in Davenport."

"We would have had turkey at home. And dressing. And mashed potatoes."

"You wanted to come, Carrie, so stop bitching." Carrie's hurt look prodded Deenie along. "Chew on your fat lip if you're hungry." She reached over and squeezed Carrie's cheek.

"Why did you do that?" Carrie squealed.

"Because you're here. Look out the window and stop complaining. Branch won't take you to Costa Rica if you act this way."

"What way?"

"Like such a wimpy baby."

"Maybe I'll call my mother in Davenport."

Her cousin was worse than she'd imagined. "If you call your mother, I'll kill you."

"How will you do that?"

Deenie pictured Carrie falling in front of the bus. She saw her flying through space like a cartoon, being run over and resurrected, a pancake version of herself. Deenie couldn't help but smile.

"What's so funny?"

"What I'm imagining."

Carrie made the "sounds like" gesture from charades.

"Sounds like gun rover," Deenie said.

"I don't understand."

"Run over." Deenie turned her body toward the aisle, away from Carrie's puzzled face. Someone had spilled a purple syrupy drink on the floor. It flowed in a foamy little rivulet toward the front of the bus. The sleeping woman's beige patent sandal was sitting in it. "Look," Deenie said, pointing to its course. "The Mississippi River."

THE THANKSGIVING RUSH at O'Hare Airport would begin the next morning. Most families were just finishing their pumpkin pies and clearing the table, or cursing over replays of the Bears' startling 31—7 loss. Sarah imagined the uniformed Greyhound ticket agent at the airport, surrounded by red luggage. What other airport scenes of loss could she conjure up to comfort her? There was the black-and-white memory of Bogart and Bergman parting forever for the good of the world. There she was, eighteen again and hopeful, leaving for NYU in a denim miniskirt and a jacket that looked like apricot poodle fur, her parents waving furtively at her indistinct shadow. Nothing evoked the devastation she felt looking at the empty departure gates all around her.

While Jeremy checked the next concourse, she decided to see if Larry had news. Pressing the buttons, she felt her anger at him increase until it pounded in her throat.

"Hello?" his impartial voice asked. No one would guess that he was anything less than reasonable.

"Hello," Sarah said blankly.

"Where did you go, Sarah?" he asked plaintively.

"We haven't found Carrie."

"You and Jeremy?"

"Right. We haven't found her. Jeremy and I," she repeated like one of them was an idiot.

"I've called all Carrie's friends and looked everywhere," Larry sighed. "I went to the Salvation Army and the YMCA and a place called End Zone that takes in street kids. It was pretty pathetic, Sarah. You should have seen the chaos there. I was waiting till morning to contact the police. I was worried about you too."

The remark hung there, and Sarah refused to pick it up. "How's Scotty?"

"He's scared."

"Let me talk to him, will you?"

"Sure."

"Hi, Scott."

"Hi."

"We're looking everywhere. Have any ideas?"

The hesitation in his voice filled her with vague hope. "Really, Scotty, if they told you anything, it's no time to keep a secret."

"I promised, Mom."

"I know, Scott." She felt she could touch each exhalation that reached the phone receiver. "Sometimes kids get carried away and do things that are pretty serious."

"They took United to Los Angeles," he said tersely.

"Do you know which flight?"

"No."

"Do you know what time?"

"No."

"Why didn't you tell Dad, Scott?"

"He didn't ask me." He hesitated. "Besides, I didn't think you'd care."

"Scott! Don't you know we love you?"

She heard more breathing. "Scott, do you hear me?" She could see his cool, downcast eyes and imagine his lips pursed in reticence.

"Yeah."

"What are they going to do when they get there?"

"They didn't tell me."

"Is Deenie going to meet her boyfriend?"

"Mom, all Carrie said was that they were flying. Deenie didn't tell me a thing. She never talked to me at all. Deenie's a real psycho."

"How long have you known about Carrie?"

"Since yesterday."

"And you weren't going to tell us?"

"I don't know . . . I *did*, didn't I?"

"Yes. Let me talk to Dad."

"So now we know." Larry's voice was a parade of tired syllables. "He sees us out of our minds and doesn't say a word."

"He made a promise."

"Big fucking deal. What the fuck is a promise?"

"I'll call Mae. If they're on United, she and Tony can intercept them. I'm already at the airport. I'll fly out there and meet Carrie."

"What will you do after you find her?"

Sarah heard fear in his voice. He probably assumed that the answer had nothing to do with him. "I'll bring Carrie back to Chicago, and we'll all talk about the future."

"I'm sorry," Larry said softly. "Does it look very bad?"

"Not for a black eye," Sarah said. "About average for a black eye."

THE MIDNIGHT FLIGHT was nearly empty, so Sarah was able to stretch out and try to rest. Curling her body in toward the seat, knees bent up, she let her head loll backward on the miniature pillow, toward Jeremy across the aisle. She kept her sore cheek in the air and tried not to think about it. Every now and then Jeremy would reach over and stroke her red hair, and she'd grasp his knuckles in response, but as she grew sleepier, she stopped acknowledging his attention and let her eyelids fall shut.

"Sarah, Sarah." Somebody was shaking her arm. Sarah couldn't believe that she'd slept through the whole plane ride. Horrible nervous energy had forced her to dream. Usually the distance from earth made her grow alert and philosophical. Flying over Iowa she'd think of the land burgeoning with invisible life: speckled fish gliding under streams, spawning and dying in season; ants building intricate hills; blind moles suckling their hairless young. Maybe all behavior was coded before birth, her movement toward Carrie, Larry's away from her, hers toward Jeremy. Smaller encumbrances too might have their origins in heredity. Was it predestined for fluorescent-lit grocery aisles to make her feel dizzy, for airports but not airplanes to frighten her? The spiraling secrets of motivation fixed her in her seat until a steward resembling the young Fred Astaire told her to position her headrest for landing. She blinked slowly at Jeremy, who had been watching her wake up.

"Was I snoring?"

"You were a perfect sleeping lady."

She didn't tell him her terrible dreams. Ivy, seated on a bale of hay in a 1940's airplane hangar, had been telling her that two of her friends were dying, but before she could hear their names, her father had interrupted. His hair was rumpled and he'd forgotten his glasses. He was telling Sarah why he'd left Ivy at sixty-seven, but he was lying about leaving her because he had died at sixty-five. Because Sarah knew he was dead in her dream, his presence was a horrifying distraction.

She was about to ask her mother to repeat herself when the scene changed. She was back with Larry in their first dismal kitchenette apartment. Standing at the stained aluminum sink, looking at snow glide past the poorly tuck-pointed wall outside the kitchen window, she was peeling tiny red potatoes, and Larry was watching. They were young again and childless, but the atmosphere wasn't comfortable. The intimate details were wrong. Larry never looked at her with such affection or waited in appreciative silence for her to finish a task. And just as her father shouldn't have been in the dream, it seemed that her children should have been.

The last time she'd been with both Scotty and Carrie was the first day of the teachers' strike in early September. She'd seen how Carrie had laid out her new clothes over the back of her rocker and how her white high-tops hadn't received their first smudge of use.

They hadn't been to Rosebud Farms for many years. About forty miles north of the city, it was a sheltered workshop for mildly retarded adults. When the kids were younger, she and Larry would drive out on fall and spring Sundays to see the farm animals and eat a country breakfast. On her butterfly chair, Carrie still kept the austere stuffed giraffe purchased on one of their visits, and Sarah remembered the texture of the large, irregular chocolate-chip cookies sold in little packets with curly blue ribbons. Until they began their silent ride, it hadn't occurred to her that the kids had agreed to go only because Sarah had seemed so urgent about it.

Both had worn their Walkmans. Sarah could hear competitive buzzing next to her, where Carrie sat, and from behind, where Scotty was stretched out. Every now and then she'd stop herself from pointing out the cows and horses that passed her urban-trained eyes like disturbances in her peripheral field. Such sights, she knew, no longer evoked wonder in the kids. She turned on the tape of the Fifth Brandenburg Concerto and let it blast. Small green hills and signs advertising motels that had been bypassed when the superhighway was built punctuated the music like a slow metronome. The deep contemplation of being alone might be reached only in the company of one's children.

The clean September air was right for Bach, and she drove faster and more happily once she'd abandoned the idea of conversation. She remembered the drives they'd taken when the children were little, she and Larry leading an endless chorus of "Row Your Boat," childhood viewed as the willing suspension of disbelief, its motive to sing as loudly as possible. She could wrap their childhoods neatly that way and include her own if she stretched the memory of cars to include a 1956 silver Chevy. Her Sunday rides had always culminated at the newly constructed Midway Airport, where her family would watch planes take off. In place of the fat propellor planes of that era, she kept visualizing stuffed airplanes, animated cartoon airplanes, and a gluey model that Scott had strung from an archway in his bedroom. If her father were still alive, she'd have asked him to describe them. She looked at her children and wondered if they had anything to ask her.

They arrived to find a crisis in progress. A llama had escaped from the petting zoo and two large, inept men were chasing it through a nearby field. Both wore green jumpsuits that had their names stitched in a yellow blur onto their pockets. The animal loped ahead, followed by the shorter of the two men, who ran faster. The second man's run was an unbalanced gait on the brink of collapse. The llama, with its superior instinct for flight, would be on a highway leading into farmland before the two found their way out of the sloping field.

"Why don't you help, Scotty?"

He'd looked at Sarah like she'd asked him to visit the moon.

"Okay," Carrie had said with enthusiasm. "Those guys will never catch up." She took off in her white high-tops and soon had caught up with the men in the chase, which involved large figure eights and crescendos of loud, nervous laughter. Scotty kicked listlessly at the gravel of the parking lot for another few seconds, smoothed back his wonderful hair, and decided to join in when the posse was close to the visitors' gate.

Sarah saw it dawn on the men that two more capable people had come to rescue them. Out of breath, both leaned against the mesh fence separating the parking lot from the field. The smaller man hunched over, clutching his knees. The larger one couldn't stop choking and grunting, but he was the first to cheer when Scotty reached the llama and held it by the muzzle. The animal stood motionless, and Sarah could see its large sides, the shape of ancient sails, blowing in and out.

By the time Carrie and Scotty had surrounded the animal, two workmen in a yellow golf cart had ridden up. They carried ropes and what looked like a cattle prod.

"Super job, Izzy and Michael," one shouted toward the fence.

Sarah wondered if this happened daily or whether they'd witnessed an event that would transform the lives of the two breathless men at the fence.

In the lunchroom, they were given seats at a round table near the window. From their vantage point, they could see the llama being led back to a special holding pen. The two men who had chased it were walking toward the main building. The taller one appeared to be lecturing the other.

"I don't know why you brought us here," Carrie was saying. "I mean, it's really . . ." She stopped to be polite when the waiter walked up to their table. The shortness of his hair made his ears stick out like dishes. He was young, perhaps sixteen, and silent. He'd chewed down his nails to the quick. Sarah saw a bandage on every cuticle.

"Plates are up there," he said pointing to the buffet lunch. Then the waiter saw the taller man who'd pursued the llama. "Shit, Izzy," he shouted across the dining room. "Shit."

Carrie tried not to laugh, but Scotty was convulsed.

"We don't talk that way, Lee," came the harsh warning from the corner where their supervisor, a young woman with waist-length brown hair, sat with a clipboard.

"Can you believe this?" Scotty asked.

"Mom sure knows how to have fun," Carrie mused.

After they'd chosen their three-bean salad, blueberry muffins, chicken à la king, and baby carrots from the buffet, the waiter was back with their drink orders. He listlessly slid Sarah's coffee and their iced teas onto the table, leaving them wherever they landed. "Nice dinner," he mumbled, and walked to the supervisor's table to join his friends.

An elderly woman at the next table was motioning to him for more coffee. Her pantomime was obvious enough, but the waiter chose to ignore it.

"Izzy's not good," the waiter was loudly commenting to the supervisor.

Izzy, legs straddled, gripping the rungs of the chairback, was defending himself. "Animals don't walk. They run." He was addressing the whole dining room.

"Can we get out of here?" Carrie asked. She drummed the table with her long fingernails and styled her hair in the window's reflection.

Sarah looked around for moral support. Except for the elderly woman and a large family of Nigerians in tribal dress, they were the only lunch patrons. "Don't you want to see the animals or buy a gift?"

"Really, Mom, let's just go after we eat. I think we're a little too old for this," Scotty said in his best long-suffering tone. "At least I'm too old," he added, and shot a glance at Carrie.

Carrie pretended to poke Scotty with her fork. Under her breath she mumbled, "Shitty Izzy, shitty Scotty, shitty teachers' strike."

"I'm going to get some shitty dessert," Scotty said.

"Stop swearing!" Sarah demanded too loudly. She watched both children go back to the buffet. They had just returned when they all were startled by Izzy's full-throated laughter.

Looking out the window, they saw the llama running toward the same field, a long rope trailing behind it. Sarah watched Carrie

focus the fancy camera she'd inherited from her grandfather and take
a picture of the llama's fading image.

When her father had died seven months earlier, Sarah had taken the
film in his camera to be developed. The entire roll was the Allerton
Hotel sign, which he could see through his high-rise window, going
through its phases. In some daytime photos it looked uninspired, a
tangle of neon and glass on a red brick background. At night, though,
it was a diffuse undecipherable blue bordering on beauty. Did the
roll of film record his interest or his ambivalence? What kind of
legacy were these abstractions? The more Sarah looked at them, the
less she had known her father.

Not that she didn't remember times they'd spent as a family on
summer vacations to Yellowstone or Sunday ballgames, where they'd
always sit up the left-field line at Comiskey Park. Once he'd gotten
them a foul ball and had two less than stellar Sox players sign it at
the next game. She didn't follow the fates of Mike Hershberger or
J. C. Martin as their names grew barely legible on the yellowing
baseball. Sarah could picture her father's wiry arm reach for a platter
of chicken at dinner. She could remember a corny joke he once told
her about being a cowboy and riding the kitchen range, but mostly
she remembered him in tableaus: at his desk grading chemistry tests,
in his less than comfortable television chair watching *The World at
War,* crying softly at the kitchen table when Kennedy was assassi-
nated, the only man in a family of women. There were few action
shots or group photos. There was one moment, though, that she had
never forgotten. She'd been jumping rope on the front sidewalk of
their house just before a tremendous summer rainstorm that ionized
the air and made their maple tree shake its silvery leaves. Instead of
shouting to her to come inside, he walked out to her on the sidewalk,
opened the passenger door to his Chevy Impala, and invited her in.
All through the storm, which was so heavy that the world smeared
into undecipherable wedges of primary color, they sat quietly in the
car, watching it batter the tree and the house. For a minute she hoped
that he was going to run away with her, maybe to Florida, but he
never even turned on the ignition. When the storm finally ended, he

simply said, "C'mon, kiddo," and led her under the dripping maple canopy and past the overflowing gutters back to the house.

Sarah spent many late hours rethinking the details of her father's death, how he had the heart attack as he got off the exit ramp at Orleans. How, after hitting a parking meter, his car ended up nestling in the brick of the Melkoff Tool-and-Die Factory. Hearing the impact, Bernie Melkoff raced downstairs to discover that his high-school friend and occasional companion of fifty years was dead. He accompanied the ambulance to the hospital, and so the duty of telling Ivy fell to him. He must have felt both honored and overwhelmed. Fate had consigned him to his cousin's factory. Suddenly he bore news worthy of a Greek tragedy.

Since her father's death, imagining his last minutes had haunted Sarah. She was sure time must stretch. Everyone has known moments of exquisite pain that rival ocean cruises. Sarah began to feel as if she might die whenever she got in her car. Her throat would fill with such anxiety that once she had to pull over to simply breathe. She hesitated to leave the house except to meet her classes and record *The Grammar Connection.* On the mornings she didn't work, she stayed in bed listening to the radio. On National Public Radio one day, a British gardening-show host named Wakefield warned listeners in a voice hushed with significance to avoid store-bought tulips in bloom before winter ends. He cited the abuse that had gone into getting the flowers to open early. He made it sound like a crime. Stressed-out tulips, he called the bulbs that would never bear more flowers. She took his warning as secret, indirect vindication for her secret collapse.

About the same time, Sarah's officemate Russell had made a remark as they stood in the lobby hallway near the vending machines. Usually Russell was tactful to the point of masochism. Sarah had heard him compliment failing writing students on their beautiful penmanship and go word by word over a term paper on General Custer's "life-style" to raise a transferring student's grade to a pass. So when he saw her buying a bag of Doritos and said to her in his soft, sometimes stammering way, "I-I-I think we're putting on a little weight this semester," Sarah knew that his friendship had forced him to an impasse where sincerity and tact collided. She recalled the time that his lover, John, had left him after a bad scene one Christmas Eve over the cost of gifts exchanged. Russell had called Sarah at midnight sounding so desperate that she'd driven over immediately. Before he wept uncontrollably onto her shoulder, he'd served her an eggnog flan and double espresso. The Christmasy apartment had been subdued by Russell's resolute terror at being abandoned. Had John taken everything with him when he'd gone? Even the tree lights seemed to be missing. Knowing Russell was always kind and well-meaning, she was careful not to meet his eyes now with her own defensive stare.

On the morning that Russell had made his comment, she rushed home to watch the first few minutes of a year-old videotape of *The Grammar Connection*. It was amazing that Sarah, who had auditioned on a whim, had gotten the job. "You're a grammar anchor-woman," her friend Rachel had quipped, toasting Sarah. Because the university had received a special grant from an obscure foundation, Sarah's TV assignment paid twice as much as her adjunct classes at what she habitually called "Larry's university." She saw herself introducing the usual cartoon man with the fedora, fat belly, and skinny legs, a cross between Bing Crosby and John Belushi. In a four-minute sequence the college television station had purchased at discount from the failing Buffalo Public Communications Network, the little pedant ran around frantically posting warning signs on every immovable object.

Sarah guessed he was supposed to be funny, but she couldn't imagine laughing at any part of the routine: the tedious Saturday-morning taping sessions, the stumbling secondhand TelePrompTer, the stupid cartoons, the opening and closing theme using minimalist music and train switchings. Finally, the caboose, which bore the show's title in angled, rickety letters, like shifting cargo, puffed onto the screen. In the smoke that trailed behind it, Sarah's name could be found in minuscule type under that of the producer, Tamara Presmanik. Tamara was a transplanted Israeli whose lively interest in Americana made her tyrannical with Americans. "Your grandparents drove an oxcart over the Midwestern plains in the early 1800's. Farmers, were they not?" she'd once asked Sarah. Before

Sarah could explain her family's relatively recent immigrant past, Tamara had moved on to another guest at the station's holiday party. As a way to display power on the set, Tamara used to make Sarah wear a child-sized Oshkosh train-engineer's cap, which Sarah had conveniently misplaced between the lesson on run-ons and fragments.

It was hard to attach the television image of herself standing in front of the blackboard to the woman who now sat on the sofa wringing her hands. She watched as the awkward segue back to the cartoon, a *Wizard of Oz* cyclone swirl, replaced her on the screen. Then she ran into the bedroom, closed her Levolor blinds, and began stripping. Standing attentively between two mirrors in a growing pile of clothing, Sarah watched herself from behind. Two rings of flesh where her upper thighs met her sagging buttocks were new to her. In an exploratory gesture made comically hesitant by disgust, she poked at one ring with her index finger. It felt like ordinary enough flesh. There was no denying it was her. She wrapped herself in her "one size fits all" terry robe and thought of how Russell had startled her into an awareness that her body was aging. It was impossible to accept the corollary, that she was aging too, since she felt she existed mainly in her mind, which seemed no older than at any other time in her life. For arbitrariness, she chose age nine, fourth grade, fat, messy red braids, a tendency toward conjunctivitis, a fascination with holiday-song lyrics, a slight stutter when called on to speak in class. Mentally, she was essentially that girl, quick to take offense but slow to show it, and quick to protect whom she loved. The person gaping at the mirror and the cheerful woman teaching grammar on the TV screen were one and the same. How could some people scare up forty personalities when just one was so unrelenting?

Later that morning she called a few doctors to ask how she might drop twenty extra pounds. One told her about a diet involving bee hormones. This "drone factor" speeded up the metabolism. If she took three pills a day, she would hike her activity rate 88 percent without putting a strain on her heart.

She had always wanted weight, like the weather, to be something that might change overnight. One morning you'd go to sleep slow and heavy as winter snow. The next morning you'd wake in the physical tropics, a smooth and sinewy you. Dr. Greer told her the bee tonic would cost her three thousand dollars for a three-month regime. That was the other problem with weight. It cost a lot of money to eat, but it cost even more to stop.

Next she called the Lifespan Center, the division of her university contrived to build enrollment by getting the community involved in learning, the same department that had made her Russell's officemate by turning her former spacious office with its coveted view of the Chicago River into a giant oven for its French-pastry seminars. The answering machine explained a full set of options in a soothing feminine voice. On Monday night you could learn to negotiate with your toddler. On Tuesday night you could eliminate back stress by learning to put less pressure on the balls of your feet. Wednesday you could learn to massage your baby. Sarah was interested in shedding about four babies. Thursday was the night for eating modification. She was all set to hang up when the voice added that Thursday was also the night for grief therapy. Suddenly in tears again about her father, she left her name and number for the recorded phone voice.

On the night that grief therapy was scheduled to start, she was assessing her family from a distance. Scotty and Carrie were almost grown. Now and then they asked her questions about homework, but mainly they hoped she wouldn't notice them. Sarah thought they looked pale and gaunt as miners in the shadowy light of the front room.

"Mom," Scotty asked, "can I have fourteen-fifty?"

"What for, my birthday?"

"Probably for drugs, Mom," Carrie offered.

"I need it for science."

"Is that with a small or a capital S?"

"What's the difference?"

"The difference is fourteen-fifty. I want to know where it's going."

"Jason and I are making crystals. I need to buy chemicals."

He handed her a list she couldn't read. Why didn't he just ask Larry, who'd look like a man regarding a showcase of passenger pigeons, unrumple some bills, and go back to his reading?

"Why doesn't Jason buy them?"

"Jason's dad just left them. His mother sits in her car all day. Jason doesn't really want to bother her, Mom."

Sarah reached into her purse. She never knew what she'd feel next. Her reactions were like a parade emerging from a tunnel. She thought of Jason's mother, Irene, a pretty immunologist she saw sometimes at school assemblies. She thought of her poor father again, suffocating in his car. She thought of the stressed-out tulips. Then she remembered a children's book Carrie had owned, where a farmer with airbrushed rosy cheeks held a lamb in his capable hands. She sucked in her breath and let out a low contorted sob.

"Something's wrong with Mom again," Carrie announced.

"Excuse me," she said, and drove off.

The Health Enhancement Floor was carpeted in heather. The walls were a calm light green. Matching wallpaper dappled the walls of the hall. If you looked closely, you could see cherries on almost invisible stems. Sarah peered into the empty room where her group was to meet. Modern gray upholstered office chairs were arranged in a circle. Sarah took her place in the last chair near the window, which looked out onto the octagon-shaped Behavioral Science Complex. She imagined desperate undergraduates trying to raise their grades by volunteering for sleep experiments. Why did she always arrive places early and spend so much of her life waiting for things to begin?

Shortly after eight, the rest of the group began assembling. A tall Native American man Sarah recognized from the campus sat two seats away from her. A small woman with mousy hair and a huge duffel bag spread out her wares near the door. Two elderly women who'd accompanied each other sat next to the mousy woman. A young couple, the rims of their eyes still red with crying, filled in between Sarah and the tall man. Next, a slender woman about ten years younger than Sarah entered. She introduced herself as Nora Sampson and wrote her qualifications on the board. They included advanced studies with Dr. Elisabeth Kübler-Ross and degrees in both psychology and music. Then she collected thirty-five-dollar checks from all the participants and wrote out neat receipts on Pepto-Bismol-pink check-shaped paper.

Sarah felt her armpits dripping sweat when she was told to introduce herself first. She said that she was Sarah Holm and was mourning the death of her father. She felt particularly bad that her father had died unexpectedly. She'd been reliving his death ever since she'd heard the news.

Next, the husband, whose name was Reed, spoke for the young couple. Reed said they'd lost their son. He stopped then and looked at his hands. Sarah kept noticing how light his eyebrows were. The silence continued, and not even the instructor could coax them from their misery. Everyone was finally relieved when she asked the next man his name.

The tall man introduced himself as Jeremy Bone Shoulder. In a quick, quiet voice he said he was mourning the fate of his people, and that it was a public grief, so he wasn't sure that he belonged.

Nora assured Mr. Shoulder that if public griefs are felt privately, they're as valid as the most personal loss.

"I beg to differ," said the smaller of the two elderly women. She appeared to be squinting with one eye only. "Every night I slept with my husband for forty-nine years. You can't share a bed with history."

Nora Sampson let her remark hang in the air without deflecting it. Then she asked the difficult woman her name.

Mrs. Pipkin's sidekick, taller and more dressed up for the occasion, was Mrs. Ramsey. She fingered a heavy gold-and-jade braided chain as she told about the loss of Sheldon, her husband of thirty-eight years.

"What's thirty-eight?" Mrs. Pipkin interrupted. "We were on our way to the Golden. My daughter-in-law was going to have a party at the purple-and-white Hyatt in Skokie, and all the family was scheduled to come. So instead of a party, it was a funeral."

"That must have been very depressing," Nora Sampson said.

"Not really," Mrs. Pipkin offered with a slight smile. "We all mourned and then we had a party." She lifted a heavy, tanned arm and with a no-nonsense gesture waved off further comments.

The small woman by the door spoke without giving her name.

Her boyfriend hadn't married her as promised after his mother died last January. Instead, he'd gone to Boston and gotten a new job.

"Run off with a woman?" Mrs. Pipkin jumped in.

"Just run off," she repeated fiercely.

Mrs. Pipkin whistled like a teapot, and Nora Sampson changed the subject.

"Name three objects you associate with your grief," she told Sarah.

Sarah said knuckles. She couldn't think of anything else for a moment. Then she added radishes and the smell of diapers.

They went around the room. Many of the people said photos or albums or a souvenir carefully explained in its context.

"We have a roomful of toys we can't even look at," the young father sighed.

"Why don't you donate them?" Mrs. Pipkin suggested. "There's plenty of needy ones, right, Mr. Shoulder?"

"I was wondering about your list, Mrs. Holm." Nora Sampson chewed on her pencil, waiting for Sarah's reply.

Sarah had no idea why she'd thought of these things. She felt her mouth quivering and a little twitch in the corner of her left eye started to move with its own birdlike pulse.

"I think knuckles because there's a picture of my father standing on a ladder about to paint our porch. I remember the ladder, and I remember my father's hands in the picture."

"And?" Nora Sampson prodded.

"And he painted the porch. And I felt proud that he did things for the family."

Then Sarah watched the couple next to her in awed silence. If her child died, she'd want time to stop and for there to be silence forever in every peopled room. She felt guilty for attracting too much attention. Why had she been so vague?

"I think I said diapers," she continued, "because they remind me of earlier years of my marriage, when things were very bad between me and my husband. He was seeing someone else."

"And radishes?"

"I don't know."

"Well," Nora began, "radishes are edible roots. They're also very bitter. Are you thinking of them in terms of their bitterness?"

"I don't think I can explain it."

Nora Sampson turned her attention to the couple. "Anything beyond your child's toys?"

"An intern holding a chart," the man said. "The night my son died I almost punched a Korean intern. She kept saying she was sorry. She kept sticking her face in mine. She didn't know Nick. She was just there on the night that he died. And the intern couldn't say it right. 'I solly,' she said, and I hit a wall."

"You'd have felt better if you had punched her," Jeremy Bone Shoulder said.

"I haven't felt better for one minute in seven months. I can't imagine how hitting that poor woman could have helped," Reed shrugged.

"Sounds like Mr. Shoulder thinks violence is a solution," the irrepressible Pipkin added summarily.

"It's fairly typical to displace anger onto any convenient person who looks different from you," Jeremy Bone Shoulder explained. "I was thinking about *The Stranger*."

"What stranger?" Pipkin queried.

"Camus's novel."

"Why were you thinking about that?" Nora asked.

"After he hears that his mother has died, he goes to the beach and kills an Arab. That's what people do. Arabs, Blacks, Indians, whoever is handy and doesn't look like them, is fair game."

"I don't get it," pouted Mrs. Pipkin.

"Let's talk about it later." Nora Sampson turned her attention to the woman closest to the door, who was getting ready to leave. She was rattling items in her large carry-all as noisily as she could. It sounded like the bag contained brass, beads, porcelain, and lead.

"Miss Sevrenson, are you leaving before our time is up?"

"My boyfriend's in Boston and you're talking about radishes." She stormed out the door and slammed it behind her.

"How did you know her name?" Mrs. Pipkin asked.

"She's been in this group before."

"We'll all be that healthy if we come every Thursday?"

• • •

Driving home, Sarah thought about doctors, who make radishes look as obvious as fire hydrants. After all, her friend Rachel had chosen a psychiatrist because he was an alcoholic and drug addict. She claimed it made him more thoughtful. She also loved his eyes, which were the color of Rob Roys. Maybe, if Rachel didn't offer the most unlikely opinions, Sarah would have confided in her more. Sarah felt calmer in the car at night, when people were obscured and objects reached eminence. She saw neon the color of violets on a hardware-store window and didn't think about her father.

"GET SOME SLEEP, SARAH. There's nothing more we can do tonight," Jeremy told her as she waited in their hotel room for her sister to answer the phone.

"Fat chance," she said. "Ever since we've gotten off the plane, all I can think is how I lost my father last spring and now I've lost Carrie." Leaning back, she closed her eyes, uninterested in the details of their temporary surroundings at the University Hilton. Her body stretched out on the harlequin bedspread, and her head found its way to the hard little pillow. "I was hoping we'd find them tonight, Jeremy."

"We will. Tomorrow."

"I'll phone Mae again."

"They're probably still out looking too. Get some rest, please."

"As soon as it's morning we'll go to Mae's."

"As soon as the sun comes up."

FRIDAY

MAE AND TONY lived in a small bungalow in Santa Monica Canyon. When they had bought it for sixty thousand dollars twenty-two years ago from a man who had made big advances in underwater photography, it had been expensive. Now the stuccoed peach-colored walls, the red Spanish tile roof, and the sprawling rhododendrons were worth at least two million.

"You may not like them," Sarah warned Jeremy as he drove their rented Ford Probe, like a gray shark, down the steep hill to their driveway.

"A public relations firm couldn't help build the image of the folks who produced Deenie the way you've described her. Which one does she get the green hair from?"

"Mae's hair's black like Deenie's. Tony's hair is salt and pepper. Green must be recessive."

"We'll get Carrie and leave."

"I hope to God she's there. What if she isn't?"

"Then she's somewhere else, Sarah. We'll find her," he said taking her hand and pressing it.

She leaned against Jeremy while they waited for someone to answer the door. It was barely six A.M. and a pale yellow haze hung over the canyon. Dew had settled over everything on the lawn. The plastic-wrapped morning paper seemed swathed in gauze. The doormat to her sister's home proclaimed SHIT HAPPENS. Sarah was about to point it out to Jeremy when they saw a car pull up in the driveway.

Tony and Mae were seated in a vintage Cadillac the color of salmon about to be thawed. The silver trim was polished to highlight the menacing sweep of its tail fins, the white vinyl top was down, and the interior was crushed gray velvet—tacky but sexual.

Sarah approached the car as if it were a bizarre throne. Leaning over Mae's side, she hugged her.

"Tony, Mae, this is Jeremy Bone Shoulder."

"I've heard so much about you!" Mae extended a long arm in Jeremy's direction and squeezed the hand he offered.

Tony opened a Heineken and took another bottle from a silver ice bucket next to him on the seat. He handed one to Jeremy in an oblique welcoming gesture.

"Want one, Sarah?"

"At six in the morning?"

Two sisters couldn't have looked less related. Mae's hair showed a little gray, but her face was young and open to things, striving to be amused. Her eyes were dark and serious but so wide-spaced that they gave her the calm gaze of a good and trusting child. Some lines around the mouth were noticeable, but more than aging her, they had pulled her frivolous mouth into unity with her eyes. Sarah's own eyes were light green and smaller. Her best feature was her mouth, which knew when to speak and how to appear about to say something. Since adolescence, she had viewed her hair as an aberration. It made a nuisance of itself by falling out of pins and spilling over collars. Remembering that Jeremy had called it the color of overripe peaches, she felt her face color.

"This is Bulletin," Mae said tapping the car door. "Don't you think that's a good name for it?"

Sarah felt nausea and fatigue rise and swell in her stomach. She had known as soon as she saw Mae that the girls were still missing. "Where are they?" she nearly wailed, checking the impulse to scream when disappointment clutched at her throat.

"They weren't on any plane all night," Tony sighed. "We just got back from the airport. An investigator from the airlines will call us in the morning. I have good connections in transportation. There'll be people monitoring all the carriers for the next twenty-four hours. I've provided a description of the girls and a photo of Deenie."

"It's not a very good photo," Mae sighed. "It shows Deenie's natural hair color."

"These people are professionals. If those girls get on or off a plane anywhere in the United States, they'll be spotted. Don't worry. Those people have found terrorists with facial corrections. They're that good, Sarah."

"Facial corrections?" Sarah asked. It was odd that language intrigued her even when it offered no hope.

"New nose, fake scars, disguises, Sarah."

"Meanwhile, I thought you'd like to see our car," Mae soothed. Her mouth held the words so long that she seemed to be talking in a fake Texas accent. It was obvious she'd been drinking. A version of "Lady Madonna" dense with strings surged through the car stereo.

"I can't stand this waiting," Sarah said hovering on the asphalt. Would Tony and Mae ever get out of their car? The meeting began to take on the dreamlike detachment of unwanted news filtered through sleeplessness.

"What are we thinking, Mae?" Mae asked of herself. "Let's go inside. Sarah, Jeremy?"

Tony lofted himself out of the car and led them into the front room through the garage.

"Have I told you my theory?" Mae asked. She was reclining on a Navajo floor pillow and playing with one of her earrings.

"What's that, Mae?" Sarah was seated on a low sofa the color of the inside of seashells. Above her was a large photo of two women, one older than the other, though otherwise identical. They both held their faces in their hands.

"Remember when we were little?"

Sarah's attention etched itself on Mae's face.

"Well, my theory's this. You were always my sidekick when we were growing up. I'd take one step and hear two behind me. I wanted to think that if I turned around it would be someone else, like Sneezy the Dwarf. But it was always you with your crazy hair and sad little mouth. If it weren't for that mouth of yours, I'd have protested to Mom. But you always looked like you were about to break into pieces around your chin. That's one nice feature, Sarah. You wear everything on your face like a message on a cake."

"I don't understand," Sarah said. She looked helplessly out of the corner of her eye at Jeremy who was seated across from her in a pale blue loveseat. His head was back, and his eyelids were trying to fight off sleep.

"She wants to know what this has to do with Deenie," Tony translated.

"I'm getting to that. It's like square roots. A number by itself can't do much. Put it next to another one and you have it to the nth power. Kids get in league with each other and do things they wouldn't do otherwise."

"Didn't you notice that Deenie was having trouble before you sent her to me?"

"Sure she was. She was seeing Dr. Weber twice a week," Mae said, shooting Tony a rather deft spiteful glance, "but I don't see much progress. He said her self-image is unmoored. He called what he was doing 'anchoring therapy.' You'd think he was a former navy man. And of course," Mae added, staring ahead and massaging her profile, "Deenie has a little eating problem too."

"Wouldn't you guess that she planned this before she left home? She had to work hard to run away, Mae. She took her plane ticket and changed the reservation. She had to help Carrie buy a ticket. They had to escape the house with luggage. They must have set it for Thanksgiving, when we'd all be distracted."

"How do you know that Carrie didn't convince her?" Tony cross-examined.

"I just know, Tony. Carrie's not an adventurous girl." Sarah pulled Carrie's note out of her pocket and handed it to Tony. "Read this."

"Where are they?" Tony demanded.

"If the girls are coming back to Los Angeles, it won't be Sycamore Drive," Jeremy said. "Someone must be meeting them. Why else would they come back?"

"I'll kill him!" Mae shouted, fists clenching in her lap.

"Mae, he's only telling us what he thinks, and I'd have to agree that Deenie has no reason to run back to us."

"I don't mean Jeremy. I mean Branch."

"Who's Branch?" Tony questioned.

"Branch is this tall person."

"That Deenie's seeing?"

"Yes."

"And you haven't mentioned him to us?"

"Who's us?"

"Me or Dr. Weber?" Tony asked shaking his head.

"Does Branch have a car?" Jeremy asked.

"What kid doesn't?" Tony said.

"How can someone you don't know exists suddenly have a car, Tony?" Mae snapped. Silence filled the room like tear gas. A few seconds later she added, "It's not easy to raise kids alone. Tony's job . . ." she began to explain to Jeremy, then looked too bored to continue. She held her head in her hands and shook it ponderously from side to side. "He does have a car, by the way."

"He's probably meeting them somewhere," Jeremy explained. "If they aren't on a plane, they'll be on a bus or a train. Our job will be to meet them first."

"I've checked on all buses and trains out of Chicago. Nothing could arrive here before Saturday night at eighteen hours," Tony said.

"Can't we have buses searched?" Sarah asked.

"Every bus in the country, Sarah?" Tony asked. "Even if we check buses heading west, it means fourteen of them over this week-end. And according to the police, the girls aren't officially missing yet, not for thirty-six hours."

Sarah went to the kitchen to pour herself some water and Mae followed her out of the room.

"Don't ever let him hit you!" she said to Sarah in a voice that juggled outrage and commiseration.

Sarah had forgotten about her cheek until Mae mentioned it. "Who?" Sarah asked.

"That Jeremy," Mae said, and broke into throaty sobs that tumbled onto the counter.

Pressing Mae's head onto her shoulder, Sarah smoothed her curls. "Jeremy didn't hit me, Mae."

"Then who did?"

"Larry. On Thanksgiving."

"That prick. Why did he do that?"

"He knows about me and Jeremy."

"So what? You know about him and a cast of thousands." Then she lowered her voice. "Tony's a world-class jerk too," Mae whispered, "but he never hit me."

Mae stared out of her kitchen window. A yellow finch was sitting on an unfruited branch of the lemon tree.

"Look, Sarah," Mae said, pointing to the bird and dabbing at her eyes with her wrist. "Nature abhors a vacuum."

Smiling at her sister's strange observation, Sarah was struck by how sad and fatigued Mae looked. It frightened Sarah to see Mae this way. "Let's have some coffee," Sarah said soothingly, taking her sister's hand and leading her into the dining room.

SARAH ADORED MAE as only little sisters can. Her own adolescence seemed altogether less substantial. Was it Mae's sense of style or Sarah's angle that provided the special lighting and the longer afterimage? Sarah remembered Mae's senior prom better than her own, how her sister's black hair was pressed into a French roll with two gardenias, one at her neck and one at her crown for emphasis, how she had painstakingly sewn blue sequins and seed pearls together to make a narrow belt for her satin gown. Ivy still kept the photo of Mae and Tony on her bookshelves in its yellowing plastic frame. Sarah would lie in bed on lazy Sunday mornings with Mae's old sketchpads, getting her index finger dirty tracing the charcoal lines of Mae's fashion designs. Mae would design women in bumblebee-striped sheaths or draw bathing suits of wolf fur. Sarah colored in the model's long torsos and legs and provided them with features, a detail Mae routinely ignored.

There'd been no jealousy between the girls, no feuds to be settled by parents or outsiders. Sarah's devotion was limitless. In fantasies of danger and rescue, Sarah would pull her sister from bedrooms where curtains blazed and smoked, or, with superhuman strength, carry her unconscious down creaking jerry-built gutters. When the Cuban missile crisis loomed and American schoolchildren sat at their slick blond desks awaiting annihilation, Sarah prayed that Mae, rather than herself, wouldn't suffer.

When Sarah was thirteen and Mae seventeen, she met Tony at a Christmas dance, where Mae had gone reluctantly with a neighbor's visiting niece. Tony attended a prestigious Catholic seminary high school that was supposed to prepare boys for the priesthood. Actually, its youthful staff, many with red Triumphs and family wealth to burn, spent their weekends taking the seniors to parties on the North Shore or driving to Lake Geneva for all-night beer blasts. They were a wild but celibate fraternity; Mae had been Tony's first girl-friend.

It was the summer before Tony was supposed to enter a seminary in Beloit that Sarah spent eavesdropping at Mae's bedroom door. At bedtime she'd rehearse even their most uninspired lines. She practiced putting her sister's dramatic inflection on her own words, and answering Mae's flirtatious queries with Tony's hesitant syllables. By the end of the summer, the door to Mae's bedroom was locked, and Tony was planning to go to Notre Dame for a degree in engineering.

Sarah guessed that it wasn't love as much as amazement that they could be lovable that had drawn Mae and Tony together. Both had spent their high-school years cloistered. Mae had too little concern for the opinions of others to be popular, so her friends had been the more interesting outcasts of the class. Sarah preferred Caroline Mouleter to Gloria Robling. Caroline, whose bowl haircut lasted through her senior graduation. Caroline's parents refused to buy a television. Instead, her father, a University of Chicago professor, took them camping on weekends. Once Sarah had joined Mae and Caroline's family for a frigid Thanksgiving weekend in Starved Rock State Park. Caroline knew all the constellations, and she helped her father take celestial measurements with a caliper Sarah later recognized as similar to an obstetrical instrument used for measuring fetal size. In the chilly tent where they could see their breath, they ate barbecued acorn squash. Then they sang an African folk song and seemed to consent, by sleepy compliance to verse after mimeographed verse, that they were having fun.

Gloria, "a change-of-life baby," as Ivy had explained to Sarah, was the only child of Gretel Robling, a widow who sweated profusely. Even on short car excursions, Gloria had to roll down the windows to offset her mother's ability to emanate heat. The Robling home was kept so cold that Gloria studied in mittens. Mrs. Robling spent her days pining for Hugo, who'd worked in a small munitions plant until his death. Her grief was so profound that Gloria had gotten lost in it. On Christmas her mother would buy her a new nightgown, which she'd place unwrapped under the Christmas tree. All the tree ornaments were memorabilia of Mrs. Robling's marriage: tiny leather canoes bought at the Wisconsin Dells, a knitted monkey from the South Pacific, where Hugo had served in the war. If Mae hadn't been handy with a sewing machine, Gloria would have worn the same brown corduroy sack jumper and orange turtleneck sweater all through high school.

Ivy's loving scrutiny served to normalize Mae's friendships. She provided pocket money for trips to the bargain basement of Marshall Field's on the condition that Sarah could tag along. Once, on a blizzardy Saturday, Sarah had watched Mae shoplift a whole purseful of sequins and odd-shaped maroon buttons. Then, in the ladies' lounge, empty on such a wretched afternoon, the girls had used Caroline's Swiss Army knife to share a day-old plum pie latticed with cinnamon icing, which they'd purchased with pooled funds. Later, Ivy treated the girls to birthday gifts of beauty-shop manicures and beaded satin dress purses in the shape of open fans for their future glamorous lives.

In the same way that Ivy engineered the girls' adolescence, Mae had shaped Tony. Though his reticence around the family was painful, it provided Mae with what she needed, room to work. After their intense summer love, Tony had been designed into what Mae wanted, a well-trained boyfriend with no former experience. He wore the clothes Mae selected, and, with no comparisons to draw upon, worshipped her simply and wholly. At Sarah's distance, their relationship seemed complete and intricate as a rose-covered trellis, blessed by cultivation as much as art.

At Mae's wedding two years later, Sarah had sprained her ankle pitching forward to snatch the bridal bouquet from Gloria's hands. Pretending that she'd marry next was immaterial. She didn't know how she'd survive her sister's absence without the flowers, which she'd planned to use as the focal point of her dresser shrine, along with peacock feathers, votive candles, and a rummage-sale incense burner. As her heel gave way, the blood left her face. She lay on the floor in perfect misery, clutching her ankle while the band played a syrupy "Moon River." Gloria, whose neck was so long that she appeared to be carrying her own head on a platter, displayed the bouquet like the spoils of war.

Soon Sarah was kissing boys' awkward lips and going to dances in stuffy gymnasiums smelling of fresh varnish and fruit punch. She dated now and then, and had a variety of gangly friends, boys and girls alike, but no real boyfriend during high school. She wasn't sure she'd be asked to the prom and didn't even start thinking about it until most of her friends had already bought their dresses. When she was asked at the last minute by Stuart Fisher, whose outrageous irrelevancies filled deadly gaps in their American history class, she thought about Mae's gown.

Ivy insisted that the waist was too low for her and the small capped sleeves were out of style. When she pointed to rips in the fabric near the zipper and coaxed one along with her thumbnail as illustration of its fragility, Sarah consented to buy a new dress. She picked the first one off the rack that fit her, a yellow chiffon with a strapless avocado lace bodice. She thought the unusual colors would highlight her hair. "I'm going to the prom with Miss Autumnal Equinox," Stuart quipped in the lunchroom when Sarah described her gown. Sarah laughed too, mainly because it was of no importance to her whatsoever what she would be wearing.

Pressing her hair into a French roll, she spent hours in her bathrobe, admiring the back of her head, where she had placed a single gardenia at her crown. Several hours before Stuart picked her up in his father's fat black Buick Electra, she found her tawdry bridesmaid's bouquet under her bed, a heap of dust and stiff ribbon. Sweeping it into the trash can, she felt how profoundly she still missed Mae.

It was obvious early in the marriage that Tony had outgrown Mae's intensive summer training. There were hints of trouble shortly after the marriage began when, to the disbelief of the entire family, Tony volunteered for a second tour of duty in Vietnam. Not even his father-in-law, a hawk on the war, had applauded Tony's zeal. He became a communications specialist for a general, an assignment with special security clearance and a certain amount of vagueness attached to it. When Sarah asked Tony what he had done in the war, he left the first person out of the reply and talked about "deployment capabilities." "Technically, I wasn't in Vietnam," he intimated to her another time. If he hadn't been "technically" in Vietnam or with Mae, where had he spent most of his twenties? Maybe in Laos, where, Mae once confided, he'd worked for Air America. It was dizzying for Sarah to believe that innocent Tony, initiated into sex in her own sister's bedroom, had worked in intelligence. Didn't CIA operatives drive Maseratis and carry vials of life-snuffing chemicals? Could Tony, in his big blue Chrysler, button-down shirts, and Timex watches, actually be a spy? Sarah tried to rationalize her brother-in-law's vocation by connecting his seminary past to his quasi-military present. After all, both are secret societies with languages women can't officially speak.

Before Mae and Tony had settled down and had Deenie, they'd lived apart for nearly seven years, years Mae stoically endured. She never admitted hurt at his absence. Instead, she defended Tony's equivocal bond and even justified it to Sarah: "Tony has a very sensitive job," she'd say, or, "Tony's a man's man." She set about to "broaden her experience," a goal she approached like a blind dart player, taking random courses from Botany and Bio-ethics to Heidegger and the Human Dilemma at the local college; by working at a Christian-owned winery and a Shriners children's hospital; and by restoring every inch of natural wood in their house, even in closets, where no one would ever see it. Tony's hair was a dignified silver at the temples the next time Sarah saw him, shortly after Deenie's birth, and he still kept his black penny loafers polished to a military brightness. She wouldn't say he was willfully aloof, but there seemed to be a learned posture, a tightness of the spine, that signified unquestionable resolve. Insignificant actions like lighting a cigarette seemed overly precise and intimidating. Sarah took it as an insult to Mae that Tony flaunted the many ways he'd transcended her training.

Sarah tried to blame Tony and his frequent absences for Mae's increasingly obvious imperfections. Beyond Mae and Tony's marriage, which had grown over the years into a series of serio-comic vignettes framed by his departures, Sarah found scant evidence that her sister existed anymore. What happened in the latest episode was recounted to Sarah on the phone in weekly set pieces that sounded like plot summaries from *TV Guide*. All that Mae would have needed was canned laughter and orchestration for a full production.

"Tony's done it again" was the refrain. Then Mae would relate how he'd tried to build a miniature greenhouse for lilies and ended up closing himself inside the geodesic dome, or how he had brought home a suitcase of women's clothes instead of his own from a recent trip to Miami.

Sometimes, without much of a response, Sarah invited Mae to talk about herself, but it would have been a breach of decorum to interrupt Mae's presentation of her life. There was a strained propriety imposed by Mae's silent command. Sarah was still the younger sister who had to respect the distance Mae inflicted upon them.

Tony's specialty for the FAA, which had hired him the same year Deenie had been born, was "human error." He was sent to disaster sites to calculate formulas for failure. It was his job to listen to the black box, assess the crew's actions, and rule on its liability. Sarah imagined his professional life to be a haunting debate between free will and determinism. He had become so expert that he frequently testified before Congress, and other countries borrowed him to investigate unusual circumstances. Mae had called Sarah in tears, when, on their twentieth anniversary, Tony was ten miles outside of Glasgow investigating the aftermath of a hostage situation in which lives had been lost. Sarah tried to have sympathy for Tony, burdened as he was. If teaching Melville to business students could depress her about human limitations, the rigors of Tony's job must tear him apart. On this occasion Mae had been less forgiving, claiming that her increasingly self-important husband loved the attention. "Whenever I picture Tony, it's not in bed with me or even sitting at the kitchen table anymore. He's inspecting a heap of bent metal with a calculator in his hand. And do you know what, Sarah? I always see him smiling. I'm married to the Grim Reaper!" When Sarah questioned further, the lid closed on the case.

Sarah did learn at one point that Tony had had a long and

serious affair with a British military attaché named Anita Lowns. "He's undressing a fucking soldier!" Mae had sobbed from the only working pay phone at a tiny Caribbean airport. This had been Mae's one emotional moment of confession to her sister all those years. Sarah assumed the affair had continued, but Mae never spoke of it. Her stories of late spun into areas that were nearly hilarious, especially since Tony, encouraged by Deenie's psychiatrist, who was a personal friend, had joined a men's group who spent weekends "discovering themselves" at an ex-Trappist monastery. On all fours, the men would cover themselves in animal dung and howl like wolves in an attempt to regain primal links to their fathers. Mae said Tony blamed his failures on his father, and on the Industrial Revolution more specifically, which had severed the bond of father to son. He'd had no mentor, he'd sobbed to Mae one night after a particularly intense male getaway weekend that included a choral reading of Whitman's "Song of Myself." Since Tony's daily failings and miscues were the only domain Mae could rule, they became her art form over the years. Sarah could see Mae on a stage, a Gracie Allen without a straight man. Sarah wondered if all storytellers aren't desperately trying to appropriate imaginary parts of people they love but can't own.

IF ADRIAN FISHBLATT'S EYES hadn't been the color of green olives, one of Deenie's formerly favorite snacks, she would have fallen asleep just over the Iowa border. As it was, her head wouldn't cooperate with her monumental effort to stay awake during his numbing conversation. Sleep was a fulcrum. While her eyes pulled her alert, her neck gave in, lurching her head forward onto her chest, where she'd steady it and refocus her eyes. She felt like she was playing catch with herself. Worse yet, much of what Adrian said meant nothing to her. Right now, for instance, he was telling her that writers couldn't be trusted, which was ironic, given that's what he planned to be in Los Angeles.

"So the woman goes up to him and sticks out her tongue. She

makes a pig nose with her fingers. She dances around him and waves her nails in his face. She makes horns on his head. Then she whispers to her companion that he certainly is blind."

Chewing his nail between thin smiling lips, he paused for a long time, too amused to continue. "And then her friend points to the door. Ved Mehta has finally arrived. The person she was making herself an ass in front of was V. S. Naipaul, who can see as well as you or I."

"Pretty funny," Deenie said without laughing. How could someone so handsome be so boring? She wanted to know his sign and whether he favored winter colors like she did. She wanted to know if he had a girlfriend.

"But the point I'm making is that the story's apocryphal. Later that semester I was talking to a visiting writer, a poet from Australia. He told the same anecdote with minor variations. Instead of a book party in New York, it was a literary conference in Melbourne."

Deenie didn't understand the meaning of *apocryphal,* but it sounded pretty negative. "Couldn't this blind guy get mistaken again and again for the guy who sees? I mean, with two Indian writers in one room, anything can happen."

Adrian looked out his window and shook his head. Maybe the Platte River was more complex than she thought, but Deenie had never seen a person smirking at a river.

"The way you interpret my story reminds me of a scene from Buñuel. A man sees a dog being mistreated. The dog is tied to a cart that another man's pulling. The wheels are turning so fast that the dog's actually being dragged along. Feeling pity for the animal, he gives the owner all the money in his wallet to buy the dog. He begins walking down the road with his new pet on a leash. Ten seconds later he sees a different man with a cart abusing a dog in the same manner." Adrian slapped his knee. "Buñuel's wicked that way."

"That's really a coincidence," Deenie said. She pointed an instructive finger at Adrian. "I told you things can repeat themselves. Take my cousin, for instance. She's running away because she knows her mother's having an affair, and her parents' marriage is ending. She thinks she can bring her parents together by doing something drastic. But it's just like the story of the dogs. If her mom doesn't leave her dad for this current guy, whose name is, *get this,* Jeremy Bone Shoulder, she'll just find someone else later, and maybe he'll be worse."

"Is this *guy* an American Indian?"

"He sure is."

"Are you running away too?"

"Not really. I'm meeting a friend in Los Angeles and going on from there."

"Do your parents know?"

"They're the ones I'm meeting." She glanced nervously at Carrie to make sure she was asleep, then warmed up to her lie. "My mom, that is. Mom's a real friend to me, and she's also an actress. She's been shooting in Europe for nearly a year. My dad died in Greece last month. He was helping to restore the Acropolis and took a terrible fall. After I meet Mom, we're going to fly back to Greece together and toss Dad's ashes into the Pacific. He loved Greece so."

"You mean the Aegean."

"What am I saying?" Deenie scratched her scalp in real confusion, then smoothed her hair in feigned composure. "I must have been thinking of California."

"I'm somewhat of a Grecophile myself, though economic considerations have restricted my travel since I got out of college. That's why I'm eager to sell this script."

"When did you get out of college?" Deenie asked, relieved she was finally going to learn something meaningful, his age.

"Two years ago I finished. I've been writing ever since."

"What's your script about?"

"It's a Surrealist-influenced love farce with Mozartian resonances. Of course, there's a lot of costuming and a play within a play involving mistaken identities like in *A Midsummer Night's Dream.* It would be considered mainstream in France. There's been some interest in it here among a small film group. Get this," he said, smiling at Deenie as he mimicked her earlier phrasing. "The group's called Quicksilver. I hope they're not a bunch of airheads still high from the sixties. Or New Age, God forbid."

"Are you French?"

"French via Fond du Lac." His laugh sounded bitter. "And you?"

"We're Alsatian," Deenie proclaimed, thinking of her dog, Breezer.

"On which side?"

Deenie considered her options as Adrian searched the contents of a canvas bag and pulled out some grapes.

"Care for some?"

"Thanks, no."

"I'll take some."

It figured that Carrie wouldn't acknowledge that she was awake until food was the issue. She pressed her fat self over Deenie and held greedy palms toward Adrian, who placed a large, sweaty bunch in her hands.

"Deenie, I wish you'd told me there were grapes."

"Adrian, this is my cousin Carrie; Carrie, Adrian. He's a scriptwriter."

"Pleased to meet you, Carrie."

"My dad's a writer too. His specialty is Rembrandt Harmenszoon van Rijn."

"Who?" Deenie asked.

"You know, Rembrandt, like in the cartoon Rembrandt van Rainbow."

"I think I remember him," Deenie nodded.

"Are you Alsatian too?"

Carrie looked at Deenie for a clue. Deenie stared resolutely ahead. "My dad's Protestant and my mom's an atheist," she finally said. "Do you happen to have more grapes, Adrian?"

BACK FROM MAE'S, in the motel room at the University Hilton, unable to take a nap though limp with fatigue, Sarah thought about Larry, who had said once that she sounded like a loon when she cried. She had never known what a loon sounded like. She had been raised in the city, and her expertise in nature was confined to dandelions and cottonwood seeds that filled the empty lots Chicagoans call prairies. When she was little, milkweed, as sticky as semen, would get on her hands. Her parents had been the children of immigrants. They couldn't afford nature, but one summer when Sarah was eleven, they had sent the girls to scout camp for a week. Sarah and Mae had ridden a school bus barely beyond the newly constructed western suburbs to a flat tract of weedy, hard dirt surrounded by pines. Sarah had her first period there, but she didn't even tell Mae. Instead, she stuffed toilet paper between her legs. Another girl, Bonnie, had stomach flu. She and Sarah were a natural pair, spending their week in the woods sequestered in the latrine, where giant carpenter ants crawled out of the floorboards reeking of pine cleaner and mildew. The cheap paper chafed her skin, making her feel wet and itchy at the same time. To Sarah, nature still had the faint odor of the latrine.

She already knew what a period was. The Body Doctor had told her. A dapper elderly man, he came to her scout troop every spring, his portable plastic model of a uterus lodged in his suit pocket. Every year she saw the same film narrated by a woman with a strange Canadian accent: "Around eleven to fifteen years old, you will notice your body filling *oot.*" Maybe *oot* was the sound a loon made.

Mae always imagined that the Body Doctor would get mugged. Together they'd enact the scene at the police station when he tried to reclaim his possession. Like the urban myths of dead cats left in shoeboxes on el trains, the surprised thief would go home with what he thought was plunder.

About the same time as scout camp, Sarah had kissed a boy. Forrest was the first black student at the Crown Grammar School. He'd been invited to Linda Gordon's twelfth birthday party as a hoax by one of the meaner boys, who knew that kissing games would be played. It happened during the freeze dance when the music stopped. The kiss was wet and more than childlike. As soon as Sarah kissed him, the game ended. The same boys who made jokes about sperm whales and *Moby Dick* carried the story home.

In school the following Monday, Miss Normandy hissed between her clenched teeth. Looking back, Sarah knew Miss Normandy was an aging virgin, which made her flirtatious with her best students, both male and female; and servile to their whims. Up until that moment, Sarah had been her favorite.

"You should have known better," Miss Normandy whispered.

At recess, from which Sarah was held back, Miss Normandy went on to explain the dangers: "First they come to your parties, then they take over your neighborhoods, and who is left?" Miss Normandy, addressing Negro children, who didn't know the first thing about Chicago history, up from the South, fresh as new pennies. And where does interracial kissing lead? To interracial dating, interracial marriage, the collapse of civilization as it was pictured in their social-studies books.

Forrest distanced himself from the other children, and the incident passed. Sarah remembered watching him standing at the playground fence kicking dust up with a pointy black slip-on shoe, different from those worn by the other boys.

She had spoken to him only one more time that year. The day her grandmother died, Stanley's mother, who was cow-eyed and eternally sad like religious statues, Sarah was playing alone in the prairie before chapel. Forrest was there with his little sister. They had found a garter snake that he held stretched between his arms like green bicycle handles. Sarah told him that her grandmother had died. *So?* he said. Then he and his sister left.

Sarah thought about Forrest at the oddest moments. When she'd first met Jeremy, she'd told him the entire story. It had been her first kiss and he had the right to know.

Until Jeremy there'd been only Larry. The worst year of her life, the year Scotty was born, they were living in a studio apartment on Arlington Street. Larry was finishing his Ph.D. on Dutch painting, and spending many nights at the library. Sarah could still see the fleur-de-lis oilcloth covering the Amvets card table she used to change the baby. She remembered picking Scotty up and carrying him, half-diapered, to the phone, when someone named Donna called one evening. From the moment she heard Donna's voice, haughty and embarrassed at the same time, Sarah knew that Larry was having an affair.

At a party a few weeks later, she saw Donna's blunt brown hair and small blue eyes and thought of the small Rouault painting of Jesus. Donna spoke in fits and starts, as if her speech were a seismographic chart of the thought process she used to arrive at it. Larry, who'd met her in a seminar on Dürer when he was a graduate as-

sistant, must have felt honored she'd chosen him, considering her
usual pained reticence. At one party there'd been endless equivocation
between beer or white wine. Then there was a summer of midnight
phone calls to Larry about which of her three fellowships to accept
for the fall. In September, award in hand, Donna vanished from their
lives. She would study art in Rome and later produce a workmanlike
study of Tintoretto. As Sarah glanced through its pages during a
miserably rainy spring many years later, she could still hear Donna's
halting miserly voice.

With Donna safely in Rome, Larry said he was sorry for the
months he'd spent at his office with her. They had enjoyed a do-
mesticity so exotic that Sarah could feel him miss it even as he told
her otherwise. He felt it honorable that they had confined their affair
to the tall faculty office building. Sarah was supposed to appreciate
the Berlin Wall of discretion that he'd built around that aspect of
his life. How could she be furious when he had been so fastidious?

In the dead of the coldest winter in fifty years, Sarah would take
insane rides down Lake Shore Drive, pushing the accelerator up to
sixty-five. Sometimes she'd blast the Rolling Stones and shout Donna's name as her car rounded the notorious S-curve. Six months
pregnant with Carrie that spring, Sarah would load Scotty in his used
infant seat and drive to the car wash, with its giant abomination of
a sign, paying her ninety-nine cents for the privilege of screaming at
the top of her lungs that she hated Larry under the pounding water
of the mechanism.

The pressure to leave Larry grew just before Carrie was born.
Sarah would walk to the newsstand and buy a variety of neighborhood papers to consider cheap apartments to sublet. It seemed that
whole areas of the city were awaiting women with lousy husbands,
small children, part-time teaching jobs, and no money. Sarah pictured
the pleasant *Sesame Street* barrio as a possible site for her new life.
She began surveying areas that she imagined resembled it. Logan
Square and Wicker Park, with their lively mixture of Polish and
Puerto Rican bakeries, bridal shops, and street gangs, were possibilities. She was about to telephone a studio that advertised free
utilities near Chicago and Ashland when her water bag broke. Standing on a soaked circle of carpet, she telephoned Larry at school. He

rushed from his office to sit with her during hours of unproductive labor that culminated in an emergency C-section because the baby was in distress.

Carrie had been born four weeks early. Although she weighed enough to go home at the end of the week, she was so small at five and a half pounds that she was constantly hungry. Carrie's need replaced Sarah's own. Nursing frantically, Carrie would gasp for breath between tugs on Sarah's swollen nipple, her round little face turning red with greedy effort. It was Sarah's fate, she reasoned, not to leave.

With Larry's pillow another galaxy, Sarah would take Carrie into their bed and nurse her, remembering those times when her heart had accelerated, hearing her parents speak angrily to each other late at night. She had wanted to think as a child that the universe had stopped when she went to sleep. Now she realized there had been a living theater in the next room. The crickets might have heard it, or the ants might have noticed as they trekked in a thin line to the garbage. Now that she was estranged from Larry, her own past had a new interpreter.

Carrie's birth made Sarah feel an exquisite pain close to martyrdom. During the previous months that Larry had been with Donna, Sarah would hold Scotty, who was barely one, and sing him her perverse lullaby: *We're all alone, we're all alone.* Now, when she looked at Carrie in rare moments of sleep in her wicker basinette, she thought how much she hated television and movies for portraying motherhood as a trivial comedy. Perhaps that was the biggest lie of her TV-viewing childhood. Motherhood is the French Foreign Legion for women, protecting a child beyond love. The two bodies that came out of her were hers to mourn forever.

She had never expressed this feeling to Larry. Even with Donna gone forever, they had lain in bed experiencing separate dream states. The space where they never collided grew larger until there was a severance beyond blame. She had been tolerant of him. They had tolerated. If they'd never had children they might have reconstructed a life together that was worthy of praise, a work of art in itself, like the exquisite closeness of Russell to John. Thriving on attention to details, her officemate's "marriage" was a four-star hotel with fresh brioche for breakfast, jonquils in crystal vases, and silk sheets to dream on. But Sarah and Larry's love had grown smaller until it was an amulet on a pillow, separate from blood and horror and the worst things she could imagine.

Before Carrie had run away, Sarah would invite panic by thinking of children lost in department stores, at beaches, to illness or war. She'd imagine a mustached general with hairy knuckles seated in her kitchen, where he'd watch her do simple things like make coffee. He was waiting for her to slip up so he could take Scotty and Carrie away. Now that Carrie was really gone, she knew that the peril couldn't have been anticipated. It had come masked as another child lost to her mother. Deenie's visit had ended Sarah's marriage to Larry. What they'd felt all those years had finally been expressed. Carrie's innocent letter had made a burlesque of their guile, without which their marriage couldn't continue.

All those years of estrangement, they'd made love amid towels and loose change and books. They'd bought dirt and transplanted things. She remembered the ceremony of unwinding the little metal tie coated in plastic that closed the bag of potting soil while Larry spread newspaper on the floor. Once she'd lifted an ivy plant out of its small, dove-shaped clay pot. Yellow as an old bruise, the leaves had been sagging, but when she'd gotten to the roots, they were tiny and unbranched. It had been a problem she couldn't detect. She recalled how, with her fingers covered in the store-bought dirt, she'd taken the plant and newspaper and stuffed them both in the garbage.

Some people are greedy for pain, Sarah thought. They chew on it until its taste is there day and night. It was possible that Larry had never loved her, and that Tony, locked in his dream of manhood, had deserted Mae long ago. How had her mother, whose own marriage appeared so stable, produced such wretched daughters? She thought of a version of *Beauty and the Beast* she used to read to the kids. She airbrushed in a beautiful and gracious mother to replace the kindly, unsuccessful father. Beauty, the blue rose, and the Beast were excised from the text. There stood Ivy, light shining off her face, between disappointing caricatures of her daughters, who couldn't marry properly or hold on to their children.

The night before in Mae and Tony's kitchen, Mae had shown Sarah a letter she'd received from Drew Ellis, a prison inmate who'd advertised in the *New York Review of Books* personals for a philosophical relationship with an MWF of any age. He was in a maximum-security prison in Nevada and they'd corresponded for seven years now. It was a wonderful irony that an armed robber, who'd wounded a gas-station attendant in a holdup when he was twenty-one, currently knew more about Mae than did Sarah. A mature thirty now, Drew specialized in advice about Tony. "Men," Drew had stated in small, perfect letters that marched straight across the lined penitentiary stationery with its forbidding logo of the impenetrable facade, "are of two kinds. Some hate the idea of women but can stand them in particular. Others hate women in particular and can't stand them in general either. Unfortunately, you seem to have chosen the latter in Mr. Tony Drucker."

Sarah looked fondly at Jeremy sleeping. She hoped that Drew's knowledge was incomplete. So as not to wake him, she peered out of the drapes. People outside the University Hilton were carrying briefcases and stopping to talk to friends. She wondered why ordinary life surprised her. She wondered why a greeting exchanged between a young man and woman on the curb seemed fraught with danger. In the courtyard of the hotel, a young woman was swimming determined laps in the tiny pool. The water seemed barely able to contain the efforts of her awkward strokes. Seven, eight, nine—Sarah counted for her until she grew bored.

It was one of those days when the moon doesn't completely vanish. A small, shadowy wedge perched in a corner of sky. Sarah remembered how as a little boy Scotty had called a streetlight the moon. Later, pointing to the real moon, high and gloomier in the sky, she had asked him to make a wish. "It's not real," Scotty had cried, shaking an angry fist.

She had told the story of Scotty's moon at the second session of grief therapy, and Nora Sampson had looked at her with amused eyes. In fact, her little parable about honesty and blame was about the only thing she remembered saying the entire evening.

The group hadn't been surprised that Miss Sevrenson didn't

return. Instead, there were two others, a Mr. Howard and Alan
Partanos, an assistant economics professor Sarah knew from some
library and environmental-safety committee work she'd done. Mr.
Howard was dignified and nicely dressed. He was the kind of man
Sarah imagined keeping a leather appointment book and riding in
taxicabs to luncheons at private clubs that probably didn't allow
women to be members. Nora Sampson looked terrific. She wore a
soft gray sweater dress that heightened the blue of her eyes.

"How are you tonight, Mr. Howard?" Nora fidgeted with some
notes after she'd introduced him to the others.

"Can't complain at the moment. But Edith's birthday's in three
weeks. We liked to go out for ice cream on her birthday. She liked
pralines and cream."

"From New Orleans," Mrs. Pipkin offered. "Very buttery. Did
she die of heart?"

"She had cancer. She died for a long time."

Jeremy Bone Shoulder shook his head and grimaced. "I hope I
go fast. Like a meteor." He imitated its curving trajectory with his
hand. "The problem with most Indians is they don't think about
dying. Being self-destructive's being optimistic, thinking you won't
die. They don't try to save themselves."

"You can only throw out ropes. If they want to drown . . ."
Pipkin looked at Jeremy with wide eyes.

"Since Linsey isn't here," Reed began, "I thought I'd tell you a
little more. One problem with Nick dying is that we hadn't planned
to have him. We both had careers. Linsey had to lower her sights to
be a good mother, and she was. She read to him before he could
hold up his head. He was a happy baby.

"A year ago he started acting funny. He was too tired to crawl
and he cried a lot. It turned out to be leukemia, not the kind that
kids catch and survive but the kind that kills you fast. You or I would
be statistically more likely to get it than Nick.

"We tried everything. We took him for experimental treatments.
We looked for a bone-marrow donor since neither of us was com-
patible. Nicky was just beginning to say words, and he was dying.
Each little word went up like a flare. It hurt so much I wanted him
to be quiet.

"After a few weeks, Linsey couldn't bring herself to visit him anymore. Nick was unconscious by then and didn't know she wasn't there, but Linsey felt awful.

"It's been four months now, and Linsey isn't leaving the house except to come here. Tonight she has a cold."

"All mothers love their children," Pipkin began. "Mothers in Chicago and mothers in Angola. Sometimes I think about that late at night. My sons are fifty. One's a salesman and homely, but he's still my boy. I don't know if I could live burying a son."

"Or a daughter," Mrs. Ramsey added. "My neighbor Charlotte lost a girl, a grown daughter. She slept on her unmade sofabed for six months. Then she got dressed and went to work."

"The nice thing," Pipkin continued, "is that you'll have another, Reed. And when he grows up, it'll be hard to remember what he did when he was small or what the first one did either. The candles blow out fast when they get older."

"I'm a bachelor," Alan Partanos began. "I don't have anyone close. When I die, no one will really care."

"You must have lots of friends." Nora smiled.

"He's lucky to be an Indian," Pipkin said, pointing at Jeremy. "He can pretend he's not alone that way."

"It's pretty selfish to grieve for your own death," Reed said to Alan.

"That's the other problem. It doesn't ennoble you. And people just sense there's something wrong with you."

"We all mourn the passing of possibilities and options. It's perfectly normal," Nora Sampson explained, "to see ourselves objectively as worthy of love and grief."

"So cheer up," Pipkin said to Alan. "Dr. Sampson says it's fine to cry your eyes out."

"Bunch of sad sacks," Alan said as he walked with Sarah to their cars.

"What did you expect of a course called 'grief therapy'?"

"To tell the truth, I expected more good-looking women. Nora Sampson's my type, but I'm not good at winning over teachers."

"I'll see you next week."

"How about getting some coffee first?"

They decided to walk over to the Student Union, a postmodern clamshell with broad concrete wings. The entire campus was poorly matched, though the Union was the most comprehensive architectural horror. Sarah wondered how such a monstrosity as her campus could dare boast an urban-planning department.

They sat at a booth in the windowless café that was open till midnight. Several groups of students, one mainly Korean and one composed of Africans, talked loudly at the opposite end of the room. Sarah watched Alan as he swished his spoon in the cup and speared cherries out of his pie, chewing furiously, then subsiding into distraction. She wondered if he moped like this on dates.

"I don't even have a suit," Alan said. "What if I died and didn't have a nice suit?"

"The group could get together and buy you one. What size?"

"Thirty-eight short."

Sarah felt eager for the evening to end. "Simply living makes us worthy of sympathy, Alan."

"But what if we have no survivors?"

Sarah thought Alan's face looked hopeful then, like she might kiss him for feeling so exquisitely awful. She patted his hand. "You have lots of friends, Alan, I'm sure."

"DAMN IT," Sarah said as she tried on sunglasses with red, elliptical frames. "I feel like we're vacationing."

"We've just hibernated for half a day. We have to do something to pass the time, Sarah."

"This is driving me crazy, Jeremy. How can we just sit here and wait?"

"You could still involve the police."

"Tony doesn't want that. His guru psychiatrist doesn't either. Do you know what Mae told me Tony and his Dr. Weber do on weekends? They go on male-bonding reconnaissance missions. They pretend they're children and 'father' each other. They pretend they're soldiers and save each other from imagined enemies. Male anatomy aside, one weekend they pretended they were giving birth to themselves. I guess Lamaze training comes in handy there. Mostly they crawl and grunt and burp and fart and reassure each other that it's great to be men."

"That's Mae's version," Jeremy said with a wry smile. "I had a feeling she couldn't stand Dr. Weber."

"From what we've heard, could you?"

"That was the one thing that Mae and I seemed to agree on."

"Mae says he's a woman-hating charlatan who specializes in eating disorders just to torture girls. She made it sound like a scene out of Dickens. Part of his therapy involves shouting at Deenie. The sessions go like this: Deenie sits silently while Weber berates her. He claims it's supposed to make her want to defend herself to the point of dropping her pretense of control."

"What does that have to do with eating?"

"Deenie thinks she controls herself by denying her body."

"So by making her lose control, he'll make her eat?"

"Something like that."

"Oh," Jeremy said. "It's pretty far-fetched. But I think they're right on the issue of the police, Sarah. Things will work out better in the long run without them."

"But what if the girls disappear forever, Jeremy?"

"Look, Sarah, they're on either a bus or a train heading this way. We'll track them down."

"But what if it crashes?"

"Why should it?"

"Because they're on it."

"The disaster's already happened. They ran away. We just have to be patient."

She knew his decisiveness was supposed to calm her, but it almost sounded smug. It wasn't fair, but she was annoyed at Jeremy for wearing his new jeans and a short-sleeved work shirt, which he'd purchased at Banana Republic while she was, finally, taking her nap. Once back from Mae and Tony's, Sarah had refused to shop when he suggested they go there together. Now they were in the hotel drugstore trying to find something she'd consent to buy. If she started

with smaller items, deodorant and sunglasses, she might work herself
into the mood for the other things she needed. She looked in the
little mirror on the sunglass display and sighed. "I've been wearing
this black dress for two days. I don't have a purse or a wallet."

"So let's go get you new ones."

"My daughter is lost and we're acting like honeymooners. Why
don't we go on a studio tour? Why don't we drive up to San Simeon?"

"We're doing all we can, Sarah. You know we are."

"If we had called the police, they could have officially worried,
and some of the pressure would be off of us."

The Chinese salesgirl was waiting for Sarah to decide. Sarah
could feel her interest as she tried not to look at them as they talked.

"I'll take these," she said with resignation. Tearing off the tag
and handing it to the girl, she put them on. Jeremy handed the girl
a twenty.

"How do I look?" she asked, cocking her head to one side.

"Like a woman who needs to take a ride."

They drove for a long time to get out of the city. The Pacific
Coast Highway was filled with late-Friday-afternoon traffic. Heat
shimmered off of bumpers and made water mirages on the highway.
The sky looked low and yellowish-green with smog. As they wound
around slow turns, they looked down at the waves, foam, and black
rocks. Usually Sarah would have called the aquamarine beautiful,
but the ocean seemed frivolous. The only feature she could appreciate
were the houses that barely clung to the cliffs of Pacific Palisades.

"We're not far from your sister's."

"Thanks anyway, Jeremy. Once in a day is enough."

Sarah couldn't help but think of the coast of Greece. There was
a plant that flowers every twenty years on a long stalk that looks
otherwise barren. She and Larry had seen it near Delphi the year it
was in bloom, a miniature flower on a treelike stem. Somewhere at
home she had photos of that flower.

"I used to run away," Jeremy said.

"Why?"

"Oh, whenever I was angry I'd get on a bus for Duluth. My
poor grandmother and someone named Uncle Jim, who wasn't really
my uncle, would always come for me."

"And what did you do when you saw them?"

"Run. That's why my grandma brought Jim. He was fast. He'd chase me around the bus terminal and sometimes into the street. Then he'd catch me."

"How many times?"

"Six or seven."

"And they never said, 'Forget you!' "

"Once they did. They let the police meet me and take me to a settlement house for the night. It was the last time I ran away."

"How would you get the money?"

"It was only four dollars or so. They had discounts for kids. And Indians. I'd steal it or make it on chores. I'd chop wood or take care of somebody's chickens. Once I raised rabbits."

"You always spent your money on running away?"

"That's all I ever saved for."

"Not toys?"

"Not even a bike."

"How old were you?"

"Nine or ten."

"That meant I was eight or nine. Do you know what I was doing the year you were running away? Sitting in my bedroom with Manhandler TV dinners I'd prepare for myself and reading James Bond. I especially liked the scenes where he was tortured."

"Want me to buy you some bamboo rods?"

"So why did you run away?"

"I hated my mother for deserting me. I hated my grandmother for being so small and abject. I hated my school and my friends."

"Do you think Carrie will run?"

"I think we should be prepared for it."

"What was your grandmother's name?"

"She didn't use one."

"Everyone has a name."

"She never called herself anything, but people called her Betty. Her real name was unpronounceable. Her parents named her after a little river in Wisconsin called Totogatic."

"What's so hard about that?"

"Nothing, really."

"But they called her Betty."

"Right."

"Where were your parents?"

"Present but unaccounted for."

"They took no interest?"

"Not much."

"They never came to Duluth to find you?"

"They never knew I was missing."

Sarah looked at herself in the car mirror. Her cheek had reached full color now. It looked like the flag of a depressed nation. "I look terrible, Jeremy. The ocean, the cliffs, everything's beautiful, but I look like a widow who's fallen on her face. I promise to behave in the next store we visit."

"Where to?"

"How about a discount store? I won't feel so guilty if I buy junk to wear."

Once they'd re-entered Los Angeles, they saw a Cost Plus, a K Mart, and a place called the Discounters across the freeway in a down-scale franchise strip on the edge of Watts. The Discounters' sign was broken. The half that was still attached to the pole shimmied in the wind. Litter blew up from the ground and circled the parking lot in small, dusty swirls.

"Does that look degraded enough to please you?"

"It's perfect."

Without trying anything on, she settled on a pair of jeans, beige chinos, a black t-shirt, two light blue oxford-cloth overblouses, a black canvas purse, a gray Velcro wallet, and gym shoes from Romania. She threw in a nightgown decorated with tiny white flowers on a white background. She stuffed them into a plastic-laminated metal basket and watched them ride down the orange check-out conveyor belt. A Hispanic woman with a handsome face rang up her purchase.

"My new wardrobe," she said. "Now wait." Finding the dressing room, she changed into jeans and the t-shirt. Everything felt stiff, like she was wearing paper. She folded her black dress into the unmarked sack and joined Jeremy at the Discounters.

He was finishing an iced tea. "How's this?"

"If you'd come for me in Duluth, I wouldn't have run away."

"What was your grandmother like?" Sarah smiled.

"She never said much to me, but I always knew she was there. She's eighty-four now, but she's never been any age. She's very solid. Kind of like geography."

"What did your grandmother wear when she came to find you?"

"Oh, a black dress like yours."

"MOVE! You're sitting with *her* now." Deenie shoved Carrie off her new seat with such force that she landed just short of her destination.

"I don't want to," Carrie began to plead from her crouch in the aisle.

"Adrian's decided to sit with me, Carrie," Deenie said slowly and instructionally. You sit across from us. It's no big deal." She moved back to the aisle, reserving the window seat for Adrian.

"You act like an idiot!" Carrie's sneer made her cheeks look all puckered and babyish. It was like her expression carried secret baggage. "Excuse me," Deenie heard her say as she climbed over her new seatmate, a peach-haired woman of perhaps seventy, who was eating a chicken-salad sandwich that she'd wrapped at home for the trip. Deenie could smell it all the way across the aisle and see how the aluminum foil held the bulging mess together. Didn't mayonnaise ever spoil? Carrie would probably like it over there. The woman had endless supplies of food.

Adrian returned from the washroom in mid-sentence. "As I was saying," he continued, settling himself next to Deenie, "monochrome makes the most important statement about art in the twentieth century. Are you familiar with the paintings of Rodchenko? His 'Pure Yellow' is one of the earliest experiments in the form, and it's brilliant. Of course, the space it occupies would do much to suggest its gesture. That's why curators are really artistic collaborators." Adrian wiped his brow and exhaled like a man who'd finished a large meal.

"So how do you *do* monochrome?"

Adrian's smile looked like the first hint of a new moon. "So what do you study, Deenie?"

"Chemistry, but I'm failing it, American history, which is totally boring, English, of course, and Photography II. I'd like that pretty much if the darkroom chemicals didn't smell so pukey."

"Do you like the work of Man Ray?"

"Man who?"

Adrian looked out the window and Deenie imitated his gesture. Evening had fallen. In one day the landscape had changed from plains to hills. Now the bus was winding through a canyon blasted out of dark rock. Deenie wondered whether Adrian's personality would thaw as the bus headed farther south and west or whether he was like that monochrome. She wondered if the new bus driver, pushing the bus toward eighty to make up for time wasted on the broken toilet, would have any effect on Adrian Fishblatt. As the bus accelerated, Adrian's mind might work more slowly. Deenie thought about word problems in geometry. She saw their interests intersecting at a distant red point in space. Their faces sat on a page smiling at each other while cloudlike thought balloons containing the same exclamation marks, asterisks, and ellipses floated over their slabs of hair.

She glanced at Carrie, who was chattering to the woman. Deenie heard her name rise and fall in their conversation.

"My boyfriend's old girlfriend's an artist." Deenie posed herself in her most important profile, lips pursed, chin jutting out.

"What medium?"

"Oh, she paints on tree bark." Deenie pulled at her chin like she had a beard.

"I guess that's easier than assaulting the whole tree. And people collect her work?"

"Oh, she does very well. She's in Costa Rica now, but a gallery in Los Angeles represents her."

"Has she shown in New York?"

"I don't know, but Branch tells me she's very dedicated. When she's busy she doesn't even stop to eat."

"Are you her follower?"

"What do you mean?"

That moon-sliver smile again and that deranged look. Who said that handsome men couldn't be crazy? Maybe the screenplay was a hoax and he was heading toward some kind of hospice for hopeless intellectuals. The West and Southwest are full of health spas. One of Mae's friends had gone to an arthritis clinic that fed her nothing but apricots. Deenie had read about a kind of ranch where you met your dead relatives again on moonlit horseback rides.

"Do you like mime?" Deenie asked. It was her favorite sophisticated entertainment. She loved how people's arms could exaggerate flying, or a white face could make laughter more expressive as silence.

"I hate its fraudulence. Don't get me wrong. All art is a fraud of sorts. It's like money. A government prints paper with pictures of old men, pyramids, and eagles, and we believe in it to the point of surrendering our lives. But mimes reek of falsehood. They tug at us. They hit us in our ribs with their sharp elbows and tell us, 'React.' The only mime I've ever liked was an anti-mime."

"What do you mean?"

"The mime pretended he was putting out a fire. The anti-mime spilled water all over him. The mime pretended he was chopping down a tree. The anti-mime got a power saw and made quick work of it."

"And where did this happen?"

"At an English circus."

"You were in England?"

"No, I was at the circus."

"Well, I like mime, and, I'm sorry to say, I think the person you're calling the anti-mime was just a hypocrite."

"On the contrary. The only art that will live must instruct itself to fail. Think about it, Deenie. If not now, then later. Your friend's friend, the artist—do you think her tree bark will last? But 'Pure Yellow' will be a marker for our era."

"Like Mount Rushmore?"

"No, that's more mime. That's a cultural hallucination on a mountain. Erosion will take care of it eventually."

"Not if people care."

"The point is that they won't. These things get sorted out over the millennia. Take my word for it."

"How do you know? Are you a few thousand years old?"

"No, I just feel like it."

Deenie thought that was funny to say. It was the first funny sentence he'd spoken since he'd made a complicated joke about recycled cans. The bad thing about humor was that it wouldn't seem funny later. It would rattle around in her brain like a window screen on a loose hinge, and she wouldn't, for the life of her, remember what made her want to kiss him. She butted her face into his, making contact at the nose. She thought this was how plants would make love if they could.

Now he was kissing her. It was like that game you played at basement birthday parties of passing a potato between partners from cheek to chin to chest to a basket. She grabbed his lower lip between her teeth and sucked on it ferociously. Adrian reached under her blouse and rubbed his hand over her ribs. She felt like a washboard. He took her tiny right breast between his fingers.

Turning to the side, she saw Carrie showing the woman something in her wallet.

"Here," she said, draping her coat over Adrian. She rotated toward him in her seat until her head was in his lap. She located his zipper in the stifling dark. She couldn't be the only traveler in the history of the world to have unzipped a man's jeans before midnight. The bus produced a loud distracting whine and a feeling of unfocused perception, like everything was happening too close to her face. Nearsighted people like her father must see life at eighty miles an hour. Would Carrie see? Would two people under a trenchcoat be more noticeable than speeded-up mountains and a sunset they were approaching like a final door?

His penis was folded into his boxer shorts. She wet her hand and stroked him hard. Then she began to suck on it, making appreciative clucks in her throat while Adrian grabbed her hair and gripped it near her scalp. She tried not to think that she'd once read in *Cosmopolitan* that an average ejaculation has ninety calories.

Adrian coaxed himself along with his hand. Having accommodated herself to the dark, she watched his fingers working themselves up and down the length of his penis, pressing the long vein at the bottom, then moving toward the top until he'd reach Deenie's face. It began to annoy her that he was laboring so hard on himself and touching no more than her scalp. She imagined that when she surfaced, her lips would be wet and smeary and she'd have a crazy look in her eyes like bowling balls fixed in space.

"Hey," she said pausing for a second. "Remember I'm here?" Adrian was gasping with pleasure, throwing his pelvis up toward the ceiling. Deenie's face was riding his stomach up and down like a wave, and nothing would break his motion, not even the momentary pause of her speech.

"I guess you don't need me!" She threw her coat off herself.

Deenie sat at attention, fully dressed, next to a masturbating man. Worse yet, he was using her coat. She decided to tell Branch that the man had been groaning and rubbing himself on a Greyhound bus.

Grabbing her purse, she pushed through the aisle to the washroom. Though the temperature had been dropping all evening, the air felt thick. She could feel her stomach clench. She thought of meeting Sarah at the airport, Aunt Sarah, whom a lion would love to eat. She thought of sitting for so many months while her mother measured her upper arm during a staged embrace or coaxed her to eat just one more baby potato. She'd live off herself. She ground her teeth together until her ears filled with her own noise and she was able to drown out the swaying of the bus.

When the door opened and a young Mexican woman with a baby exited, Deenie lunged inside, stooped over the silver bowl, and, clutching it with both hands, tried to vomit. Then she threw water into her eyes. She drank deep gulps from the tap, found her flask, and used her Jim Beam as mouthwash. The bathroom mirror wasn't glass. She looked at her streaky self with her cheeks full and spat at it twice. The liquid ran into the sink. God, she hated everything and everyone—him and her parents and herself and her whole stupid life. A pain gripped her middle, like her stomach could touch her back with emptiness.

Stumbling back up the aisle, she heard sounds of sleep come from the seats on both sides.

"Deenie, I want you to meet someone," Carrie was saying to her as she stood in the dark by her seat. The peach-haired woman was staring at her too. "This is Reena Fishblatt."

Deenie felt faint. She held on to the back of her chair and lowered herself into it slowly. "You said Fishblatt."

"A funny name, isn't it? Before Adrian was born, I couldn't think of something that could join that last name. Then I looked at him and the names just belonged together. They sounded so pure."

"You're his mom?" Waiting for her answer, Deenie felt herself color with stupidity.

"I heard my son telling you that we're traveling to Los Angeles. I'm acting as his agent, you might say. My son knows all the right words, but I'm afraid he's no businessman." She sighed wearily. "Sit down with me, honey. Would you like some grapes or a sweater? It was so nice of you to share your coat with Adrian. Selfish boy, he's fallen asleep with it now. Poor you, you have nothing."

SARAH WOKE UP in the middle of the night thinking about the vacation when they'd found something dead. It had gotten tangled up on Larry's fishing line and had been so heavy that the whole family had to help haul it in. When Sarah saw the bloated, decaying beaver carcass, she had gagged in front of the children. Without looking at anyone, she'd run into the bushes and vomited.

Now she looked at Jeremy's sleeping face and wondered why he couldn't protect her from the memory of it. Picking up a glass of water to calm herself, she noticed how the glass was wet on the outside and appeared to be breathing with her. Blood drummed in her wrists. She tried to slow herself down by taking deep, calculated breaths between swallows. Counting deliberately, exhaling fiercely, she was an instrument of breath, blue blood inside made red by rage and love. Pinching the sheet fabric, she chewed on a corner of her mouth until a poignant, salty taste glazed her tongue.

SATURDAY

WITH SARAH AND CARRIE GONE and Scotty staying at a friend's, Larry decided to spend a rare Saturday at school. The campus would be deserted, and he'd be able to concentrate on something other than Carrie. As he drove down Lake Shore Drive, the lake looked gray and nondescript. He was glad it wasn't a morning when light shimmered off the water and seemed to beg praise. He preferred the insularity of being in practically the only car on the road. Knowing he was about to lose everything he'd come to expect, he felt a strange calm. He wistfully remembered Sarah sagging away from him in bed, Sarah tumbling toward him in the morning. Shaking her out of his head, he inhaled deeply. Without her, he'd be himself again, not part of the storm of human activity that had sucked him in and batted him about like a tree limb.

Only when he was alone or with a woman other than Sarah did he feel separate and grounded. At times, while walking on campus, he'd touch his own pants leg, or, watching his calf stride, see his foot make contact with the earth. Sometimes, when he sat on the john, he'd simply stare at his toes. He guessed it was childish to affirm that his body was his, but constantly through the day he'd look for its reflection in glass or car fenders and feel serene. It belonged to him like nothing else. Throwing his pelvis into the shared rhythm of fucking, he'd think of its arc in the air, the mottled grain of his own flesh. He was sure that Sarah didn't understand that intimacy had cost him a great deal. Could she imagine that it was pleasant to disappear into a marriage, then get buried under the obligations that family brought? Why did love have to be so fucking selfless? And why had children intruded so soon? Given ten years alone with Sarah, he might have figured out his location and latitude, and how to satisfy her without feeling used up.

As it was, as soon as he heard he was to be a father, he'd found Donna. She was so insubstantial, so expressionless, that it was easy to love her. As he swelled with significance, she disappeared into their love. She'd listen to him for hours and never pose a single question. Her presence didn't breathe down his neck. But Sarah never vanished. She peppered his monologues with indelicate questions and made him accountable for positions he didn't know he'd formed. "Why?" she'd ask in the middle of an account of his fierce interrogation of a job candidate. Why in the fuck did she want to know what he'd never considered? She was always solid, always substantial. On a map he imagined that she was a continent, maybe Australia, and he was the Bering Strait.

As soon as Carrie was found, he could begin his new life away from Sarah. He'd think of the right questions to ask the woman of the nineties, questions about the subtlety of shades of black clothing and whether the Brazilian rain forest might be saved now that Sting was involved in the issue. The women would be too young to have thought much about death, a topic that increasingly occupied him. Lying in bed, he'd imagine the blue-veined inside of his throat closing, or, seeing a car round a corner, he'd picture it hurtling his body through the air like a board. On dates, he certainly wouldn't mention his own youth, a sure sign of fogyism, or naive religious art or Samuel Barber or Campari, tastes acquired later in life. He'd watch more of those entertainment-news shows anchored by well-polished lowbrows and designed for young audiences. Just last week he'd learned about a new craze called vogueing, where dancers freeze onstage in mannequin stillness, chins jutting out, cheeks sucked hollow. Maybe Deenie, he suddenly thought, had cultivated her look for aesthetic impact. There was an African model, thin as bamboo, whom he'd recently seen interviewed on a talk show.

He knew he was a young thirty-nine but thought he could add to his assets with a little thoughtful redesigning: some fawn-colored suede shoes from Milan, an expensive resale-store overcoat. He could resurrect the little gold hoop he used to wear. When Carrie came back, they'd go on an outing. He'd ask her to take him to a store in the mall where he could get his ear double-pierced. She could pick out the stud for him. Maybe he'd buy her a suede skirt. He thought he'd heard her asking Sarah for one unsuccessfully a while back.

On campus he saw women in denim jackets and long black

shapeless overcoats, some with pouty lips, some with delicate brows. One hundred feet away at the periodicals desk was the librarian he'd slept with a few times last March. Despite the allure of Rita Cellbridge's Welsh accent, her long, freckled legs, and her ruddy cheeks that burned after sex, her inflections were finally an annoyance. Her "Care for tea?" post-coital remark made him feel like he was sleeping with Jessica Mitford—only Jessica Mitford, he was sure, had a sense of humor. Tamara Presmanik had called him a few times lately, but he was tired of women with strong accents who probably moaned theatrically in bed.

Better prospects were among his own students, like that devastating blonde named Amy, whose little breasts made radish-sized distractions under her batik t-shirt. During a discussion of one of her assignments in the student coffeehouse, she'd arched her back, thrusting herself forward from a murky, unsure canvas while fiddling with a long, shiny Moroccan scarf belt that jingled with coins. On an uncommonly warm May day, she'd asked him if he wanted to go to the beach, and he'd told her that sun was among the million other hazards that sensible people should avoid. Her invitation had made him picture Sarah at the ocean with the family on a previous summer vacation. The color of nature herself, she had pointed at his pale, veiny legs while she did a Chaplinesque penguin walk in the sand. Amy would look wraithlike beside her. He'd have to put a ton of sunscreen on her scrawny little bones to protect her from burning. Larry guessed she looked better in her flawlessly hip clothes than naked. Actually he was afraid to fuck someone who looked like she might break under the eagerness of his body.

His desk was a hopeless mess. The kids' old school photos were buried in an avalanche of galleys, slides of Dutch art, and unclaimed term papers spanning what felt like a century of teaching. He began to worry that by being at the office he'd miss some important news, but the answering machine was on at home. If any word of Carrie came through, the red light would flash obsessively. Instead of cleaning his desk like he'd planned, he passed the time lying on his couch, a beat-up leather luxury he'd bought years ago when he was seeing Donna. They'd had sex maybe a hundred times on that couch. He'd once read an article on how the fall of empires is related to decadent styles of architecture and household furnishings. As people grow more comfortable, they also grow more licentious.

He had spent weeks of inertia here staring blankly out of the twenty-fourth-floor corner window at the Eisenhower Expressway below. He loved the discord—its ugly gray industrial smoke and ancient iron bridges with frozen gears to the west, the backside of downtown to the east. He'd put on some Glenn Gould and watch cars move to tortured music. Once, during a rainstorm, there'd been an amazingly elegant chain-reaction accident. From his height it was merely a prism of wet colors separating: green into yellow into red accompanied by the flashing of blue police lights. Later, he'd heard two people had died, but that hardly made sense from this pleasant impersonal distance.

Eyes focused on the unrelieved white of the acoustic ceiling tile, he couldn't help thinking of Donna. Once, after an inept game of racquetball, they'd sneaked into the men's showers and made love there. He remembered Scotty's sweet aroma, a mixture of milk and baby talc, and Sarah's clean perspiration. During the Donna years, his life had reached an apex of fulfillment.

He wondered if his last meeting with Sarah would be a battle, or if seventeen years of comings and goings, of absentminded kisses amid laundry, of terrible, bruising words and forgiveness, would just fizzle out like heat lightning. Could he locate Donna and tell her of his new status? Fourteen years was a long time. The last time he'd heard, she was living with a documentary filmmaker in Munich. Germany had a tremendous arts budget, and Larry figured that Donna's boyfriend was one of the many who lived on the dole. Larry had taken Sarah to a viewing of the man's films at the Art Institute Film Center. Donna's boyfriend was into Nordic-looking skiers juxtaposed with street scenes in Calcutta. Mother Teresa scuttled over the scene speaking into a hand-held mike, followed by more skiers and the Wagnerian music of German pageantry. Donna had probably tired of his sophomoric vision by now.

He'd look for a place downtown with a view, maybe with a swimming pool. He'd have the floor carpeted a neutral color that didn't show dirt, buy a couple of futons for himself and Scotty, and give Carrie the bedroom. The kids would like a pool and a sauna. They'd want to visit him. Of course, if he could find Donna, it wouldn't matter as much if the kids liked to visit or not. Most of all, he didn't want to be a lonely man cooking linguine with Paul Newman sauce. Even with Sarah so distant from him, she'd been a warm presence in bed. How did that country song go? "My Woman, My Buffer, My Wife."

When the phone rang, Larry jumped off the couch.

"When I got your machine, I thought you might be hiding out here," Ivy said. "Any word?"

"Your daughter's staying at the Hilton waiting for buses and trains. No word beyond that, Ivy."

"I know. I talked to Mae. Sarah and that man . . ." Her voice trailed off. "What do you think of him?"

"Of whom?"

"The Indian. I guess I shouldn't ask."

"Probably not."

"I was thinking, Larry. How people live today. When I tell my own daughter that Deenie looks like something out of Dachau, she says that thinness is healthy. She says I could stand to shed some pounds. Is emaciation beautiful?"

"Deenie's in therapy, Ivy."

"And I've been thinking about Stanley. Everything's been wrong since the day he retired. First it was bike-riding. He'd take long rides on his shiny new three-speed past the ridiculous flamingos in their steamy glass dome at the zoo. He'd stop and throw bread crumbs to swans. Now that man hadn't looked at a bird in the forty years I knew him, Larry. He'd lock his bike and walk into the overheated air of the conservatory and see ordinary houseplants grown to extraordinary height. He'd come home and point, asking why all our plants were dwarfed. He virtually accused me of mistreating them."

"I'm sure it wasn't your fault."

"Then he began nature photography. He bought a Japanese camera, a tripod, lots of film. How could someone with a tripod and a college degree in science fail to understand a shutter? The petals were blurred, the stems looked like someone had smeared them with grease. Many of the close-ups reminded me of pubic hair, if you'll excuse my frankness, Larry.

"The morning he died he had just bought a sketchpad. What do you think he was going to do with that?"

"Make sketches?"

"Larry, use your noodle. What was he going to sketch?"

"Flamingos?"

"What do men sketch, Larry?"

"I give up."

"Don't tell the girls, but I think he had a mistress. The bike and the birds were an excuse, believe me. There were a few ladies at the funeral that I just couldn't place. And someone was plenty guilty too. Just ask Sarah. On my kitchen table there must have been eight fruit baskets, all from an anonymous donor. It was disgusting to see them brimming with all those apples and pears. Poor Sarah had to carry them two at a time to the veterans' hospital down the street. She said the men would enjoy them."

"They probably did."

"And I keep thinking, Larry, what if he was thinking of her when he died?"

"Thinking of whom?"

"Oh, I know it's probably nonsense, Larry, but it drives me crazy at night imagining him thinking in that car of some Dolores instead of me."

"Why would you worry about that, Ivy? Don't torture yourself. I never heard Stanley say one thing ever to indicate there was someone else. And besides, you two were happy. I sometimes think Sarah would have been more pleased with me if you and Stanley hadn't set such a good example."

"I just think his death set a tone."

"What do you mean?"

"Oh, just that things stopped making sense. The universe changed. Kids stopped eating. My one daughter took her inheritance and spent it on a Cadillac fit for a pimp. My other one started sleeping with an Indian."

"You can't blame that all on Stanley."

"I think his aspirations survived him, Larry. And I don't mean the sketchpad and charcoal. I gave them to Edda Eddie's little granddaughter down the hall. I mean things that seem solid fall apart. I mean girls are supposed to stay home, not wander around the country like gypsies. I mean one minute I'm looking in Stanley's eyes—maybe we're arguing as usual—and the next minute Bernie is telling me he's dead. How can this be? I'll tell you, Larry. There's a sinister spirit loose in the world."

"Stanley's haunting us?"

"No, no, he didn't intend all of this. It just happened and now he can't stop it. What is it Hamlet says?"

"Plenty of things."

"Well, one of them pertains, Larry. Or maybe it's King Lear."

"What passage are you thinking of?"

"Oh, something about the times being out of joint."

"That's *Hamlet*."

"Fine, fine. Is it as foggy away from the lake as it is by me?"

"No, it's just drizzly here. Kind of bleak."

"I can't see out of my window. And with what I pay for the view . . ." Her voice trailed off. "Call me, honey, if you hear more about Carrie and Deenie."

CARRIE WAS THINKING about a movie she had seen where a kidnapped housewife left lipstick instructions on how to save her in every washroom she visited. The woman got killed by the bleached-blond psychopath with the Cool Hand Luke glasses anyway, but she must have felt better knowing that at least she'd made an effort.

Because one of the toilets on the bus was out of order, they were taking an unscheduled ten-minute rest stop in North Platte. A pit stop, the bus driver had called it. Adrian was talking to Deenie as usual, but her body was turned away from his and she didn't seem to be listening. He was telling her about something called instress in someone named Hopkins. With Adrian having so much to say, Deenie might be the most self-improved anorectic on the bus by the

time they reached Los Angeles. Maybe the bus driver could give her
a little diploma and a gift certificate for mineral water.

Deenie and Adrian, who was shorter when he stood than he
appeared to be seated, had their backs to each other. Both were
leaning on a picnic table in front of the comfort station. They seemed
to be posing for a black-and-white fashion layout for a perfume with
an ironic name. Despite the chilly air, Deenie had left her black rayon
trenchcoat on the bus. She had put on her little French hat and white
gloves and lots of maroon lipstick. Adrian was wearing a rumpled
white shirt and longish jeans that were tight at his ankles. He was
eating more grapes and Deenie wasn't. They were concentrating so
fiercely on ignoring each other that they didn't see Carrie as she
jogged behind them to the opposite side of the building, past the gas
pumps and the semis and the special disabled unisex washroom,
whose doors were as wide as a field.

She stopped at a pop machine and bought a grape Crush. Taking
a long swig, she imagined her parents exchanging grateful glances
and coming together in a long, slow embrace when they heard her
alive on the phone. Her mother's pretty upper lip would quiver, and
her father would stare, just stare, like he did when touched by beauty
or sadness. Carrie took a fistful of change from the bottom of her
purse and dropped it onto the metal shelf that had once held a phone
book. Her stomach turning over in anticipation of their bereft voices,
she pressed the buttons in sequence. She'd always liked the antici-
patory jingle of phone keys. She thought the word for it was *dis-
cordant*. She smiled to think she knew bigger words than Deenie,
who was so sophisticated. The problem with Deenie's intellect was
that her parents weren't professors like Carrie's. What was Tony?
Some kind of spy, and Mae was just a professional nut. She spent
more time nursing orphan blue jays and corresponding with life-term
inmates than she did watching Deenie disappear. It was an odd
comfort to Carrie that even when her mother had decided to cheat
on her father she hadn't left the academic community. She'd chosen
a social scientist. She remembered a joke her dad had made pre-
Jeremy, that social scientists are to academia what sanitation engi-
neers are to urban planning. Well, now her mother was in love with
a garbage man.

The computerized phone voice said, "A-dollar-eighty-five-please." It talked like it was on sedation. Her grandmother Ivy took sleeping pills, and when Carrie was younger and liked staying at Ivy's overnight, she'd have trouble waking her up in the morning. Until she drank a few cups of coffee with fake sugar, Ivy would talk like the robotoid voice on the phone.

Carrie dropped in five quarters and six dimes. It took her a long time to count all the change, especially the thin dimes, so hard to pick up with her false nail tips. "Thank-you," the phone voice said, affectless, indifferent.

At the fourth ring, Carrie knew no one was home. It would make just as good an impression on her parents to hear her on the machine when they returned from wherever. She waited for her own recorded voice to finish the polite instructions. It figured they wouldn't be home. They were sitting at a police station under a noisy clock, weeping in each other's arms and whispering her name.

"Hi, Mom and Dad. I just wanted to tell you that I'm alive and well. Greyhound's pretty nice, except our toilet is broken. I'll probably see you soon, guys. Um . . ."

What more? She thought of *Lassie* reruns where the little boy reacts to the feelings he pretends to read in his dog's inscrutable, walnut-sized brain.

"C'mon, Mom, cheer up. Dad, don't look so droopy. Scotty, stay out of my room."

The tape ran out before she could say good-bye, but they'd understand her spirit was undaunted. She was pretty sure that was the word.

ON THE CHEAP TRANSISTOR that Jeremy had bought for their motel room, Sarah heard the most haunting songs, longer and more sonorous than whale music. A spokesman for a manufacturing conglomerate went on to explain that it was the sound that a foot-thick piece of ice makes fifteen hundred feet below the sea. It was the music of cracking, of coming apart at a rate that is centuries slow. It was a constant unchanging tone that mankind had only recently learned to measure.

All that previous spring she had trained her ear to hear what had fallen apart invisibly. Using the grief-therapy sessions as her probe, she sat silent while the others told their stories, but in the amorphous glow of human company, she began to feel a strangely detached sympathy for herself. Sometimes she thought of herself in the third person. "Poor Sarah," she consoled as she waited on the steps for Alan Partanos to pick her up for the third session. "Poor Sarah." What luxury two meager words had begun to afford her.

"Did you see Nora's necklace?" Alan asked Sarah in the car.

"Didn't notice."

"One banana, one apple, one orange. She's a minimalist Carmen Miranda. I've thought about her all week."

"Why don't you ask her out?"

"Well, Miss Right Hemisphere, you obviously don't understand. There's a time and a place. She has to appreciate my gesture intellectually and aesthetically. How will she be able to resist a man who's gone beyond grief into healing?"

"You're a fraud."

"I'm a pragmatist. I know how to assuage my grief. I'm about to do it."

"Good luck. Just let me pretend I don't know you."

"And what are your plans for tonight?"

"Oh, to talk more about my father. Maybe my kids and my marriage."

"I don't know your husband well, but I've seen him around. He's very friendly to students."

"You mean that he sleeps with his students?"

"I didn't say that." Alan smiled in brisk consolation, and then they entered the room.

It was a smaller crew. Pipkin was there, Anselm Howard, Jeremy Bone Shoulder, and, of course, Nora Sampson. She was dressed in a fuzzy black Orlon sweater dress with a large, ornate cross defining her breasts.

Jeremy looked especially attractive. He'd cut his blue-black hair and was wearing a black pocket t-shirt. Reed and Linsey were absent, and so was Pipkin's sidekick, Lil.

Nora began the session by telling the group that it would be her last. Her mother was to have heart surgery, and she'd be in New York for a month. Sarah watched Alan, who looked like his train had left the station without him.

Just as Pipkin was beginning to speak, Linsey and Reed walked in. Linsey had a new haircut, and Reed was holding her hand. Pipkin greeted them, explaining why Lil was absent. "Phlebitis again. Just like Nixon." Then she passed around a get-well card with two baby lambs and a duck in a sailor hat for all of them to sign.

Alan jumped right in. "Don't you find," he said, addressing Nora, "that we need to move beyond grief for grief to be meaningful?"

"First we need to explore our grief fully. If we let it go too soon, we find ourselves missing it. Then guilt grows like weeds to fill in what's missing."

"Well, I'm a hard worker, Nora. I'd guess it's not common to move beyond grief in one short week, but I have."

"So why are you back, then?" Pipkin challenged.

"I want to explore my healing."

"Exploring your healing is a different night. This is plain grief."

"Let him continue, Mrs. Pipkin," Nora said with some irritation.

"Thank you, Nora," Alan said. "It's a little embarrassing to tell the whole group this, but it's your leadership that's healed me."

Sarah felt ready to do a Pipkin on Alan. She shook her head and caught Jeremy's sympathetic glance.

"What I have to say, Nora, is very private, and I don't really want to take up the group's time. How about a quick drink afterward?"

"I'm not against a drink, Alan, but you diminish the credit you deserve by assigning too much power to me."

"But I want to thank you."

"You just did." Nora flashed a smile that could have stopped a freight train. Then she turned her attention to Linsey and Reed.

"We'd like to talk less and listen more," Linsey said. "We're tired of hearing ourselves."

"Okay," Jeremy began. "I've had a rotten week. Jess, who works at the Indian Center, had a massive stroke. He drank for years and gave it up. He quit smoking. He made a go of it with his family again. Now he can't walk or talk."

"Where's there to go? What's there to say?" Pipkin asked.

Sarah waited for Nora to strike a blow for sensitivity.

Instead, Reed countered, "Mrs. Pipkin's right. Renouncing the world negates grief. That's what Linsey and I have decided to do. We've sent away for information to a Zen center in Taos. We're thinking of joining. We've lost our son. If we give up the world, we've lost nothing."

"If you give up the world, you've lost everything," Sarah said.

"I'd have to agree," Anselm Howard said. "I've decided to travel. I won't miss Edith less, but I'll be distracted."

"Just a minute. Wherever you go there's grief. Where are you traveling to?" Pipkin paused, ready to throw her instructive dart at whatever location he'd chosen.

"India," Anselm smiled.

"Okay," Pipkin said. "You'll see street beggars in Calcutta. You'll see children with flies in their eyes. You'll see lepers. And what will you think? You'll think about Edith. Save money. Be miserable at home."

"I'll miss her everywhere, I agree," Anselm said.

"Let's have some drinks," Pipkin said. "It's Nora's last night, Anselm's going to India, Mr. Shoulder's friend and Lil are sick, Alan is healed, Sarah's still thinking about radishes, and Reed and Linsey are renouncing the world. Let's *do* something."

They walked in a silent cortège the two blocks to O'Grady's, a brightly lit, Christmasy place where two ex–chainsaw murderers flanked the door for the protection of the clientele. They knew the regulars and were directed to screen out under-age drinkers, bikers, and bumpkins. According to Alan, O'Grady's had so many rules that a person might be barred entrance on the basis of cologne—too much or too little—profane language, t-shirts, bow ties, cowlicks, swimmer's ear, too many Ph.D.'s, pimples, boutonnières, facial hair, whatever pleased Nathan and Desmond, the bouncers, whom Alan greeted by name.

They took a large, U-shaped booth. On their right were two skinny, uniformed men who were whispering to each other. Exterminators, Sarah guessed. On their left a woolly elderly man with a huge diamond pinkie ring was caressing a blond woman whose hairdo suggested a different era. Through the smoke and the talk and the dimly lit bar wood, it was hard to make out others. Now and then an anonymous drinker would shout a greeting to Alan. Sarah had never expected him to have so many acquaintances.

The Alan she knew was making his move. Announcing he'd pay for the first round, he slipped closer to Nora. A waitress took the order, which included Scotch and water for Alan, a Heineken for Jeremy, a double Gibson straight up for Anselm, and Irish coffee for Nora and Sarah. Reed and Linsey wanted Perrier. Pipkin ordered a Singapore sling.

"Wait till I tell Lil what she missed," she said after the first long slurp of her drink.

The conversation crept along once they were settled. Sarah talked about a surgeon she knew whose specialty was removing pennies from children's windpipes. Anselm told them about a friend whose depression had begun when he missed Christmas by crossing the international date line. Mrs. Pipkin told them that when her grandson went to see Santa, he'd gotten off Santa's lap announcing that Santa had a penis.

Whenever Sarah looked at Alan, he was edging Nora farther away from the group. His strategy seemed to be working. Talking softly at a distance, they reminded Sarah of conspirators.

After they'd had three rounds, they learned that Mrs. Pipkin's first name was Loretta.

"To Loretta," they said, exchanging different Pipkinesque slogans all at once.

When Nora went to the washroom, Alan rejoined the group. "I'll drive you home right now, Sarah."

"I'm not planning to leave yet."

Alan gave her a smiting look.

"When I am ready, I'll take a cab."

"That'll be fine," he beamed.

Nora and Alan were the second pair to leave, right after Reed and
Linsey. Linsey thanked them for being cheerful and took Reed's hand.
Anselm, slurring his speech, said he had business in the morning.
Sarah was left with Pipkin, who was humming something with gusto,
and Jeremy, who was tracing wet circles on the table counter with
his finger.

"Just the hardcore alcoholics," Mrs. Pipkin said. "I haven't had
so much alcohol since my second son got married."

Jeremy and Sarah had been drinking more slowly. Still, she felt
her legs were leaden.

"May I drive either of you home?"

"I think the question is *can you*," Pipkin said. "Besides, don't
you think old ladies can drive?"

"This old lady has had a lot to drink."

"When I was young during World War Two, I'd go with my
boss, an ugly guy always with a cigar, and have a few quick ones
after work. I can drink like a Teamster. It's late, though, so I'll leave
you kids alone. What was it I used to drink?" She held her index
finger in the air as she rose and pulled the answer out of space.
"Perfect Manhattans."

Jeremy scooted closer to Sarah in the booth, closing the gap that
the six had vacated.

"Pipkin's something," Jeremy said.

Sarah agreed. They both stared at their drinks.

"I should get home."

"It's only eleven-thirty."

"I don't really want to go yet," she confessed.

"Are people expecting you?"

"Yes and no."

"More yes or more no?"

"Are you married?"

"I lived with a woman for a long time. She's in Austin now.
Lurene's a textile designer."

"I've been married sixteen years."

"If Lurene had stayed, I'd still be with her."

"Why did she leave?"

"Money, jobs, sex—you know."

Sarah watched Jeremy's hand encircle her shoulder. "Can you believe Alan?" Sarah asked.

"I can't believe that Nora believes Alan. It spoils her credibility as a psychologist."

"People believe what they want."

"I guess," Jeremy said, and took her chin in his hand.

Jeremy's face was very pleasant. His eyes were large and his skin looked soft, like a woman's skin. Staring at her, he drew her toward his face. The kiss began slowly, like they had a century to occupy the orange torn booth. Then he kissed her again, slipping his tongue into her mouth, and she kissed him back.

"Come home with me." He rubbed her knee under the booth. He smelled like ginger.

"I'd better not."

He pressed even closer, pushing into her with his hip, which was surprisingly sharp for a man whose skin looked so smooth.

Driving home with Jeremy, Sarah tried to make wifely conversation. Larry this and that, she said. Larry says and does, she said.

Jeremy pulled his ancient silver Fairlane into the beach parking lot at Greenleaf. "Let's talk more."

The grass was too dark to see, but the walk by the lake was floodlit. Lights were bobbing in the water's reflection like lemons. She could hear the expanse of the lake practicing *R*'s.

He turned off the engine but left on the radio. Dick Buckley's jazz show was on WBEZ. A saxophone played a long, serious riff.

"I've liked you since the first week I saw you, Sarah. You look so smart." He touched her hair and put it close to his face.

"If I were smart, I'd have taken a cab home."

"Now you sound like Pipkin," he said, "but I'll take you home now." He made no effort to move.

They listened to Dick Buckley sell a jazz tour of Europe. It would be their fault if not enough people registered and it had to be canceled.

"He's disappointed." Jeremy's smile revealed even teeth that looked friendly. Through the half-open window, Sarah could hear the April air, as if it were still blue from the beautiful day, over the gray sound of the lake. She saw dim stars veiled in rolling clouds. Resting her head on his arm, she thought of the perfect reasons why she shouldn't be here.

"I don't know you," she said. But her words sank. She knew very well why she'd consented to listen to the sad, strange vocals of Sarah Vaughan. Sarah leaned against Jeremy's neck and shoulder and touched his chest in a way that said, unmistakably, now.

Jeremy leaned from his shadow to kiss her. At first they were clumsy and thoughtful; then, as if caught in the same curious dream, they began clawing at each other's clothes. She thrust against his hand as he slid his finger inside. Excited by her own boldness, she put her hand between his legs, and as she worked to loosen his belt, they looked at each other like children entering a building with hammers and matches. He removed her underpants and politely set them aside. The casual, yet terrible, intimacy of these preparations began to break her heart. It had not been this way with Larry, not for years. Perhaps never. Busy with consent, they removed their clothing like teenagers. Then, holding him in both hands, she straddled him, arching her back and shaking her hair. It was the playground where she used to take the kids, now safely empty. The curious air, having entered the car, breathed against her shoulder.

"No one else is here," she whispered.

"That's good."

And then he was in her. Rocking in his lap, she was sweaty and wild, drowning in the strange and suddenly familiar odors of just plain fucking.

"Oh," she said again and again as Jeremy licked her neck. Jeremy's whistling breath was a taut string of assent. As he came, his back arched and her head hit the roof of the car.

"Ow."

They both laughed and settled into an awareness of what they had done. Despite the open window, the windshield was steamy with breath; the cars of strangers sat in strict rows. Sleepily, his voice creaking deep inside him, Jeremy exhaled and mumbled something.

"What?"

"I said I love you."

"You do?"

When she finally moved off him, they kissed conspiratorially yet neatly, as if at a cousin's wedding. The small kiss confirmed everything they'd done. There would be no downcast glances and apologies. Regarding each other with clear eyes, they dressed like practiced lovers. When each button was back in place, she stroked him again as they kissed. From the corner of her eye, Sarah saw the moon slide in the sky. Then she understood that a man was passing the car, walking a statuesque dog. Its muzzle slipped past the window.

"Holy shit," Jeremy said.

"He didn't see?"

"No way," he said, "but let's go." He started the car, which guiltily sputtered to life. "Have everything?" he asked, like they were going on vacation, and then they drove off.

In front of the house, she thanked him for the ride. They laughed at the understatement, but hers was nervous laughter. She was watching the windows of the house.

"I'm thirty-nine," she said.

"Happy birthday."

"I mean all year."

When she got out of the car, he said, "Call me. I'm the only Bone Shoulder in the book."

He was saying more, but she opened the front door and was inside.

She looked around her darkened front room at the only light Larry had left on. It looked like a seashell and had stood near the front door since they first moved into the house eight years ago. When she and Larry first met, it was their bedside lamp. They'd turn it off before they made love, then turn it on again and read before they fell asleep. It was the kind of thing that their kids would keep someday or throw away without much thought. She sat in the near dark for quite a long time and then turned on the television.

In the earlier years of her marriage, she'd tell people about their furniture with great enthusiasm, as if their lives might be altered by knowing that their coffee table had once been part of a bowling alley or that their rice-paper lampshade was purchased in Holland. Most people went on with their conversations, and Sarah began to ignore her surroundings with practiced indifference. When furniture wore out, they replaced it. They took care to buy paintings that they'd like forever and to keep books from too much humidity.

With her eyes closed, she listened to the sound track of *Zulu*, the midnight movie, to block out the memory of her excited breathing in Jeremy's car. The cat joined her on the sofa and examined her warily, jerking her head away from Sarah's unfamiliar smell. She thought of Jeremy's satisfied moaning. On the television screen, white men were shooting Africans with dubbed-in British accents. One fell, then another. If she'd just gone into the bedroom and concentrated on sleep, if she'd just put her leg over Larry's or whispered anything into his ear, she could have changed what had happened to her.

When *Zulu* was over, she looked up Jeremy's name and said the numbers to herself as she dialed them.

"Hello," he said.

"I can't sleep."

"Neither can I."

"I was wondering what kind of Indian you are."

"A happy Indian. When can I see you again?"

"How about tomorrow afternoon?"

"That'll have to be soon enough. Why don't you come by my apartment at two?"

"Okay."

"What color is your phone?"

"This one's light blue."

"I have a black phone with a dial."

"An antique."

"Where are you standing?"

"In the hallway."

"Can you see outside?"

"Yes. Alan Partanos is walking out of some bushes with Nora Sampson."

They both laughed.

After they talked, she dozed on the couch for a while. She looked out her picture window at the sky, the color of a dirty undershirt. Then she took a shower and fell asleep.

"How was grief last night?" Larry asked.

"Fine," Sarah said tentatively.

"Is sleeping on the couch part of the therapy?"

"I came in late. The class went to a bar."

"I stayed up late watching a PBS special on the plate-sized toads of Australia. They can be boiled down and their juice drunk for psychedelic effects. The Aborigines get high on them all the time. Want some toad?" Larry asked handing her a half-filled cup of coffee. He brushed her wrist as he passed the mug to her. "Don't miss your class," he said. "It's eight-thirty already."

Sipping the lukewarm coffee that Larry had made for himself, she imagined that he knew. A strange panic marched up her veins and made her head fill with happiness.

IN HER LECTURE on Hawthorne and Melville that morning, she had said *surreptitiously* more times than she had in her entire life. Dwelling on the intensity of the friendship between the two men, she noticed how her good students were becoming uncomfortable and her poor ones uninterested, but she felt uncontrollably effusive. Like the Sarah on *The Grammar Connection,* she pumped her voice through the entire script. At one point she made a joke about colored chalk and used the board to sketch the toreador outfit that Melville had worn to woo Hawthorne on one of their famous picnics in the Berkshires. With some giddiness, she imagined her students reviewing for finals, trying to make sense of their April 17th notes. Maybe Hilda Smock, her most serious literature major, had written in her sensible hand, *Dr. Holm is out of character today.*

She had never inflicted herself on her students before, and once outside of class, she was embarrassed by her excesses. A cloud of guilt seemed to follow her car through the vibrant spring sky. She drove to Jeremy's apartment thinking about her mother. Who were the members of the previous generation, unselfish women in aprons, who, if they had private lives, kept them in hiding? She remembered their bathroom vanity stocked with contingencies. She had grown up in a household where soap, toilet paper, kitchen cleanser, sanitary napkins, and toothpaste would never be missing. She couldn't remember one moment of discomfort her mother had caused her.

She doubted that Ivy had ever been with another man. She began to recall the men she'd known when her mother was young—vegetable men, knife-sharpeners, Fuller Brush salesmen. It had been more difficult to meet men when most items were brought to the kitchen. She remembered Larry's colleague Dan, whose pregnant wife had run off with the Gourmet Pantry chef from Dominick's the Tuesday before they were supposed to go to Belgium on a Fulbright. But Mae and Sarah had always been in the house underfoot. While Sarah had built a tower of McCormick spice containers, she could see Mae cutting Campbell's soup paper dolls on the kitchen's black linoleum floor peppered with glitter. Of course, Ivy could have sent them to their rooms or the playground across Godfrey Boulevard, but Sarah didn't remember that happening.

The man Ivy seemed to like most was old enough to be her grandfather. Mr. Harz repaired vacuums and other small appliances. He was frightening to Sarah because arthritis had bent him over. When he offered her candy, she'd hide. She could still see the careless bow of her mother's morning-glory-print apron. There would have been several years when Mae was already in school, and Sarah, afraid of the sound of the vacuum, would have fled to her room. But she couldn't imagine Ivy wanting to be touched by his gnarled nicotine hands. The egg man had beautiful palomino-colored hair that swirled like a conch shell, but his uniform was unpressed and his fingernails were dirty. Sarah and Mae weren't allowed to keep the unwrapped pastel candy hearts he'd hand them. Otherwise, he might have been a possibility.

She remembered calling her mother years ago, when Larry began seeing Donna. She hadn't exactly told Ivy about Donna, since that would have meant reporting on her own cowardice, but judging from the hints Ivy had dropped, she understood very well that Sarah was miserable. Sarah, confiding in no one, had deflected the help she offered. Instead, she'd held her breath all these years, watching the little altar she'd erected to her martyrdom wobble in space. Her grief-therapy class, a group of strangers, had been the first human beings who'd heard about her marriage, and that obliquely, through her remark about soiled diapers.

Since the apartment numbers climbed more slowly than she'd expected, it turned out that she had parked the car several blocks away from Jeremy's and had to walk in the unfamiliar neighborhood. It was surprisingly warm for April. A subtle breeze stirred the trees. People sat on the stoops of their apartment houses, the types you see more in New York than Chicago, with no back stairs and flimsy fire escapes attached here and there. A woman with a towel wrapped around her hair called upstairs to an open, unscreened window, "Take a nap, Donny. Lie down." The weather reminded her more of late autumn than spring. In October people would take to their porches in fervent appreciation of the last few days of warmth before cold weather set in. She remembered how dark the world had seemed after her father had died.

On the lawn adjoining Jeremy's on Dover, two boys feigned combat while one of their German shepherds, a partisan, sincerely barked. On the porch of the six-flat, a heavy man in a sleeveless t-shirt was drinking beer, ignoring the tumult. The children continued pounding each other, and the dog changed its focus to a man in a battered, rust-colored Pinto that looked like it had survived a collision with a gas tanker. The man was listening to Ray Charles sing "Georgia." When the dog continued barking at his car window, the man gave it the finger.

Jeremy had been watching television from his sofabed in the center of a living room with enameled white walls facing bare bricks, Oriental rugs, stripped woodwork, and sheer breezy curtains. He was wearing khaki pants and no shirt. His chest had a small patch of hair that was lighter than Sarah had expected. His nipples were dark and slightly puckered. His entire surface glowed, as if polished from shiny brown stone.

He handed her a glass of red wine and they sat in bed. Phil

Donahue was interviewing a transsexual who looked a little like Phil Donahue but was taller and had a weaker chin. She wore severely short hair and small pearl earrings. "No, I wouldn't have the operation done in the United States, not even if Johns Hopkins had approved it. American expertise in genital restoration is far behind that of European surgeons, particularly the Scandinavians."

Jeremy clicked the off button on the remote, and they began to unbutton themselves silently and solemnly. Today would confirm a course of action, Sarah thought, as Jeremy took Sarah's clothes from her and placed them neatly on his bentwood rocker.

"Let's talk," he said.

He'd been raised in Red Lake, Minnesota, but had come to Chicago for college on a full scholarship. In 1968 he was one of three Native Americans at the University of Chicago. It drove him crazy that several members of the Committee for Social Thought, SDS, and his British Marxist sociology professor thought it his obligation to be political. If he'd have told them what he really thought of their half-assed best efforts to change the world, they might never have spoken to him again. Besides, he'd left Minnesota to be a person, and he wasn't going to waste his time trying to please others by acting like their concept of a socially committed Indian.

Before he'd found his first assistant professorship, he'd been a social worker for the Department of Children and Family Services. He investigated families who wanted to adopt children and filed reports on their suitability. Making discreet inquiries about their attitudes toward race and religion, he used a numerical code to rate their openness and stability. Other than making him feel like a spy, the job was interesting and paid decently. Besides, it satisfied him that kids without a home would be able to receive a proper one due to his powers of observation. If he had had no grandmother when his mother gave him up, some smug, unpracticed U of C graduate like himself might have been trying to peddle him to a nice middle-class couple. Like the rest, they'd have preferred a blue-eyed boy, but if they were getting too old waiting to qualify for one, they might have chosen him. Sometimes, reacting to this notion, he gave a couple high marks in all the meaningful categories, regardless of what they said.

The winter he broke up with his girlfriend, a rich girl named Anne from Chester, Pennsylvania, who was studying medieval theology at the U of C Divinity School, he moved from Hyde Park to Uptown and stopped reporting to work. He stayed home smoking huge bars of hash and Thai sticks and reading Dostoevsky. He had about a thousand dollars saved up, enough to get him through the summer. He figured he'd get high and read or fish off Montrose Harbor all summer, but when he started drinking too much and couldn't account for hours at a time, he got frightened and considered being an Indian more seriously.

He went back to Red Lake and lived with his grandmother all spring. He helped her plant her garden that year, tilling the narrow rows of the nearly frozen soil with her old hoe, no larger than a child's shovel. He watched her cook things from dented cans and Mason jars that tasted good when they reached the table. Observing her eat silently at the table, eyes averted even in conversation, he found that he didn't hate her anymore for having been so kind.

He spent some time with the men he'd grown up with, many of whom had served in Vietnam or were destined to serve there. Others, including his older cousin Ted, had already been killed in the war. He remembered being envious of Ted's all-American bedroom full of baseball pennants, of his thick-wheeled dirt bike as it circled in a field near his house, of his stable, plodding, good-natured parents. Summer after summer, Ted would drop in and nod his head as a cue. Then they'd silently toss a baseball back and forth in the yard until an unexpected wind or silhouette on the horizon caught someone's attention and broke the spell. He could remember his cousin's tanned scalp through his summer flat-top and his secondhand baseball spikes, tied together by the shoelaces, and slung over his shoulder. Now he'd never see Ted again. In their small community alone, there'd been three deaths in Vietnam. There were more names on the War Memorial than boys he'd known who'd finished college. He was lucky to have gotten a high lottery number.

At home some of them called him the Prize Indian and the Great White Hope, but in many ways he felt the same as he always had with them, reticent and unable to show his concern for them or enjoy the aimless fun they sometimes had. He'd go joy-riding in someone's rusty, broken-down Chevy and watch them steal highway signs or splatter metal mailboxes with shells from a thirty aught six. They'd pass around fifths of off-brand bourbon and joints and fall asleep in bars that had country music on their juke boxes. They'd laugh and sing along with the chorus of "Okie from Muskogee" on the car radio, unanimously giving Merle Haggard the finger on the final note. Once he and Roland, a quiet high-school dropout who later became a missionary, took some windowpane acid and just sat by the lake watching the air vibrate for what seemed like days. When he went home at sunrise to sleep, he had been covered with dew.

When an acquaintance named Carl, just back from Vietnam, wanted to fight for no particular reason and Jeremy refused, he'd gotten beat up. High on speed, Carl was ferocious, landing random punches even as three men tried to pull him off. After Jeremy's welts and bruises healed, his grandmother urged him to go back to Chicago. Her eyes met his, and for the first time he could remember she raised her voice to him. He used his last savings to buy an old motorcycle and drive back to Uptown. The first night he parked it in front of his building on Leland it had gotten stolen.

"Did you feel guilty you didn't go?" Sarah asked.

"No, the innocent were slaughtered. I'd read books, Sarah. I knew how to prevent myself from being a fucking sacrifice."

"What would have happened if you were drafted?"

"Canada's very near Red Lake. I could have lived there with no problem at all."

They took a shower together and made love standing up in the stall. Jeremy was as slippery as a bar of soap. Sarah took him into her hands, mouth, and body. It ended with her legs comfortably wrapped around his waist. Her agility made her feel like a teenager, but when she saw herself in the fogged mirror she looked about the same.

"We'll have to try a bed next time," Sarah said as Jeremy dried her off.

"Just for variety," Jeremy smiled.

They dozed for a while, leaving off their clothes. Every now and then Jeremy reached over and leisurely touched her.

"I have to go home, make dinner, be a mom."

"Stay." He watched Sarah getting dressed. "Can I see you to-morrow?" His voice was small and hopeful.

The afternoon had made Sarah weak. It took great effort to collect her clothes. Jeremy remained naked on the covers, watching her. "I'll walk you to the car," he said, rushing to put on his clothes.

They walked hand in hand down Dover Street. Twilight was descending. Kids raced up and down stairways, frantically rode bikes, squeezed in one more game of double Dutch before dinner. Jeremy nodded a hello to two paunchy Indians about his age who sat on a bench drinking out of cans of beer in paper bags in a cul-de-sac at the end of his street. "My buddies," Jeremy sighed, and pressed her hand more tightly.

They hovered around her car, reluctant to say good-bye, watching the weather change as clouds speeded up. Trains whizzed by on the el track above the stone Graceland Cemetery wall covered in Latin Kings emblems. One car probably held Larry coming home to Sarah.

When Sarah unlocked their door, Larry was resting his feet on their bowling-alley table and watching the TV they'd bought last year when the bigger one would receive only UHF. For a few weeks they'd tried a diet of *Yugoslavia Live*, dancers in laced-up bodices and puffy sleeves, and commentators talking in front of red-tinted maps with Cyrillic letters, but they missed the news in English and settled for a smaller color set. A public-television news analyst was speaking to an Arab Herman Munster with a British accent.

Sarah joined him on the couch, and Larry leaned his head back on Sarah's arm.

"Your mother called."

"What did she say?"

"That marriage is a bond."

"Sounds reasonable."

"That maybe she'll die soon."

"I'd better call her."

Sarah sat at the kitchen table stirring some warmed-over coffee and dialed Ivy's number.

"Hello?"

"It's me."

"My preoccupation," Ivy sighed.

Sarah could see her mother lying on her plaid couch with a triangular snack tray beside her. She'd have a cigarette lit and Stanley's photos tacked over the couch unevenly, the way a child hangs schoolwork.

"I put my legs up on the couch so all my veins show like I'm a map and watch *The Honeymooners*. I'm only wearing a nightgown and I think, what if they find me like this?"

"Mom, you're not going to die."

"That's why I like talking to you, Tharry. You're so realistic. Listen, I don't want people staring at me. I want decorum. A closed casket. White flowers. A short service. Maybe some Perry Como."

"How about classical music?"

"That's a better idea. You're right."

"Anything else new?"

"Larry thinks you're in a phase. He says you're awfully quiet. Is everything okay?"

"Sure, Mom. You know, I've been in a group lately. Maybe that's why I'm quiet."

"What do you mean, 'a group'?"

"Group therapy."

"You get together and talk about what?"

"About grief."

Ivy chuckled.

"What, Mom?"

"The modern solution, Sarah. Talking it out. I'm fed up with talking myself. Anyway, I told Larry that everything's a phase. Dad had his baseball phase, his transistor-radio phase, his bike phase, his art phase, a very brief dying phase. He also had his separate-attic-cot phase and his separate-bath-towel phase, but I won't bore you with those."

"What did Larry say to that?"

"Not much. You know how he is."

"Mom, do you remember Mr. Harz? Did you ever . . . well, it's too bizarre, forget it."

"Did I ever what?"

"Sleep with him?"

"Don't you think I could have gotten something better? But I was loyal to Stanley. I'm practically the Virgin Queen. Why do you ask?"

"I was just wondering."

"Why?"

"Because."

"Are you seeing someone else, Sarah?"

"Yes." There. She'd said it. To her mother, of all people.

After a long pause, Ivy's voice resurfaced, clearer than usual. "You know what I think of sleeping around."

"Right."

"Do you love him?"

"Maybe. Yes."

There was a long silence. "Listen, Sarah, I think I'll put my chickeny feet up now and think about this development. Are you okay, honey?"

"Sure."

"Honest?"

"I'll call tomorrow when Larry isn't home."

"That was my mother," Sarah said nervously.

"I know. I told you to call her."

On TV two policemen were chasing a thief in a three-piece suit. Television gunfire broke out. The white-collar criminal was dead.

"It would have been nice to be alone forever," Larry sighed.

"Not according to Alan Partanos. It's even affected the way he eats pie."

"That little guy who teaches economics? He looks like a whippet."

"One and the same."

"How do you know him?"

"From grief therapy."

"Someone told me he once saw Alan kick a pigeon that got in his way."

"I'd believe it. Guess I'll start dinner."

The dead criminal's brother chased the policemen into the same warehouse policemen always wind up in. People hid behind barrels and fired rounds into each other.

Sarah thought of Alan never having anyone to ask him if he was hungry, eating his cherry pie slowly. She remembered that her father used to carry notes on jokes he'd heard in his wallet. He probably had one for Sarah and Larry, for Ivy's fear of death, for the occasion of Alan eating pie.

"Where are the kids?" Sarah called.

Larry had joined her in the kitchen. "Studying. What I meant before," he said, walking slowly toward her and putting his hands on the small of her back, "is that we're sandwiched between generations. Just imagine. No kids. No parents. Doesn't it drive you crazy being who you are?"

Yesterday afternoon she would have agreed with him. She didn't say anything for a long time. She silently chopped peppers and avocado into the salad. She added some herbed goat cheese and dried Italian olives that looked like miniature shrunken heads. Larry took two beers out of the refrigerator, taking care to pour them so that a minimum of foam got into their glasses.

"Dinner's ready," she said, and preceded him into the dining room. Before she called Carrie and Scotty, she thought of telling Larry about Jeremy. She could feel the pressure to speak as she tossed the salad and sliced some bread. It would have been easy to blurt out, "I'm seeing someone, Larry," but then he was grinding pepper into the salad and chopping a hard-boiled egg. She felt a sickness filling her chest as she imagined him faltering upon hearing the news. "Carrie, Scott, dinner," she said, and forced the moment to pass.

BY FALL, the affair hadn't ended as Ivy had predicted. Sarah saw Jeremy on the days she taught, and sometimes on weekends if Larry and the kids were busy. In just a month, Deenie would be coming to visit for Thanksgiving, but Sarah was unwilling for her life to change in any way. What could she say to Mae, who sounded more desperate than usual on the phone, to discourage the visit? "She wants to see us that badly?" Sarah asked, trying to imagine why.

"She claims she does. Maybe because of me and Tony."

"What do you mean?"

"We're not exactly good company."

"Are we ever good company for our kids when they're more than four feet tall?"

"Some parents probably are. Tony and I just clam up when Deenie's around. I sometimes think she'd benefit from knowing a little about us, even if the news is disturbing. But Tony's always wanted to shelter her from life. Does he think life won't find her?"

"So what does Deenie want to do here?"

"You'll have to ask her. She hasn't revealed a plan to me in the last century."

"I have to torture Scotty on the wheel to discover that he needs field-trip money. He's a master of subterfuge too."

"So is Tony," Mae laughed bitterly.

"Jeremy's been to my house, Mae." Since their relationship began, Sarah had become a non-sequitress.

"How did you manage that?"

"Larry was lecturing at Notre Dame. The kids were at school, but it was so disorienting to walk over that threshold together that we sat on the couch behaving like actors on a rather tame *Masterpiece Theatre.* Then we more or less fled."

"I bet it helps to have Jeremy. All I do is think about Deenie or Tony. And every night I dream about Dad. I haven't lived in his house for twenty-five years."

"So do I, Mae." They were both silent for a moment.

Sarah didn't elaborate about all the time she spent mourning Stanley. Usually it overtook her when she was driving alone or taking a shower. Hot mist would mingle with her heavy tears. Sometimes, looking at Larry's fine cheekbones, she'd transfer the fear. Imagining him dying, she'd still feel a rush of nostalgia or maybe even love.

But that morning Sarah didn't think about Larry or her father as she drove to the park and sat on a bench, turning her face to the sky. It was important to acknowledge Jeremy's existence before Deenie descended for Thanksgiving. Knowing that she was going to tell Rachel about Jeremy made her feel giddy. Then Rachel, her emissary to the larger world, could spread the news or not, and Jeremy would be admitted as existing in her life beyond his apartment or her phone conversations with Ivy and Mae. She wondered what Mae really thought of her affair. Her sister's responses were bland, almost therapeutic. How many lovers had Mae concealed from her? Sarah thought about the truth-in-lending clause that banks attach to loans. Didn't reporting on one's marriage, even as it was failing, require some scrupulosity?

She knew that Rachel, whose insights were sometimes uncanny, wouldn't mince words. She was the one who had told her how bad her marriage was before she had even inquired. She was also the only person on earth she knew who watched *The Grammar Connection* regularly. On various occasions she had instructed Sarah to speak up, slow down, and not wear red. She had even taped the show and threatened to coach Sarah in meaningful eye contact. Her concentration on Sarah had lapsed when she'd become involved with her new love interest, a big investor in soy futures and pork bellies, abstract Midwestern riches that remained a mystery to Sarah. Now, when Rachel wasn't teaching classics or Latin I to premed students, she spent her viewing hours reading the stock ticker on Channel 60.

Warm for late October, the park was still filled with sturdy flowers: geraniums, chrysanthemums, and marigolds. Reds, oranges, and yellows have a staying power that softer, less aggressive colors lack. Sarah couldn't say they were her favorites, but she respected their ability to endure as the calendar edged into November. When only the cockroaches were left on earth, they'd be surrounded by resilient flowers like these.

Sarah saw dried leaves blowing across the grass. The wind picked up some newspaper and sent aluminum cans skittering along the bicycle path. The whole park rattled like a chime and Sarah closed her eyes. She wondered why some leaves become brown while others take on more color. She wondered what she'd miss most about Larry.

"Caught you sleeping in public," she heard Rachel's cheerful voice saying.

Opening her eyes, she saw a well-groomed woman in a gray jogging suit and new Reeboks. "Rach, you look so proper."

"You mean I don't look like a British eccentric for once? You mean my clothes match? You mean I've given up Barbara Pym for self-help books on redoing my closet? The book calls it 'an environment,' you'll be happy to know."

"You look like an official jogger," Sarah smiled.

"I look like a corporate lawyer with twins named Spencer and Kate. Or is that too incestuous?"

They laughed, and Rachel joined her on the bench, pecking her on the cheek as she lowered herself to be seated.

As soon as Rachel got comfortable, Sarah suggested that they walk. It wasn't that she thought the elderly man on the next bench would listen, but she'd feel his presence just the same.

"But I'm so happy here!" Rachel protested, but not too strongly, closing her eyes to take in a few seconds of the lethargic autumn sun.

"I'll tell you why we need to walk later," Sarah whispered, tugging at Rachel's arm.

"Do we have to walk continuously or just to a destination? Jogging outfit aside, I prefer breakfast to health."

They headed across the park to Whoppi's, a small mom-and-pop espresso bar. Despite the levity of its name, the mom and pop who ran it were members of a sect who wore white turbans and gave their profits to a guru with a degree in physics who lived in New Hampshire. Sarah couldn't remember if it was that guru or one in Massachusetts who had been cross-examined on *60 Minutes* a few months earlier.

The six tables were taken when they arrived, mostly by young mothers with yacht-sized buggies who'd come to renew their sanity in public. One was just finishing her croissant and tea. "Now we'll go to the park, Mitchell," she was telling her sleeping infant, whose amazingly long, curly black hair spilled out of his woven bonnet. "Mitchell loves the park," she announced. Sarah remembered how she used to talk to her kids in public with fuller sentences and better diction than at home.

"Looks like you need a carriage to be admitted," Rachel smiled.

Everywhere they went lately, children were inevitable. When Carrie and Scotty were little, before most of their contemporaries started having children, Sarah could walk for blocks and would have been more likely to see a Frenchman with a wooden leg than another woman with a child.

"Can you loan me some baby pictures if they card us?"

Fatisha, a turbaned woman who was rumored to have been a dancer with Twyla Tharp before she married into the sect, weaved through the infants toward their table. They ordered two cranberry-orange muffins and cappuccino.

"You're probably wondering why I needed to see you."

"I thought for breakfast."

"Well, that and something more."

"You want the name of a detective."

"Why would I want that?"

"I was just reading in the grocery about an actress whose name I've already forgotten. She hired a detective to watch her husband. The detective found him in bed with the left-handed drummer from God's Dogs. It spoiled a happy illusion for her."

"About dogs or God?"

"About the left-handed." Rachel rolled her eyes.

"Well, I want to tell you about Jeremy," Sarah said, clutching at her own wrist, smoothing her hair, winking. She wasn't sure how she was supposed to continue. There were so many scenes that would have been too intimate, but to simply say she was in love would rob her of the pleasure of narrating it to Rachel. "You remember I mentioned him before? I met him in grief therapy after my father died," she said solemnly.

"Sure, I remember. You're in love." Rachel smiled.

"How do you know that?" Sarah asked fiercely.

"It's obvious, Sarah. I'm surprised you think I don't know, after, what, these six months?"

"Do you think Larry knows?"

"Not necessarily. I doubt you gloat around the house. I doubt you take him to breakfast for portentous announcements. I doubt you've practically stopped talking to him."

"I've stopped talking to you?"

"Not really. It's just that you confine yourself to politics and religion. It's a bad sign in friends."

"So Larry doesn't know even though you do?"

"Why should he? Pardon me for saying this, Sarah, but if Larry noticed a change in you it would have to be real obvious, like no respiration. I've wondered why you haven't been living it up all these years. You could have gotten away with murder if you'd wanted."

Sarah felt the waters had parted. Fear-abatement was Rachel's specialty. She could mediate hostage crises, reassure world leaders.

"Then I have nothing to explain?"

"Maybe to Russell. He's interested in how heterosexuality works. He wonders especially about generic fucking. He's seen it in movies, of course, but it always looks better or worse in movies."

"Russell knows too?"

"Sarah, your most remedial English student probably knows. The one who begins every essay, 'In our modern society of today.' The ancient man who trims the vines on campus probably knows. You walk around practically beaming."

Sarah looked disappointed and Rachel patted her on the back.

"I know, Sarah, you poor, egregious woman. You wanted to explain it slowly, slowly, slowly, and spare no details, right? How he rubbed his index finger over a vein in your wrist. How you kissed for the first time under a dim, wobbly chandelier. You wanted to be dramatic and make me see how the process has involved suffering. How you've suffered keeping yourself from him. How you suffered that first time, wherever it happened. How you continued to suffer even when your pleasure was as deep as a fucking river.

"That's what I hate about people in love. They want to graft some pain onto it. They don't want to admit they're simply happy. It reminds me of something I once read about poor Mark Twain. The man never thought he was funny. And people in love don't either."

Fatisha brought the second round of muffins Sarah had ordered.

"Thanks for nothing," Rachel said, piling some spare crumbs into her mouth and giving the plate a harsh look. "Now I'll have to jog home too. By the way, I'm not seeing Rodney anymore."

Almost afraid to speak, Sarah asked why.

"It turns out he isn't very flexible about small matters like sex and sex. But he has me investing in high-yield bonds. We're not going to be underpaid university lackeys forever, Sarah." Rachel dug inside her purse and handed Sarah a brochure from an annuity fund.

The jig is up, Sarah thought, sitting at her kitchen table after breakfast with Rachel. Maybe she should talk to Larry before bed. She could introduce the topic by saying she'd met Rachel for breakfast and bring the conversation around to what they had discussed. The information would convey less meaning as an anecdote in a larger story, but could she be so coy? When she did tell him, she'd need a funeral dirge and perfect candor. Maybe she'd wait for the weather to get cold. Funerals are unsettling without chilling rain and wind that stings your face. She looked at her dime-store gingham-chicken tea cozy, her fern plant, her austere gray coffee mug with the indelible brown swirls. She thought of their kitchen empty of its familiar objects. She'd drive around and formulate how to tell Larry. First she'd put a few small things she knew she wanted into her car. That way she would be able to keep them.

"I'm surprised to see you," Russell said, stepping out onto the stoop of his ancient graystone to hug Sarah. He was wearing black jeans, a soft white cotton shirt with long tails, and beige moccasins. He looked like a model with a headache. "Come in," he said shading his eyes from the sun. He took her hand and led her into the dark foyer.

"The weather's so nice," Sarah said. "I've had breakfast with Rachel and been down to the lake and driven around the block a couple of hundred times, but I don't want to go home yet. Have you been outside, Russ?"

He gave her a look of incredulity. "Didn't you miss me at work yesterday? I had a migraine, so I'm photosensitive. Before I get one, I see halos and meteor showers. The man who invented fireworks must have gotten migraines. Too bad John's not home. He'll be sorry he missed you. He's so greedy about company. Except when Tamara visits. Then John flees." He motioned her into the front room.

"My producer is a case," Sarah agreed. "I think Tamara's one of a handful of women whom Larry's refused."

"How do you know that?"

"For no reason I can explain, she was spitting angry at me for about a month after we'd all been at a party together. She was wearing leather pants and had Larry cornered on the rather ghastly roof of this industrial loft on Loomis. When a bat flew from a pipe near a rafter, she nearly jumped him. Larry spent a week imitating her accent."

"I ahm ah Zabra," Russell said in heavily German-tinged English. "Kee smee meet filling." Sarah sat on his beige leather couch laughing. She absentmindedly touched the translucent beak of his end-table goose lamp.

"You like it?" Russell said with real surprise.

"Sure."

"John says my lamp's the indoor equivalent of lawn flamingos."

"I like lawn flamingos too." They laughed.

"He limits the number of hanging baskets I can put out in summer. If it were up to me, the deck would be full of fuchsia." He made a sweeping gesture toward the partially obscured kitchen and the deck beyond it.

"John's funny."

"He's a decorating fascist."

He offered Sarah coffee, tea, wine, and finally beer, which she accepted. A huge stein of weissbier appeared on the elegantly curved black marble coffee table. The Dow Jones average gave way to a percussive version of *The Grand Canyon Suite*.

"Is Ferde Grofé the only modern composer? Every time I listen to a classical station, I hear hooves going clip clop clip clop," Sarah said.

Russell's eyes went sanpaku, and he smiled mysteriously. Sarah thought of Chinese art, of Buddhas, of the Mona Lisa, of archetypal female inscrutability on his handsome male face.

"So what do you want to know?"

"About what?"

"About me and Jeremy."

"As much as you want me to know."

"Well, in that case . . ." Sarah began talking, weaving a long skein of connections, and interlacing it with some color: Mrs. Pipkin, Reed, Alan Partanos coming on to Nora Sampson.

"I'd always thought Alan was of my persuasion."

When she got to the subject of Jeremy, she felt strangely reticent. Her story slowed, then came to a full stop. Maybe she was doomed not to tell it after all. She drank her beer slowly and ate some shelled pistachios that had magically appeared on the table.

Russell brought more drinks, straightened the coffee-table clutter, dusted off a copy of *Art in America,* offered her beer nuts, looked at the neat half-moons of his cuticles. "I only have till five, Sarah. Then I'll need to ungoo the okra and and start a jambalaya. It's my day to cook."

"The first time, I made love in Jeremy's car," Sarah blurted out.

"And then?"

"And then I told him I was thirty-nine and went home and sat in the dark."

They laughed for a long time.

"Have more beer," Russell said.

"I can't. I need to go home and tell Larry."

"Why would you want to do that?" Russell asked, turning his face self-consciously up to hers.

"Because you very discreetly told me I was fat, remember? My father had died and I was eating like mad. I thought of going to a weight-loss class."

"You were eating Doritos."

"Right. So I went to grief therapy and met Jeremy."

"So why are you crying, Sarah?"

"Because I still miss my father."

"Sh-sh-sh," Russell stammered, patting Sarah's back. "I shouldn't have given you so much beer. You've turned soggy on me."

Sarah wiped her face on her sleeve as a child would and tried to smile.

"You can lie down till John gets home if you're feeling bad. He can drive you. I wouldn't take our lives in my hands myself, what with my auras."

"You *are* a bad driver," Sarah laughed, thinking of Russell's habit of testing his brakes long before an intersection. "I think I'm better now, though." She kissed him on the cheek and made her way toward the door.

"See you at the orifice tomorrow." He opened the door for her and waved as she walked down his steps.

She was elated that the world knew, and drunk, stinking drunk. Odd sensations crowded her head: the smell of Larry's shirts, the color of the sky the day her father died, Mae telling her at seventeen that she didn't like how semen flowed down the insides of her thighs after sex. She called it snail trail, a code name that dotted their conversations for a decade. Sarah scanned her rearview mirror and saw a bald man who was singing and a woman whose station wagon contained three empty infant seats.

Standing at her threshold, vertiginous as Grendel after the Mead Hall, she heard rock music down the hall.

"Is everything fine, Carrie, Scotty?" she called to each child in turn.

"Did you know that Carrie wants to get a tattoo on her ass?"

"That'll be very pretty," Sarah answered. "Good night."

She wondered if drunkenness required depth perception. If she closed one eye, she didn't spin. She remembered playing Ping-Pong with Larry and a Mexican economist aboard a cruise ship off Crete. That the missed ball wound up in the ocean provided the game with a comic urgency. It was a pleasure to think of the blue moonlit deck as she did blinking experiments. She squinted into the half-light, realized how comfortable the world was consigned to a nine-by-twelve frame, and made one more effort to close both eyes.

AFTER SHE'D FINISHED talking to Larry, Ivy walked to her corner. She stood at Sheridan and Granville adjusting her paisley scarf so that it would cover the back of her neck and turned her profile away from the wind. The lake, which she could hear from her usual bus stop, was in an uproar. Now and then, as she imagined a whitecap crashing against the breakwater, she wondered if Mae remembered that Lake Michigan had whitecaps. Her California daughter probably considered it pretty tame compared to her ocean. Feeling the wind pierce three layers of clothing, she thought of Sarah in California and the girls somewhere in the West. She conjured up a benign yellow sun high in the sky over a bald, perfectly symmetrical mountain. She'd driven west once with Stan when the kids were young and visited the usual sights.

Squinting into the distance, she could see the green outline of the bus at the curve near Mundelein College. As soon as she got out of the cold, she'd begin talking to Stan as she always did when she was alone. She smiled to think how much could be said without speaking. "I'm a ventriloquist," she wanted to tell the dignified black woman in the white uniform who was coming off her shift at the nursing home. Thank God Stan had escaped a long illness and confinement. He'd have hated being cooped up, Ivy thought, as she slowly ascended the three-grooved rubber-and-metal stairs of the bus and showed the driver her senior citizen's pass. As soon as she found her seat at a window near the driver, she could begin.

Stanley, it's foolish to prepare so early with Christmas a month away, but it's a way to avoid my darkest thoughts about what's happened to Carrie and Deenie. The 147 Sheridan bus is full of grandmothers, just like me, the blue-hairs, I call them, going to waste a Saturday shopping. Life's just too long: It's outlived you. Look. That old man is smiling. His lip is so high on his gums that he looks like a frightened old dog. Who's he looking at, I wonder, and how many women are talking inside of themselves like I do? My new theory of longevity's this: Men die first because women are the ones who talk. We talk to our babies when they're swimming blindly inside us and to our children even when they stop listening. Day in, day out, we talk to our husbands. You used to watch the Sox, and I'd tell you things. Once I said I hated you just to test, and you said, "Uh huh." Imagine the silence if you'd lived beyond me. It's less lonely this way, Stan.

We all watch the lake, so gray and temporary, making its mark on the world. The actual water's different all the time, I think, like my face in the mirror; and the wind is so strong that the bus travels on a slight diagonal almost like a sailboat over Lake Shore Drive. The waves are so high that the two easternmost lanes are flooded. You would say, "Quite a storm," and adjust your collar up with a quick little turn of your wrist that card dealers make. I'd agree, and we'd talk about the weather. What we said was never important, Stan.

Without a lake, how do people know seasons? When winter descends they can't sense anything's wrong. Look at Mae and Tony, basking in endless summer in that foolish state where women wear mink coats when it's sixty degrees. Palm trees rising like three-story buildings. We know who we are because of our needs: hunger, shelter, thirst. Like the elements of your classroom chemistry chart that had such beautiful names and made up everything we ever touched.

The State Street Mall's crowded with people already carrying cheery bundles, dropping coins into Salvation Army kettles. On the corner in front of the Washington Street entrance to Field's, two women wearing military caps are doing a Punch and Judy show. The puppets are old and raggy like a couple who've been together many years. A crowd has gathered to watch them perform, but they're too coy for me. They act like they don't mean a word they say.

So I go for a bite at the Field's cafeteria before what? Buying one bran muffin in the bakery section or a box of Frango mints to eat alone in bed? Were our lives this slow? Yes, we ate things and read magazines. You liked wool socks in winter. I was a mediocre cook. Chicken salad on a croissant, a pot of tea, and a blueberry cobbler that I should resist. I show my charge card

to the listless clerk—it still says your name—and find a
table with no particular view. And all the time I'm thinking this: The nerve of these people to be alive when
you're not. There's a portly Italian every bit your age at
the next table who's brought a sandwich from home.
He's bought coffee to wash it down. There's an ancient
woman at the next table drinking hot water and eating
raisin toast. When did people our age become so depressing? Here's a little secret: People hardly amount to much
anymore.

Should I have visited you instead? Regained my tol-
erance by touching your stone? That's what I do there,
Stan. Last week I treated myself to a cab. It was a rainy
day, and I packed some extra sweaters, a tuna sandwich
on toast, a coffee thermos, and some pink geraniums I'd
grown on our balcony. They won't last long in the blast-
ing cold, but I wanted you to have them. I sat on your
ground and thought about Thanksgiving. I thought about
Sarah and Larry and tried to understand it. After all, we
want the right person next to us when we die.

You're not flying from place to place like a leaf or
an invisible light, Stan, but you're privy to information.
Why has everyone gone so wrong? That's the trouble
with you dead. Even when I dream you just sit there
watching whatever happens to me. I wish you'd lift your
hand to help us out somehow.

I find myself talking to you all the time. I have to
make sure my lips aren't moving in the book-check-out
line at the library or on the bus like today. It happens
when I have a joke to share. When I saw the man with
the chicken on his head on State Street, I wanted to tug
your arm and roll my eyes in a friendly direction.

From where I'm sitting now I see one side of the
giant Christmas tree. It's just the way you remember.
Going to Field's isn't much different from going to
church. I think of life and death here. What else is reli-

gion but inspiring architecture, noble views? I admit I close my eyes sometimes and wish. I've always done that, and a few times I spoke to God when I felt slighted: When the Depression kept me from buying the three white uniforms and the watch with a second hand I needed to be a nurse. When you were drafted three weeks before Mae was born, and I had to go with Papa to the hospital. He was so afraid that his daughter was going to embarrass him by giving birth in the lobby. "Wait, Ivy, wait!" he was shouting as I pulled against nature to hold Mae inside me. Do you know what Sarah asked me last spring? If I ever had lovers. Sometimes I wished for that too, Stan. There's no reason you shouldn't know.

When I think of Christmas, my mind keeps returning to this: If God had had a daughter, it might have worked out better. I could have spoken to God on more friendly terms. I could have said everything on my mind instead of keeping it all inside like I do. When I think about it, Stan, I find myself, no matter who's around, talking to you, moving my lips.

CARRIE HEARD Deenie's voice, as loud and insistent as a Chinese gong. The whole bus was going to know that her mother didn't love her and her father didn't care. Carrie heard a country singer playing her ballad on a nervous guitar. She thought of the poems about loneliness that her friends wrote in lower-case letters. They had grown gardens of it and built towers. The sea, the stars, everything whispered it. What could they mean? It seemed that the universe was too full, that people bumped into each other and stuck or fell apart whether they wanted to or not. She thought of a beach full of starfish coupling on the sand. She wasn't sure that was how they did it, but the image of all those arms satisfied her. While Carrie had been

absorbed in her view, everything had shifted again. More people had
fallen in or out of love right under her nose. First her mother and
Jeremy. Now Deenie and Adrian. Was there a code they used, a
secret language spoken to merge and dissolve? Watching Deenie and
Reena Fishblatt pressing their faces together now, punctuating their
words with harmonious laughter, she guessed they were a little in
love too. Now and then Mrs. Fishblatt would pat Deenie's tangly
hair or exclaim, "My poor dear," as if she were traveling cross-
country with a Dickens orphan robbed of her inheritance. The way
Carrie saw it, Deenie had robbed herself, Deenie, who stared straight
ahead, refusing to look at either Carrie or Adrian.

She was Carrie Holm and he was Adrian Fishblatt. He was
twenty-four and traveling with his mother. She was fourteen and
alone. Her face was probably on milk cartons by now, "Last seen
on Thanksgiving, five feet three." In the world of coupling bodies,
she was invisible as the air they traveled through. Now and then an
older man like that skinny, rat-bearded clerk at the North Platte
comfort station might take notice of her, but he'd shake her out of
his head like a bad idea.

Carrie rubbed her cheek. She liked touching her own face.
The skin was so firm. Not like Adrian's, peppered with stubble, or
Mrs. Fishblatt's, with a craggy geography of its own. Her skin was
more like her mother's. She looked smooth as water. She remembered
her grandmother saying that you can tell when people are honest:
Look in their eyes, Ivy would say, but Carrie knew it was in the
skin.

The best words were already used up. *Majestic* would describe
Utah if it had any meaning beyond Majestic Rug Cleaners, Majestic
Burgers with extra cheese, hold the relish. Carrie wished that she
had lived when language was fresher. How would she make anyone
believe the purplish night sky and the flood of jack rabbits that had
poured across the road just in front of the bus headlights? She was
seeing for the first time. Being with her parents had blurred her vision.
They faced her in a direction and told her how to name the view.
They gave her old words and told her to believe in them. Now that
there was Jeremy, what should she call her father? Love hadn't failed
her; words had.

• • •

"WHAT SHALL WE DO this afternoon?" Jeremy asked.

"Oh, I don't know. Los Angeles just seems like a big waiting room to me."

"I've always wanted to see the La Brea Tar Pits."

Sarah warmed up some water on the washroom hot plate and stirred in a package of instant coffee. She watched Jeremy's hand adding powdered creamer and stirring. It was a good hand, an object of her life that had become as familiar as a coffee cup. She thought of it abstractedly like a sponge or a pocket watch. She thought of it holding a spoon. She imagined Jeremy eating in a spare kitchen with his grandmother, putting beans on a fork and sharing a remark with her about the weather.

"I keep wondering what Pipkin and the others would think of us."

"She'd fully approve, I'm sure."

"I've always suspected that people join self-help groups for this to happen, Jeremy."

"I've thought about that too, Sarah, but it's hard for me to accept that I'm just Alan Partanos with better manners."

"He came to our group with the express intention of meeting women. He complained to me that there wasn't a better sample to choose from."

"Isn't the cure ancillary to love?"

"I guess if Larry and I hadn't been falling apart, I wouldn't have sought out a group of strangers. Do you think everyone was there looking for someone? Like at a singles bar?"

"Everyone except Reed and Linsey, maybe. They can't ever replace what they lost."

Outside it had changed overnight. Rain fell in short, heavy bursts. They bought a cheap black umbrella in the hotel drugstore and walked out to the car.

"Maybe we should go to the Discounters for raincoats."

"Or get pith helmets at Banana Republic."

"It never rains in California," Jeremy sang as they stepped into the drizzle. She remembered being caught in a fierce downpour near Wrigley Field when the kids were little. She had picked up Carrie, who was crying that she couldn't breathe, as the rain beat on her face.

They stopped at an Italian deli and got two submarine sandwiches to go and two bottles of Coke. They ate the sandwiches wrapped in heavy paper in the front seat of the Ford Probe in the Tar Pits parking lot. Rain on the roof was a comforting sound reminding them of home. If Sarah didn't look at the battered palm trees, she could pretend nothing unusual was happening.

She was obsessed with the image of Carrie stepping off the bus and extending her hand. Then Sarah would take Carrie to a restaurant and offer her the Thanksgiving dinner that she'd missed.

Jeremy said that he didn't want to sound too ominous, but comforting phone call or not, they should prepare themselves for her running away, pretending simply not to recognize them. Jeremy, like his Uncle Jim, would be ready to give chase if necessary.

The rain was beating down more heavily, making a sheet of water that blurred everything around them. They couldn't even see out the window.

"I can't believe she'll run when I've come all this way to find her."

"You can't expect her to be grateful, Sarah." Sarah knew Jeremy was right.

"I have an idea. Let's go to the bus station and case it. You know, like detectives would."

"I guess it's better than the Tar Pits on a day like today."

Jeremy and Sarah sat on turquoise plastic chairs and watched couples reunite. They heard buses departing for Reno, for Tucson, for Cheyenne. They watched an ample Mexican mother kiss her small, sinewy, middle-aged son good-bye. Buses were leaving for Coos Bay, for Tacoma, for Alberta. She shared a 7-Up with Jeremy and imagined Carrie stepping through the arrival door between the Youth for Christ and the Japanese grandmother, outrunning the sailor who was making a beeline for his girlfriend and falling into her arms.

. . .

LARRY WAS SO RELIEVED that Carrie had left the message, that he was actually enjoying himself at dinner. He looked at his son affectionately. Their bodies were so much alike that he could interpret Scotty's emotions by the way he pressed his wrist to his high-boned cheek or the way one angular shoulder blade perched lower than the other in enthusiasm.

The tuba player and the banjo player wore Gay Nineties outfits: red-striped vests, black arm garters, and jaunty hats. One had a real mustache. Larry couldn't tell about the other. His nose looked a little crooked, making his face appear haphazardly constructed, like a cubist painting. Maybe there was only one duo who strolled from table to table at every restaurant in the city, changing their forms and symbolism to suit the diners' needs. Musical holograms, the stuff of science fiction. Maybe he could poke his finger through the blushing tuba player or change his angle of perception, making the banjoist disappear. It was a good omen that the men were hooting and stomping through a rather sedate version of "La Bamba" and that Scotty was clapping his narrow, tenative hands.

Larry wadded two dollars into their pockets when they finished. "Fun, huh?" he asked Scotty.

"Yeah, I guess so."

"You looked like you were having fun."

"Dad, you're acting creepy."

"What do you mean?"

"It's like you want to impress me."

"I just want to cheer you up." Larry looked helplessly at his pants, retied his shoe, ordered another glass of Chardonnay. He was afraid to look at Scotty's clear intelligent eyes. "Do you know what you want to eat?"

"How about a steak?"

"Once, when I was a kid, I went to dinner with my parents. It was someone's birthday, but I don't remember whose anymore. When it came time to order, I said I wanted lobster. My dad didn't want me to get it because it was too expensive. He said, 'I didn't drive this far to argue with you,' and I said, 'I didn't drive this far to eat crap.' "

"How old were you?"

"About eight."

"What did your dad do then?"

"Not much. He had this way of not looking at the whole family, like he was trying to cut his losses."

"I never knew him."

"He's been dead a long time, but I still think about him a lot."

"It feels like Carrie and Mom are dead too."

"Oh, they'll be back with us soon, Scott. Mom said she'll bring Carrie home when her bus arrives."

"Not really. Mom won't be back home with you."

"Why do you say that?"

"Carrie and I are both pretty old, so the judge will let us choose. But before we choose, you and Mom have to decide what you want."

"Don't you think we both want you?"

Scotty didn't answer.

The food had arrived, but Larry wasn't hungry. Sarah had a way of sensing when things were wrong. She was always right about the kids being sick. "She's getting a fever," she'd predict before Carrie's eyes went glassy and her cheeks colored. But Sarah's eyes had been fidgety long before Thanksgiving. He retreated into a memory of a summer when his parents had almost ended their marriage over plans for a vacation.

"How can you be too tired to go on a vacation?" his father had asked.

"All the driving, Larry, you, the sights. I just can't bear it."

"Vacations are for resting. You'll sit in the goddamn Buick. You'll see the goddamn Capitol building. The waitress will bring us rare roast beef and hot rolls with sweet butter. How can you be too tired for that?"

Then his mother had burst into tears. She crossed her legs and stared fiercely into her lap like a child refusing to speak.

His father was silent for a few seconds. Then he walked up to a small mahogany table with lion's-claw legs and hurled a maroon portable radio to the floor. Before his mother picked it up, she got a rag and dusted it carefully. She didn't try playing it then, but later that afternoon, Larry, drinking lemonade and peeling the paint off the curved wooden porch, remembered hearing "The Wayward Wind" and knowing he'd stay with his mother if it came to choosing sides.

"When do you think Mom started seeing Jeremy?" Larry asked.

"Around spring."

"How do you know?"

"She was on the phone a lot, and she seemed crazy."

"How was she crazy?"

"She was too talkative."

Larry squirmed in his seat, feeling his body fill with anger. "And you knew Carrie was going to leave and didn't tell us that either!" His chest burned and his hands felt fat. "How come you know so much, and I know nothing?"

"Dad, quiet down," Scotty whispered. His voice was aimed at his glass of water and he wouldn't move his eyes, not for anything.

"Was this the first time Mom, well, saw someone else?" Larry asked, trying to sound calm.

"I think so. And what about you?" Scotty asked, fixing Larry with his eyes.

Should Larry tell him that he couldn't stay home with Sarah even when Scotty was a baby? There had been something wrong from the start that he never could name. Maybe they'd gotten married too young. Maybe they weren't right for each other. Larry remembered the cold winter he was seeing Donna. He'd come home at midnight. Frost would be covering the windows and the wind would be howling. Sarah would be sitting up clutching Scotty, who had fallen asleep. Poor Sarah. She looked like a refugee holding her worldly goods. Larry knew that if he had loved her better, she would have put the baby down in his crib and simply gone to bed.

· · ·

WHILE THE OVERHEATED RADIATOR was cooling down, Deenie's first inclination had been to wait inside when Carrie and Adrian and Mrs. Fishblatt wanted to go exploring. It was funny that Reena knew so much about buses. She had convinced Deenie that a radiator problem could take a long time, so Deenie had consented to join the group as they made their way to the front of the bus.

Standing on gray, mountainous land with mesquite scratching at her legs, Deenie thought about the dolls she used to play with when she was eight. Because they were all girls, the plot was predetermined. The tallest doll would be the mother, widowed in an Indian attack. She was trying to get her family safely west on the rickety Conestoga wagon that pitched and buckled over snaky trails and dry gullies. She was the doll whose hair had been cut in a fit of pique over something that Deenie had forgotten. She wore a pink gingham dress. Her children, six to twelve in all, were fairly useless. While she sat on the arm of the couch holding the reins, they huddled on the cushion behind her, eyes vacant. It was up to her to drive the wagon, make their food, take care of their clothes, and, of course, nurse those that fell ill. In one version of the story, she lost them all to a virulent fever that lasted for days and had to dig dusty graves marked by stick crosses before she moved on alone. If she gave in to her emotions, they'd all be lost. Most of the time, she got them through with good sense and invention. Yes, they'd eat broiled iguanas to live. Yes, they'd boil yellow water if they had to.

The imaginary West of the saga she enacted with her dolls seemed more real to her than where she'd lived her entire life. All those years in California, she'd ignored the yellow daytime heat and black night of the desert. When Tony and Mae drove to Palm Springs for holidays, Deenie would sit with her back to the window reading movie-magazine gossip or dozing. Then she'd do her best to plant herself in the hotel lobby drinking virgin margaritas. She had no interest in the special winds or hearty water-conserving flowers or animals equipped to adapt to extremes of heat and cold. She'd seen pictures of foxes with exaggerated ears, of mice whose feet had become genetically enlarged with the exertion of travel.

Carrie and Adrian had walked on ahead. Thank God he was concentrating on her now instead of Deenie. No doubt he'd be on to "the dance," the only art he hadn't covered in his endless lectures. Deenie watched as they crested a rather steep hill, shoulders touching. Once Carrie had taken Adrian's arm for support and Deenie had felt a quick stab of jealousy. She was stuck with Reena Fishblatt, whose heavy legs ached, who couldn't climb hills, who was, at this moment, settling herself on a flat smooth stone and kneading her fat red toes.

"I thought a desert would be warmer," Reena said adjusting her sweater over her shoulders.

"We're up in the mountains too, and it's getting late."

"What town are we near?"

"I think the driver said a woman's name, maybe Jean."

"I hope we're not near a nuclear-testing site. Nevada has one, you know."

"I doubt a bus would go somewhere radioactive."

"Too bad this didn't happen in Las Vegas. We could have doubled our money."

"I bet you don't gamble."

"You never know where desperation can lead."

Deenie was bored to death. Reena was nice, but she longed to be with Branch. He never talked her to sleep. Everything he said was important. She couldn't see Carrie and Adrian anymore. She liked the bitterness of imagining them screwing in some ravine but knew it wasn't true. They might French a few times, but judging from Adrian's performance on the bus, he wouldn't try. And if he did, Carrie would be chicken. She'd come back real fast, faster than Deenie could say *shitfuckpiss*.

Having to pee, she wandered away from Reena and found a nearly bare bush attached to a rock. Crouching alongside it, she heard her urine tinkle onto the flat stone. In her doll games, no one ever peed. What would Reena do if she had to urinate? She'd never survive in the mountains like Deenie could. She needed sweaters and nail clippers. Deenie needed hardly any food and little water, and she wasn't afraid of a thing. Maybe if they were stranded, she'd trap an animal and cook it for Reena. She'd take a picture of it first, though, and send it to Dr. Weber. He had pictures of birds of prey on his office walls. Some were historical etchings of falconry. One was a painting of an owl swooping down on a mouse in the snow. Other less clear images seemed to have been taken by an inept photographer like her grandfather.

"Feel better?" Reena smiled when Deenie reappeared.

Reena was combing her hair with one hand and holding a pocket toothbrush and an aqua cup that unfolded like an accordion in the other. She looked like a vendor at Woolworth's.

"All I need is my vanity mirror with the circle lights, and I'll feel right at home."

"How long do you think we have?"

"The driver said half an hour. He has to add water and some kind of a sealant. I heard him telling that nice Mexican man."

"And how long have we been here?"

"Maybe ten minutes?"

Deenie shivered and wrapped her hands around her shoulders. By evening it would be cold, and Deenie would want the stupid trenchcoat that Adrian had ruined. Branch had told her that Costa Rica was warm and green. She wouldn't need it there.

When she saw Branch, she'd give him the best kiss ever. She'd tackle his legs and squirm all over the bus station and then they'd be off without Carrie. She'd give Carrie her mother's phone number but make her promise not to call for six or eight hours. Carrie was so dumb that she kept her promises. By the time Carrie called Mae, Deenie and Branch would be gone. She imagined them lying on a beach in Costa Rica. The sand was pink and a fat red sunset perched over their shoulders.

Many yards away over several gray hills, Deenie could hear a remnant of Carrie's laugh. Deenie stared relentlessly ahead. Watching an old woman applying cream to her feet was enough to make her want to puke.

"I was forty-two when I had Adrian," Reena began. "I didn't think I'd be able to reproduce anymore, Deenie, but suddenly I was pregnant."

"What were you doing until then? I mean when you were young."

"Oh, this and that. First there was the war. I was just a kid, but New York was filled with sailors, and to tell you the truth, I was a pretty wild girl. I saw lots of men, Deenie. I met one named Darian. Isn't that a wonderful name? I had a passionate time. He was a lot older than me. His family lived in the South. He had a voice that was very low and sweet at the same time. It mortified my family that I was seeing this strapping fellow with a fine square jaw. They thought that everyone from Louisiana was in the Ku Klux Klan. 'Don't bring that goy here again,' my mother warned. 'Papa will kill him.' "

"Would he have?" Deenie felt her heart accelerate. She hadn't thought much about what her dad would do about Branch. Mainly she hoped he wouldn't notice.

"Maybe. Papa was so angry to be in America. He'd been privileged in Germany. Here he handled produce all day. His hands got dirty, especially from the potatoes. And no one knew his name. So I'd meet Darian. We'd go to movies and ride on the Staten Island Ferry, wherever it would get dark."

Reena looked all around her and, in one swift gesture, removed her cardigan, pulled off her flower-print blouse, and replaced it with a similar one that had been folded on her lap. She reached inside her blouse and dusted talcum from a little container onto her chest.

"After the war, Darian went back home. He had a girlfriend there, and they were engaged. Her name was something like Lolly. I went on to college at NYU. I majored in botany and did research in a greenhouse right in the middle of Manhattan. It was wonderful in winter to work in that humid place. The air was so warm. It made me happy to be alone all day. I was through my master's degree and living like a nun. I'd come home every night and make canned soup and play my little radio. I figured I'd had enough fun in my teens to justify a pretty quiet life.

"I was twenty-nine when I met my first husband. He was a businessman my cousins knew, older and pretty well-off. His wife had died in Europe in the war. We married and bought a little house in Scarsdale. Except for his thick accent, we looked like an ad for a friendly bank. Anyway, it didn't work out. I should have known more before we married." Reena looked down at the ground, appearing to brush the memory away with her hand.

"Why?"

"Well, he wasn't, let's just say, a very good husband."

"What did he do?"

"He saw other people. He stayed away for days at a time. I'd sit in the kitchen smoking, wanting to burn down the house. He didn't want children, he didn't want me to work, and he certainly didn't want me, so I finally left him.

"I wasn't feeling very well at the time. I went to a doctor who found about fifteen things wrong with me. I moved to Chicago and found a doctor who told me I was depressed. Then he became my husband. Dr. Fishblatt was already an elderly man when we met. He had a heavy accent. He wasn't much to look at, but I was thirty-seven and desperate not to be alone."

"How old was he?"

"Nearly seventy."

"Adrian's father was an old man?"

"Yes."

"When did he die?"

"When Adrian was seven. He was very kind, Deenie. I hope your Branch is half as kind."

"What was it like, being with an old man?"

"Oh, in some ways like you'd expect. He was saggy in his skin and very hairy like a white bear, but it worked fine for us. We loved each other."

"Didn't you think of that first guy?"

"Of Darian, sure. I think about him now. Once I looked in a New Orleans phone book for his name."

"Was it there?"

"It was at the time."

"Did you call him?"

"No, but I imagined him better. I can still see his face. Of course, as a young man. No doubt he looks better in my memory."

"We'd better be getting back to the bus."

"Okay, honey. I feel nice and refreshed now. I guess the kids'll make it back themselves."

· · ·

The first hill they'd climbed revealed a narrow valley that was greener than anything else around. A little creek ran through it. Carrie ran toward the creek feeling untroubled that their bus was stranded between Las Vegas and the California border. When she had looked on the map, she saw there were hardly any names for where they were. Many lakes were called Dry Lakes and somewhere not so far west of them was a place called the Devil's Playground. The West seemed infinite and spare. You'd reach the crest of one hill and realize that its companions were everywhere, each as anonymous as the other. Nothing had an address. Everything was nameless. She thought of the view from her father's office, where every square inch above sidewalk level was named. Other than mesquite and a few quick lizards under rocks, they could have been on the moon. That's why the little valley had made her so happy. She crawled down the steep ledge to the creek and put her feet into water that was colder than she'd imagined. There must be an underground spring that fed it and provided the acre or so of green. In the city green was so tame; here it looked strange.

Perched on the slope, Adrian shouted "Don't drink the water" through megaphone hands.

"I won't," Carrie laughed. Adrian wasn't that bad. She'd watched him sleep and thought him very appealing. There was a secret that Deenie had missed about his nervous speech. If Carrie blabbed away about most anything, he was content to listen. She'd told him about her parents and Jeremy. She'd told him about all her friends at school, even Justin Parsons, who'd tried to kill himself last summer. He knew about Mr. Pinktotoen, the blind music teacher who came on Tuesdays and sang a cappella to a pitch pipe.

"Come down!" Carrie called.

"I don't think so."

"Why not?"

"We won't be able to climb back up. Then what?"

"Where's your sense of adventure? Besides, the water's wonderful. I'm thinking of taking a bath."

"Go ahead."

"Promise you won't look?"

Carrie rolled her jeans up and carefully folded her shirt over her stomach. She threw water on her legs. If Adrian hadn't been there, she'd have taken off her clothes and sat in the creek. She remembered her mother telling her how she loved to roll in the waves at the beach, while Scotty huddled on a towel shaking his head in resistance, afraid to touch the sand.

"Okay," Adrian said. "I'll come down."

He climbed down the rock on his behind, using the soles of his Nikes for traction. He was puffing and sweaty when he reached the bottom. "Now you're going to have to not mind what I'm about to do. I'm going to take off my shirt and pants and have a little shower. You can close your eyes if you'd like."

"I've seen men naked."

"Who?"

"My brother and father."

"Relatives don't count."

"And boys at camp. They'd swim nude all the time at night, especially when there was a moon. We'd watch from our cabins."

"Not the same."

Adrian laid his clothes out on the edge of the rock he'd just climbed down. He put his shirt, pants, and shoes in order to give the appearance that a body was lying there.

"You're silly," Carrie said, rearranging his shirt so that the right arm pointed up.

"That's how hands point on old gravestones. Ever seen them?"

Carrie was lying in the green ground cover next to his clothes. There was something luxurious about feeling so much sun at once. "My grandpa's grave just says his name."

Adrian had taken off all but his shorts and was throwing water onto his legs and chest. Carrie watched him from behind. He was shorter than Larry annd Scotty but more muscled. It was odd that someone who had no use for his body had such a good one. She watched the tendons in the back of his legs and his buttocks tighten as he squatted to throw water on his face.

"So what do you think of Deenie?"

"She's pretty confused."

"Can you believe how skinny she is?"

"She's anorectic."

"I know. Adrian, you're not the only person in the world who has a vocabulary."

"I just think I am."

When he finished washing himelf, he sat on a stone and pulled at a succulent's leaves. Carrie watched them darken as he flattened them between his fingers, removing their water.

"Should we get back?"

"Probably. Hand me my clothes, will you?"

Carrie piled his shirt and pants on top of his shoes and dumped them in his lap.

When she turned to climb back up the ledge, she wondered if she should have kissed him.

"Give me a hand," Adrian said. He grabbed her wrist and hoisted himself up the rocks. "Let's find the happy crew."

When they crested the next hill, they saw the empty spot where they'd left Deenie and Mrs. Fishblatt.

"They must have gone back to the bus." Adrian shrugged.

A feeling of terror made Carrie take off in a run that Adrian would never be able to sustain. She saw the ground blur under her as she flapped her arms and kicked her feet wildly up to her behind. Now and then a rock reached up or a root from a distant tree made her miss a step. Her sides ached and one of her ankles felt like it was straining to stay together. When she sprinted the last few yards up the hill back to the highway, she already knew.

It was a scene from a complicated tragedy. Deenie was sitting on the side of the road digging with a stick, a murderous expression on her face. Mrs. Fishblatt, inexplicably wearing a different shirt than before, was sitting on her suitcase and holding her face in her hands. The sun was just beginning to set, swathing them all in an Arctic pink glow. The bus was gone and the empty road looked strangely beautiful. Was that a mirage or the painterly light of the highway receding from them even as they sat at its side?

"Where in the fuck were you?"

"We went for a walk."

"Where's Adrian?" Mrs. Fishblatt asked, squinting past Carrie, combing the landscape for him.

"Oh, he'll be here soon. I think I hear him now. I ran back."

"Why did you run?"

"I had a feeling we were late."

"You *were* late, damn it," Deenie shrieked just as Adrian arrived. "We asked them to wait fifteen more minutes, but they already had waited forty." She waved her arms wildly for emphasis. "We're fucking stranded, Carrie, and when the bus gets in, I won't be on it. What will Branch think?" Her voice was a knot of misery.

Carrie didn't know what to say. "We found a green place with a stream. I guess we lost track of time."

"Damn," Adrian shouted as he panted and wiped sweat from his upper lip. "Mom, why didn't you make them wait?"

"Can I change bus schedules for you? The way you think the world works, Adrian."

"Where's my script?"

"Right here, right here." Reena smoothed her skirt with her fingers and pointed at his satchel. "I guess we'll just have to sit tight. They phoned a dispatcher. Another bus will be here in an hour or so and take us back to Las Vegas. They'll even put us up for the night. We can make connections to Los Angeles in the morning."

"I'm not waiting!" Deenie asserted, pressing against Reena with her entire meager body.

"You have to wait!" Reena demanded, waving a cautionary finger in her face. "It's almost night, for heaven's sake."

"C'mon, Carrie," Deenie said, and tugged at her shoulder.

"Can't we just call?" Carrie asked timidly.

"Can't we just call?" Deenie mimicked in a falsetto whine. She started walking away from the group.

"Where are you going in the dark?" Reena asked desperately.

"We're going to hitchhike. I can't go back to fucking Las Vegas. I have to get to Los Angeles when that bus does!"

"You're not going anywhere!" Reena shouted, but Deenie had already dragged her suitcase several yards down the highway and Carrie was reluctantly following.

"Carrie, stop her!" Reena pleaded into the vague darkness ahead of her. She could barely see the girls anymore.

"Adrian, can't you do something? I feel responsible for those girls."

"My meeting's tomorrow and I won't be at it," Adrian said flatly.

Reena watched desperately as the girls grew smaller in the distance. "Adrian, please," she pleaded, but when she saw him hunched over his suitcase at the side of the road, her resolve dissipated.

MAE'S BLOCK looked better to Sarah than it had the day before. The moon, backed into a corner of the sky, looked unsubstantial. Birds were silent on telephone lines. Sarah preferred the distracting noise of her own city neighborhood, where Korean and Puerto Rican kids on skateboards and old Chinese women hunched over shopping carts vied for the sidewalk. You'd hardly expect anyone to be alive on Sycamore.

She and Jeremy hesitated at Mae and Tony's threshold.

"Ready?" Jeremy asked before ringing the bell.

Sarah nodded tentatively. "Maybe we shouldn't do this," she whispered.

"You say that a lot," he said, pushing her ahead of him.

Tony, wearing a pink LaCoste shirt, was talking to a small man with a low hairline. His eyebrows nearly met his scalp, and everything about him was miniature. Sarah had trouble imagining his prim body rolling in primeval mud or his diminutive hands setting rabbit traps during Tony's manhood weekends. He was dressed in a pinstriped suit, a starched blue shirt with a white collar, and a blue paisley tie. Both men rose together when Mae, carrying a pitcher of Bloody Marys, ushered Sarah and Jeremy into the front room, pointing them toward the loveseat. Mae was wearing a black jumpsuit. A large onyx owl perched on her left breast.

"Jeremy and Sarah, this is Dr. Frank Weber."

He half-bowed in greeting but didn't come forward to shake their hands. Sarah couldn't help watching how his small eyes seemed greedy to take them in. At a much earlier age, his unabashed stare would have made her nervous. Now she figured it was a glance certified by his advanced degree in human nature. He was doing long-distance phrenology on them.

They all settled in with drinks, and Dr. Weber began. "I hear Deenie's with your daughter."

"Correct," Sarah said, wondering why such obvious trivia was necessary.

"Would you like some hors d'oeuvres?" Mae said in her best formal tone, pointing to a tray of cream-cheese-stuffed olives, celery, and cherry tomatoes. Sarah thought about variations on Mae's voice. Her signature, too, differed from letter to letter and message to message. It could be strident or unnerved in its small, downward slant.

Tony lined up some celery symmetrically on his plate, then cleared his throat and began. Sarah saw his face become animated with significance. New lines appeared in his brow, and his chin, jutting forward, seemed to bear responsibility for the world.

"This is a difficult situation, and we have a lot to say, so I guess we'd better begin." He picked up a sesame breadstick and waved it like a wand toward Jeremy and Sarah before crunching it self-consciously. "Frank has some ideas he'd like to share," he said chewing.

It was odd how everybody was getting younger, Sarah thought, looking at Dr. Weber, whose first name rang uncomfortably in her ears.

"It's important that we all act rationally tomorrow at the bus terminal. We want the best for everyone concerned." His delivery was slightly nasal and quietly assertive.

"Are you coming?" Jeremy asked.

"I had intended to." Dr. Weber's eyes flashed quick irritation.

"We've asked Frank to join us for support, Jeremy. Deenie is a pretty troubled little girl."

Where was Mae? Sarah peered down the hall. She saw her staring out the kitchen window. Except for her cheeks, which quivered up and down as she chewed on her lower lip, her body was completely still.

"It's important that we provide a show of force without being overly forceful. We need to catch Deenie without causing further injury."

"What do you plan to do about her boyfriend?" Jeremy asked. "She must be meeting him, you know."

"We're trying to locate him now. We feel we can convince him of the therapeutic necessity of an alternate plan." Dr. Weber looked at Jeremy with eyes full of certainty.

"He's not going to be convinced," Jeremy insisted. "They think they're in love. They're running away together."

"We can resort to legal means if we have to. You know that Deenie's a minor."

"You'll have her boyfriend arrested, Tony? That's very subtle. If you do, she'll just run away again. Or worse."

"Jeremy's right, Tony," Mae's voice interrupted from the kitchen.

"I . . . agree," Sarah was about to say, when Dr. Weber snapped, "We'll do what's necessary to intercept the child and separate her from non-adaptive influences. We understand the situation, thank you." Dr. Weber stared down Jeremy.

Jeremy held his hands up in surrender. "We want to deal with Carrie. Deenie's yours." He smiled. Sarah could sense the annoyance he was straining to contain in his face.

"Well, Jeremy, I see no reason why our strategies need to correspond. You're apprehending a well-grounded child who's given you little trouble. We're dealing with a poorly anchored ego."

"Mae's explained your anchoring therapy to us," Jeremy replied. From the look on Weber's face, Sarah could tell he thought that a bad sign.

We're dealing with a poorly anchored ego. Sarah found herself echoing his words in silent parody. Why did psychiatrists have to sound so portentous, as if the mind were a terrorist's plastic explosive?

"We have no reason to believe that Carrie will give us any trouble, but the appearance of trouble might scare her away," Jeremy explained.

"You have our word that no force will be used against either girl."

"When I used to run away, I just resisted more when there was something to resist."

"That's perfectly normal," Dr. Weber assured him. "Non-intervention is the best intervention."

"Together they love her like a father." Mae's caustic voice rang out from the dining room, where she was holding a large platter overflowing with food. "Dinner's ready, *mesdames et messieurs.*"

The rack of lamb was surrounded by curried rice with walnuts, raisins, and curled apple skins. Sarah imagined Deenie sitting in front of such elaborate meals, tapping her dirty nails in defiance. Across the table from Jeremy, she felt lost. She thought of the hyperbolic flowers, imitation Georgia O'Keeffe, that hung over their hotel bed, and missed being next to him.

"We know a stunt man named Rip," Mae said like a straight man.

"That's an appropriate name," Sarah replied.

"He's gotten out of the business because he says there's too much compromise. He was willing to do anything to create the illusion of danger, but there are so many clauses in contracts nowadays that even stunt men use stunt men."

"I'd think he'd appreciate the protection he's receiving."

"People tend to think that, Sarah. The more the government interferes, the more some people feel protected." Tony suddenly became animated with tension. He looked like he wanted to step on her.

"He said he used formulas to calculate the exact trajectory of his leaps," Mae continued. "He had standards the directors refused to consider in their decisions about his body. He would have done anything to control his artistic situation."

"I can't help smiling," Sarah said. "The man was what? Jumping out of cars? Pretending to be washed overboard?"

"Rip's a pretty special fellow," Tony asserted. "In my line of work, I've come to respect craftsmanship and dedication. You don't know how many accidents happen due to lack of planning."

"Who does the more dangerous stunts now?"

"Who else? The Japanese," Tony snorted.

Some time passed while everyone chewed silently. Dr. Weber filled the wine glasses and whispered something to Tony.

"Back to tomorrow," Sarah said. "I still don't know how you're going to handle Deenie."

"With anchors and long ropes," Mae quipped.

"We have it under control," Dr. Weber asserted.

Sarah looked from Tony to Mae, who had resumed her enthusiastic eating.

"Jeremy and I plan to split up. I'll be near the arrival gate. If Carrie sees me and accepts that I'm there, he won't intervene at all, but if I need him, he'll be ready."

"I've always admired cowboys," Mae said.

"Jeremy's not a cowboy, Mae."

"I know that." She wrinkled her nose in a perplexed smile.

Sarah watched Mae inspect her lamb-chop bone. She turned it over slowly and picked at it with her fingernails. Her sister was drunk again, that was clear.

"How do you know Rip?" Jeremy asked.

"We're both in a kind of investment club slash political-action caucus slash men's group. So's Dr. Weber. If you were staying longer, Jeremy, I'd invite you to one of our weekend seminars. Some of our initiation paradigms have been adapted from Native American and tribal practices. We've discovered quite a few cultures that handle all this better than we do. We've sanitized coming-of-age. You buy the right aftershave and you're a man, right, Frank?"

Mouth full, Frank assented enthusiastically by widening his pale eyes.

"This has implications for women too. We're thinking of starting a ladies' auxiliary," Tony added sincerely.

Mae rolled her eyes sarcastically. "As soon as girls reach puberty, a shaman puts them in a tent and makes a circle of chicken blood around it. No one can enter or exit. If their families don't sneak them food, they sometimes starve."

"Only in Cameroon, Mae. They go for depth in the more primitive societies in general. There may be pain and some deprivation, but there's great dignity too."

When Tony seemed to be fixing on Jeremy for the next question, Sarah changed the subject. "I didn't realize you were active in politics, Tony."

"We're trying to modify the Bill of Rights."

"How's that?" Jeremy asked.

"Less government interference."

"For example?" Sarah asked.

"Well, for instance, if someone like me wanted to keep a horse in my yard, would the government let me?"

"Zoning laws are local, aren't they, Tony?"

"What if someone like me wanted to kill that horse?"

"Animal-cruelty laws."

"What if someone like me wanted to process and sell its hide?"

"Small-business regulations and environmental laws."

"And what if someone like me made a profit from that sale?"

"Taxes."

"Right. We plan to change all that." Beaming at Dr. Weber, Tony did funny squints that looked like facial calisthenics.

"It's getting late," Jeremy sighed.

Sarah looked at her watch and swallowed a grin. They'd been there less than an hour.

"Wait! I've made a special dessert for Sarah."

Mae hurried around the table and into the next room. She came back with a large bowl of orange liquid in which something icy was floating.

"What is it?" Sarah asked.

"An apricot ocean with a daiquiri sherbet ice floe."

"Why's it for me?"

"I was thinking about your Lillian Gish mouth. You look like you need to be rescued. You remember that movie where she's on an ice floe?"

Mae took a little Guatemalan worry doll and put it on the sherbet. "That's Sarah."

Everyone chuckled nervously.

"I have a Jeremy doll too." Mae removed another worry doll from the palm of her hand. She pretended it was swimming through the apricot goo. It picked up the Sarah doll and carried it to the periphery of the bowl. "Well, help yourselves." She smiled. "These raspberries can go on top."

After Mae served them, they added spoonfuls of raspberries. Sarah hid the Sarah doll, which sat on her serving, under the coffee saucer. The concoction tasted good.

"You're a good cook, Mae," Jeremy said.

"Do you think so?"

A cardinal was perching on the dining-room windowsill preening itself. Sarah thought of female cardinals, at a distance drab as dried blood.

Mae's eyes were upturned, as if gazing at a cloud. "If I were Deenie, I'd get off that bus and disappear," she said, firing a pretend pistol at Frank Weber.

Everyone looked at her with confusion on their faces.

UNABLE TO FALL ASLEEP after Mae's unsettling dinner, Sarah watched the digital blips of light on her clock, their vague greenish yellow making her think of time bending and refracting like light. She remembered the slow clock face on the wall of the bedroom she'd shared with Mae when they were little. Mae could tell time years before Sarah but was never interested in facts. "Is it time to get up?" Sarah would ask. "If you want to," Mae would groan before sleep took hold of her again. Sarah, waiting for Mae's breathing to even out, would climb unnoticed into her bed to share the last half-hour before dawn.

Earlier, she had imagined herself talking to Scotty and Carrie, saying that she loved them and hoped they'd forgive her. It was something she repeated every night like a mantra. Was there a special dispensation for loving your children? Mrs. Pipkin had thought so. "Hitler didn't have children" had been her worst epithet, and the entire group had agreed that the love that Linsey and Reed bore for Nicky could balance any mourner's scale.

While she had been attending the class, Sarah's grief had actually grown. She had allowed herself to understand how much Stanley

must have loved her and to feel guilty for how little contact they'd
had. She remembered the Saturday several years ago when she had
joined him at his high-rise pool for a swim. Looking at his gray,
hairy back and fragile chest, she'd realized with some horror that
her father had become an old man. And for that she had loved him
less. Why hadn't he warned her this would happen? Then she might
have been especially attentive. Maybe she could have saved him. She
knew how foolish it was to think she could reverse death like Super-
man. But if she could have him back for just one afternoon, it might
somehow clear her mind of the image of her father dying alone in
his Chevy Malibu.

It didn't help to visit his grave either, as she had on occasion
with Ivy. The small stone and grassy plot seemed extraneous to all
the incarnations she imagined of him: Stanley as a little boy in a
Humboldt Park photographer's studio, pouting in a striped sailor
suit; as a nonchalant father, infant Sarah propped on his lap on the
just-shoveled steps; in a tuxedo, hair nicely graying, giving Sarah
away to Larry; as an old man swimming slow laps that Saturday
afternoon. Sarah saw things in a haze of compassion whenever she
thought of her father: Ivy trekking in her beige oxfords to Stanley's
grave with tulips and geraniums in season and sturdy wreaths in
winter, talking to him through the snow; Mae, in her tight black
pants suit, Bloody Mary tumbler in hand, spinning through space
like a crazy astronaut; poor Larry, so alone in their marriage, unable
to love her completely. Still, she and Larry had one thing in common,
their mutual love for their children. Had Carrie and Scotty felt it
vibrating toward them?

Sarah wondered how childless people spent sleepless pre-dawn
hours. Probably like Alan Partanos, wondering how soon history
would wipe out their tracks. Shuddering in the chilly hotel room,
she wondered what Jeremy regretted.

It was five-forty. In the near dark she remembered lying beside
little Carrie in her oceanic bed. "It's so lonely in my room," Carrie
would cry. Why were kids made to sleep in the dark? "Hug a doll,"
Sarah had told her, offering a plastic baby whose eyes were permanently closed. Carrie had turned her serious back to Sarah. Guilt
had always been everywhere, little traps set for her, leaving no marks.

Maybe they weren't traps but hazards, like on Scotty's game boards, requiring three hasty steps backward as penalty: *Go to jail. Go directly to jail.* When she saw Carrie again, she'd tell her the truth: Sleep with a flashlight to remind yourself that there's no permanent comfort.

For the first time since she had met Jeremy, she wished she were alone. What had caused the atmosphere to change overnight? Driving back to the hotel after Mae's, she'd felt the air itself chill. In Los Angeles it was nearly winter. Though no snow would fall, the season had snapped into place like a new stage set. Maybe it was all Jeremy's fault, after all. If it hadn't been for him, Carrie would never have gone. Mae was wrong about Sarah needing rescue. She could have swum away from Larry to safety herself. Or was she a coward, a greedy coward, wanting the world to accommodate her weakness?

She took the small transistor radio Jeremy had purchased at Discounters into the washroom and found a classical station. Who would be up before six wanting to be improved? Widows, the ill, the insane? Voices were reciting lines from what must have been a play:

> *For swifter than wings of the morning*
> *the pathways of the heart!*
> *Over ten thousands of miles.*

Then a second voice:

> *Is the little bowl empty, Nita?*

What if love and pain were like those voices, so similar that they converged?

Stop this, she thought. Do something useful. She blasted the shower until the room filled with smoky steam. Stepping into it, she hoped the morning would disappear. She felt the water beat over her head and held her face up to receive it. Why would Jeremy want to look at her? She was pale and had spidery wrinkles by her eyes that were magnified when she smiled. She stared at her freckly, imperfect arms and legs, at her dimpled thighs and bony kneecaps. Didn't Jeremy see what a disaster she was? She had a surfeit of everything: children, men, freckles, wrinkles, worries. She pinched her flabby arm. How could she imagine that Carrie would want her, Carrie, who'd signaled plainly that their life was to be escaped? Maybe Mae's attitude was right after all: Stare straight ahead. Block out conversation. Fuck a stunt man. Pour some vodka and swallow.

Across from the hotel-room bed hung an overly expressive blue cow, smiling compassionately, wedged between trees. Above the trees suspended in air was a little cottage. Title: *Heaven*. It was the first thing Sarah had seen every morning of their stay. Today the simplicity of the image annoyed her. She was barred from understanding it. She was too complicated, too self-righteous, fickle—an adultress, a child-deserter.

"Are you in there?" Jeremy opened the bathroom door, unleashing a blast of cooler air, clearing the steam in the room.

"It's me," Sarah said, but she tried not to look at him. He stumbled sleepily to the toilet and urinated.

"Sleep well?"

"Not really."

"Why?"

"I couldn't stop thinking about Mae or you or Carrie long enough to sleep."

"Mae could keep a team of serious thinkers awake for a century."

"All those years on the phone talking to her, Jeremy, sharing my darkest thoughts, I couldn't tell that Mae is always drunk."

"Sullen drunks make good listeners."

"She never told me she wasn't doing well. She only let information leak out about Tony now and then. She let me be her little sister. I feel so guilty for not having guessed."

"Maybe she'll be better when Deenie's back. But she'll still be married to the libertarian horse-butcher."

"He wasn't always that way either. I remember when Tony was deferential, like a good Catholic boy talking to nuns."

"He's mutated somehow."

"Don't we all?"

"I thought we're supposed to mellow with age."

"Some of us spoil."

When he reached to hug her, she knew she'd have to tell him.

"Jeremy, something's bothering me, but I don't know how to say it."

"Say what?"

"Maybe I should meet Carrie alone. She ran away because she knew about us. How will having you there improve matters?"

Jeremy sighed deeply. She couldn't look at his face.

"I mean," she continued, prodded by his silence, "it's our fault she ran away in the first place."

"She doesn't know anything about me, Sarah."

"That's what I mean, Jeremy. You're practically a stranger."

"You're thinking out loud because you're nervous."

She was horrified to feel a tense smile turning her face cruel. "Maybe I don't love you."

"Is the *maybe* supposed to keep this cordial?" He looked stricken.

She was suddenly so sleepy that she could barely continue. "I don't know."

"Send me a message when you decide." He slammed the bathroom door behind him. She hesitated a moment, then followed him out.

Sitting on the bed, she watched him dress. He hadn't showered, but his hair looked damp from the steamy room. Sweat paraded down his forehead.

"What are you doing?"

"Getting dressed."

"Why?"

He didn't answer.

"Why?" she shouted, fear making her voice shrill.

He was tying his gym shoes, pretending she wasn't there. He went to the door and slammed it behind him.

Every muscle in her body contracted in alarm as she sat on the bed listening. She heard his footsteps disappearing. Then, to her great relief, it seemed they were returning.

He opened the door and flung the car keys onto the bed. "You'll need them later."

"Please, Jeremy, don't go," she said, but he was already out the door.

SUNDAY

I F THEY ASK YOU questions in hell, the first will be what you fear. Because they are purely literal, they'll believe whatever you say. If you say snakes, they'll produce a roomful and place you among them forever. If you say heights, hell will become the highest, sheerest cliff you can imagine. Say snakes if it's heights you fear. Say death or hell, and there's nothing they can do.

It was one of Jeremy's favorite parables. He used it now to defuse his anger at Sarah. He knew that Sarah was simply overwrought, afraid of how the final day of waiting would unfold. Who wanted an audience for possible misery? Maybe the Greyhound trip was a decoy, and Jeremy and Sarah had sat like obedient dummies for seventy-two hours while the girls had distanced themselves forever. Maybe Carrie would meet someone too, a friend of Branch's or a boy from music camp whom Sarah didn't know. Sarah was proud, but she'd need him later if not now.

He unfolded from his wallet the letter he'd never sent her last spring and read it again.

Dear Sarah,
    Call me Mesmer. I've led you here by focusing your eyes and it worked. I wasn't amazed, because I wanted you. It was my strategy. I made the earth move a millisecond faster, and I caught you. No, you say, nodding your logical head. There isn't any time, and the stars can't move faster than light. But I don't mean scientific time. You can accelerate human time, and the funny thing is that no one else notices or minds. Why do people call the farthest object they see the limit? You have a whole galaxy, and you diffuse your energy into it, yet you're as undiscovered as those planets beyond Pluto.
    It's your duty to change human time. Not to harm

*people—though they may first see your intercession on
their behalf as a threat—but to captivate them. Think of
the life of a "captive," the marvelous freedom of being
directed by someone who, through an act of imagination
or empathy, can understand what's best for you better
than you do. Think of a spiritual usher with a giant
flashlight.*

*Was it Galileo who established the Law of Falling
Bodies? I left open a space for you, and you've fallen
through the air, slowed by your mental resistance and
gravity, into the space I arranged. And you don't even
know I arranged it. You think we met and made love in
a car. You think we came together by accident. But I had
a pillow waiting for you. And I've learned to rub your
back when you sleep between what I call your wings
without waking you up.*

*Do you know that I once visited France? I placed a
flower on the grave of Guillaume Apollinaire. I ate horse
brains in a restaurant while a woman whom Lautrec
might have painted looked on with hands on her hips. I
went to the Louvre and saw "The Winged Victory." I
stood with the Japanese tourists in the Bois de Boulogne
and watched an old dog wearing a clown hat jump onto
the back of a llama with matted fur, and even then, before I saw you, I knew I'd meet a woman who sleeps on
her face.*

The coffee shop had a three-egg breakfast. He sat at the counter next
to an elderly businessman with stubble on his nose and drank his
coffee slowly and listlessly poked at his eggs. He'd give Sarah a few
hours to recover, and then he'd go back to her, relentlessly faithful.

He doused his poached eggs in Tabasco and spooned them onto
toast. He wondered what Sarah was doing. Maybe she'd call Mae.
Maybe she'd sleep. He could see her forehead tucked in the pillow
and her arms curved underneath her. She burrowed into sleep like
some slow-breathing animal.

He thought of the winters in Minnesota. It would have been better to hibernate than suffer the winds that nearly blew the coats off their backs. He remembered the lake, where he'd cut a small, perfect hole in the ice and wait for fish all day. He'd chew on the salty beef jerky his grandmother cured. Warming his hands on a kerosene heater, he'd watch his Uncle Jim's face, rather than the hole itself, for signs of success.

Jim must have been his grandmother's lover. Jeremy didn't think much about where Jim slept on the nights he stayed with them. Sleeping on the old sofa in his secondhand sleeping bag, he never heard a sound from his grandmother's bedroom, where he usually slept on a cot. It was to be expected that his grandmother would be quiet in love.

Jim had a family somewhere, but as long as there were odd jobs and good fishing, he'd stayed in Red Lake. Jeremy remembered an unusually warm spring when Jim had gone back home and his grandmother's customary silence filled with anger. She'd snap at him about the smallest things and look at him with disgust. Where would he live now that his grandmother didn't want him anymore? It wouldn't matter much in summer. He could sleep outside and hunt for rabbits to eat, but when winter came, what would he do? Maybe the school-teacher, Mrs. Benchard, or the overworked minister with the poorly shaven neck, would find a place for him. He'd seen plenty of foster kids get big, candy-stuffed stockings at Christmas.

In late May Jim came back. His daughter had been ill in Duluth but was over the worst of it. Jim had his fishing gear and a new pair of water wings for Jeremy, the only gift Jim ever gave him. Jeremy remembered wearing them over his clothes, padding around his grandmother's kitchen in a state as close to joy as childhood had ever moved him. His grandmother had mussed his crewcut with her palm and given him a quarter to spend on Coke and candy. That night they all sat on the porch swing outside of the general store. When his grandmother asked him to sing a song, he recited one he'd learned in school about February being the shortest month.

On the walk home Jeremy had followed them, kicking at stones and listening to crickets scratch their legs together. He watched Jim take his grandmother's arm as the evening darkened and steady shadows lengthened onto the road. Before they went home, they stood at the edge of a swampy, reedy pond that buzzed with mosquitoes in summer. They were so quiet they could hear the frogs singing and the insects hovering on top of the water, wings beating. Jim asked Jeremy where his water wings were, then pretended he was about to push Jeremy into the pond. Jeremy's eyes had gone squinty with pleasure, and later, his head on the hard arm of the couch, he'd cried a little before falling asleep and hadn't known why.

IT WAS UNLIKELY that Jeremy would walk anywhere, and it was too early to take a cab. Sarah held her breath as the elevator, thankfully unwired for music, slowly descended and opened. The coffee shop was crowded with people, a good sign, but she didn't see Jeremy at the nearby tables. She quickly inspected the booths and entered the room with the long, S-shaped counter. Seeing Jeremy's shirt, his arms, his hair, she felt her mouth quivering with relief and had to force it still with her hand.

She took the seat next to him and asked the waitress for coffee.
"I'm sure now," she said, taking Jeremy's hand.
He looked at her wryly. "You're sure you don't love me?"
"No."
"You're sure you do?"
"Right."
"Good."
They exchanged uneasy smiles.
"I'm sorry."
"Let's see the Tar Pits while we still have a chance."
She gulped her coffee.
"Have breakfast first. It's not an emergency."
"I'm not very hungry."

Because it was drizzling again, it was easy to find parking. They followed the signs across the sodden grass, stopping every so often to watch gaps where millennial tar still bubbled up. Jeremy feigned being stuck in it, and Sarah, admiring the finesse of his pantomime, pretended to pull him out with great labor. The placard in front of the mastodon statue told of unsuspecting animals looking for water and getting caught in the tar. Predators would eat them in the morning.

A young man in art-gallery black with a hennaed Mohawk and an old Polaroid strung around his neck approached.

"Care for a photo?"

"How much?"

"Five bucks."

They chose the statue of the giant sloth as the backdrop, and as they tried out different poses, Sarah strained to connect the young man's features with how Branch might appear. Why hadn't she asked Mae for more details about him?

Jeremy put his arm around Sarah, who tilted her head back on his chest and tried to look amused. She wondered whether the umbrella Jeremy was holding would shade their faces. They held the pose for an eternity while the young man aimed and re-aimed. Maybe he had never used a camera before.

"I don't think I smiled," Jeremy said as they waited for the results.

"We can be serious. It's our official Tar Pits portrait."

The photographer held the snapshot between his thumbs as they stood at his side watching themselves solidify on the slick, grayed-out paper.

"Pretty good likeness, huh?" he asked.

After he had walked away, they took turns laughing. Jeremy's eyes were closed. Sarah's were red pinholes.

"Dawn of the dead," Jeremy said as they walked back to the car.

DEENIE THOUGHT RAY H. DUBAR looked like someone on television whom her mom liked—was it Stacy Keach with about fifty

extra pounds at his midriff? He had picked them up returning from
a little vacation in Las Vegas, where he'd done so well on the slot
machines that he was thinking of quitting his job.

He handed Deenie his billfold. It was black but thick as a woman's wallet, filled with money and credit cards and a foldout photo
enclosure. "See this?" he said, stretching the photos out like a path
between them. Deenie couldn't stop observing how his heavy arm
hair stopped abruptly at his wrists, leaving his reddish hands looking
shiny and bare.

She saw a photo of a billboard that said COKE. "Why do you
have that?"

"It's the first sign I ever painted. I'm much better at it now. See
that little squiggle in the corner?"

"No."

"Well, it's where I had to paint over a little problem. I guess
it's hard to see."

"Don't you get nervous up in the air?"

"Some people like adventure," Ray H. Dubar said, winking and
grinning at Deenie and Carrie in turn.

Deenie hated when people turned around in their seats to talk
as they drove. All you needed was a damn prairie dog on the road
or an error in your vision and you'd be in a ditch. "Look out!"
Deenie cautioned as the car veered momentarily. "These are the
mountains." She craned her neck to see how the road cut away from
the bluish-gray rock. Could anyone survive a fall? She searched for
a soft-looking meadow but saw sheer cliffs, jagged boulders, and
scrubby bushes everywhere.

"Hey," Ray said, "don't worry about my driving. I'll take care
of that, honey."

"Okay," Deenie said.

"You girls in college?"

"Yeah," Deenie said. "Harvard."

"Taking time off to do some traveling?"

"Sure."

"I went to the College of Marin for a while last year when I
was living in the Bay Area. Let's see. I took beginning chemistry,
beginning business law, beginning African-American history, and

advanced photography. Maybe later in the trip I'll show you some photos I took."

Deenie watched his passive face as they crossed the California border. It was the same state where Branch lived, where she'd see him later in the day. She felt so happy that she reached behind her, grabbed Carrie's hand, and squeezed it as hard as she could.

"I've always liked college girls," Ray continued. "I've dated a few, but there'll never be another one like Loretta. I bet you think Loretta's an old-fashioned name."

Deenie watched his face sweat with the exertion of speaking. His scuffed black loafers were as wide as barges and run-down at the heels.

"So?" Ray said. "I'm waiting."

"For what?" Deenie asked.

"You're supposed to tell him whether Loretta's an old-fashioned name," Carrie said.

"Kind of. Not that it matters what you're called. You can't help it anyway. My parents named me Henrietta, but I don't look like a Henrietta, so I call myself Star."

"Right, and I'm Cecily," Carrie added.

"Didn't you tell me something else before?"

Carrie burst out laughing. "We're just kidding. She's Deenie and I'm Carrie."

"Well, Loretta wasn't old-fashioned. She was modern in the best sense of the word. She had a little boy named Patrick?" he said like a question, "and no husband I ever saw, but that didn't slow her down." Ray choked and laughed and Carrie joined in. "Well, I'm seeing Loretta," he continued. "It's not serious at first, but then I take some real arty shots, and we get pretty close. Patrick's about a year and a half old, and damned if he doesn't start calling me Daddy. I bring him little toys. There's one he really likes. It's a little rubber statue of Ronald Reagan that I bought at Fisherman's Wharf. Patrick chews on it, and every time he bites it in the center, it lets out a big quack.

"We're dating for some months. Loretta lives all in the way in Novato in a trailer, and I'm way in the hell down in Marin City in a studio. Do you know Northern California?"

"No," Carrie said, "but I hope to live there one day if not in the desert, maybe in Arizona."

"I got there almost every night, and we drink a little, we lie around, we watch Disney videos with Patrick. He has red hair and is fat, fat, fat. Whenever he goes to sleep, we take these photos. Loretta thinks that if they're good, she can get a high-fashion job or model lingerie.

"This goes on for a few months, and I learn a lot about her. For one, she's Ukrainian, which explains why she has this gingerbread embroidery everywhere and these wide cheekbones. It's like her eyes are lost in her face, but that's also what makes her interesting. That's something about beauty. It has to be a little ugly to shine out.

"Another thing's her job. She works at a health-food store and has all these potions and health tonics around. When she wants to get sexy, she mixes some sandy-looking powder with pineapple and carrot juice, slugs it down, and puts Tiger Balm on her forehead.

"After a while her portfolio's complete. It's wonderful to look at her in all the poses, horizontal, vertical, and everything in between. We've taken some of her in a pretty flowered dress with Patrick too in case they need models to pose with children.

"I show them to her and she says, 'Great job, Ray,' but then she won't look at me. I haven't seen her in a week because I've been so busy developing them. And guess what's happened in that week? It's the oldest story in the book."

Carrie noticed that Deenie had fallen asleep. Her head was straight back, her eyelids were pale and veiny, her nostrils were flaring, and some spittle was collecting between her cheek and the cowl-necked sweater that Reena Fishblatt had given her.

"Loretta's found a new boyfriend. This fat Samoan named Wesley's hanging around. He has a big Harley and lots of cash. I see some new toys when I come in. Instead of my Ronald Reagan doll, Patrick's dragging around this stuffed clown with red hair just like his own. Oh, Wesley's all right for a Samoan, but let me tell you something about them. I've had some experience in the restaurant trade, and next to Iranians, Samoans are the worst. They'll rent a hall for a wedding, say, and play some Don Ho, but by the end of the night, there'll be a brawl. Samoans will be throwing other Samoans over their heads. People will be using chairs as weapons. And try to collect later.

"Anyway, Wesley's no stranger. He's from the college too, which is where I met Loretta, in the financial-aid office. Wesley was in my humanities class, and I sat next to him once on a field trip to San Jose to see an art exhibit."

"What kind of art?"

"Oh, paintings and things. Mostly paintings.

"The three of us look at the photos, and I can see a little embarrassment between Wesley and Loretta like it's not the first time he's seen her in the buff. We drink for a while. She's bought some mixer and is making something fancy in the blender that tastes like orange juice and licorice with a cherry afterbite. Around midnight I start wondering who's going to leave for the night. We smoke a few joints, but no one's relaxed. Around one o'clock I say I'd better go, and Loretta tells me about Hawaii and all. She and Wesley are going there in a few days. The baby will stay at her mom's. So I tell them good luck, and I'm about to leave just like that.

"But why do I want to be a chump? I look around and see that she's left the portfolio by her bed. So I make a little detour and walk out with all the photos. It was real luck that I did, too. A guy near where I live now, his name is Victor, says he'll buy all of them for $300. That's about ten bucks a photo, which is fair considering the materials were free at the college. Fine, I say. It'll pay back some of the time that I've spent in the darkroom spilling those lousy chemicals all over my hands. He's about to write me a check when I start thinking. Maybe I want to keep those photos. So I've had them in my trunk for a few months now. Sometimes I bring them into my bedroom, prop them up like mirrors all over the place, and just stare.

"It didn't work out with the Samoan, by the way. Loretta says he has more relatives there than the pope has followers, and every single one of them is fat and ugly. If you have kids with a guy like that, it can cause you real harm."

"Do you still see Loretta?"

"We talk now and then. She says she's going to invite me to Patrick's third birthday.

"I forgot one point. Wesley's in jail."

"Why?"

"The guy goes to a Labor Day party at this bar in Novato called the Brew House. He sees an old friend, they get to talking, and for a reason that no one knows, they start banging each other around. Wesley knocks the guy unconscious and lands in jail for assault and property damage. Loretta goes to bail him out, but Wesley says no. He's proud that way. Samoans are like that."

"I've never met a Samoan."

"I've never met one I liked."

"My mom's seeing an Indian. They met at my mom and dad's university."

"Does he like fishing?"

"I don't know."

"Indians like fishing, I know that. I once knew an Indian named Pete, just Pete, and if you needed to find him, you'd look in his boat. A lot of successful ones sell insurance. Does your mom's friend?"

"He's a professor."

"Yeah, some are that too. Fisherman, insurance agents, professors. There used to be a few ball players too, like Early Wynn, who played for the White Sox."

Carrie yawned. Out the window she saw signs advertising a farmers' market in Yermo and a turnoff for the Goldstone Deep Space Tracking Station.

"What do you suppose they do there?" she asked.

"Where?"

She leaned forward from the back seat and pointed out the sign. Her cheek was close by Ray's. She could see small veins in his ear and a patch of hair he'd missed in shaving. She liked how he smelled, like coconuts mixed with sweat.

"Oh, Captain Kirk and Spock check out the black holes."

Carrie smiled, wondering how old Ray was. Maybe as old as her dad, but being kind of dumb made him seem younger. She wished he were driving all the way to Los Angeles. He was pretty nice to talk to.

"Your friend is sawing logs here."

"We're both tired."

"Want to come with me to Glendora? My sister has a nice little

house where you girls can rest. Her name's Penny. Did you ever see
Sky King?"

"No."

"It was a Saturday-morning TV show when I was a kid. My
mom named her after that Penny, Sky King's niece. She was as cute
as a bug's ass. So you want to stay at Penny's?"

"Thanks, Ray, but Deenie needs to be in Los Angeles by late
this afternoon."

"Well, get some sleep now. We have about two more hours
before your ride's up. Why's your friend in such a hurry, anyway?"

"She has to meet her boyfriend."

"I hope he's a good guy."

"I've never met him, but he's not a Samoan."

"That's lucky for starters. She'd better make sure he's not Iranian
either. I once saw an Iranian throw his girlfriend right off a balcony.
No kidding. Lucky there was a car hood to land on and break her
fall. She was an American. I kept thinking he wouldn't do that to
one of his own."

"I think I'll sleep now," Carrie said.

"I don't suppose you're interested in seeing the photos."

"I think I'll just sleep."

"Well, I can understand. When we took that bus trip, some
people, me for one, didn't like the paintings at all. Others thought
they were terrific. If photography isn't for you, I understand."

"What were the paintings of?"

"Oh, snakes and lizards and shit. And a dog screwing a big red
rock, at least that's how it looked to me."

THEY STOOD ON THE ROADSIDE at Glendora with a sign saying
LOS ANGELES that Ray had hand-lettered for them in thick felt-tip
marker when they'd stopped for a burger. Deenie didn't understand
why she had felt hungry ever since they lost the bus in Nevada. She
had liked the taste of Reena's leftover grapes and had devoured the
quarter-pounder with cheese that Ray had bought her in Claremont.
She could eat everything but the pickle, which tasted slimy. Maybe,

when she went to Costa Rica with Branch, she could make eating
part of her life again. Not that she'd be gulping down mouthfuls of
whatever landed in her hand, like Carrie did, but she might manage
a little fruit with granola for breakfast, a sandwich for lunch, and a
salad at dinner. For some reason, she thought of turnips, faded beige
and purple on top. She could cut them like potato chips in a little
salad and make a nice vinaigrette dressing. Then she'd garnish it with
watercress. She loved its bitter taste, how fresh it seemed in your
mouth after being refrigerated for days on end.

Maybe there was something philosophical about not eating. Her
mother's refrigerator was like a secret morgue. You could look behind new orange juice, cherries, bottles of olives, boxes of chocolates,
and see grapefruits speckled green and white with mold, chicken fat
separated from the gravy and frozen to its bowl, forgotten hamburger
patties a raw surreal red from contact with the air. If her mother
had respected food, Deenie might have eaten it. As it was, Mae's
wastefulness reminded her of death and decay. If Deenie saw Dr.
Weber again, first she'd tell him that she wanted to be cremated,
thank you. Then she'd tell him that she'd decided to eat again, but
not from her mother's refrigerator, where food was embalmed out
of negligence.

"I wish I had some watercress," she told Carrie, who was sucking
on the straw from her strawberry milkshake.

"How about some cucumber sandwiches?"

"Yeah. That would taste good too. You know what I wish more?
That somebody would pick us up. Ray said this was a busy intersection, but other than mothers in mini-vans, I haven't seen anyone
since he dropped us off."

"How much time do we have?"

"About three hours."

"If anything, the bus will be late. Branch knows to call the
station, doesn't he?"

"How do I know what Branch knows?"

"You could call him and tell him where you are."

"Get this. He doesn't have a phone. The phone company said
he owed three hundred dollars, which wasn't true. This guy named
Billy, who was staying with him for a while, decided to call his

girlfriend every day. The only problem was that she lived in SoHo."

"Was she an artist?"

"She was a cocktail waitress. They took out Branch's phone. If he wants it back, he has to make a two-hundred-dollar deposit, plus pay off his bill. The company called to tell him they were shutting it off and Branch said, 'Fuck that!' You know what else he did?"

"What?"

"He went to a public phone and called Billy's girlfriend, reversing the charges. He told Kate that Billy had been seeing this girl named Jenni that Kate sincerely hates from high school. Jenni's a real fashion slut."

"That wasn't very nice."

"It wasn't nice of Billy to use Branch."

"How did you meet Branch, Deenie?"

"He used to hang out at the high school. I saw him around. One day we started talking, and we realized we had a lot in common. For one, he hates the same music I do, all that English and Irish shit like the Pet Shop Boys and U-2. I think Americans should be for American music just like American cars. My dad would kill me if I drove home a Toyota or a Hyundai. What kind of name is that for a car? It sounds like someone barfing in Korean."

"Then how did you fall in love?"

"That was pretty easy. We went to his apartment and liked what we did."

"That's it?"

"What do you mean that's it?"

"There should be more of a story. Didn't you say things to each other? When I fall in love, we're going to do a lot of talking, I know that."

"Sure. He said, 'Touch it,' and I did." She laughed.

"Look! Someone's stopping."

Thirty feet ahead Carrie saw a blue Volkswagen pulling over. She hadn't been watching the road, so she didn't know what to expect as she ran, bag in hand, over the dusty gravel. The highway glistened as far as she could see.

"Need a ride?" a woman was asking.

"We need to get to the Los Angeles Greyhound terminal."

"Hop in."

This time it was Carrie's turn to ride in front. Deenie slid in back and shut the door. Carrie handed Deenie her suitcase, which Deenie stowed next to her without complaining for once.

"My name's Lois. Where are you girls from?"

Lois had short gray hair, matching eyes, a blue-and-white collarless striped shirt, and a denim skirt. Carrie guessed she was about her mom's age, but because she didn't wear make-up, she could look younger or older, depending on how the afternoon light hit her face.

"We're from Chicago, at least I am. Deenie's from right here. Well, not right here like the middle of the road. Right here like Santa Monica."

"I'm from La Jolla. I was visiting a friend for the weekend, but I have to get back to work tomorrow."

"What do you do?"

"I'm an agronomist. I analyze soil."

Deenie laughed. "Soil's pretty deep."

"I see what's in it and what's missing from it."

"Then you're a scientist?"

"Yep, Lois Tercelli, lady scientist. I got my degree at Texas A and M, and I've studied soil all over the world."

"Where have you lived?" Carrie asked.

"Tanzania. Pretty rotten soil there. Hungary. An interesting mix. And La Jolla."

Carrie looked out the window at the California she'd imagined before she saw the desert, the one with shopping centers at every corner and little dives to eat in called Lucy's Lunch and Daily Bread. She saw a sign saying PERSIAN RUGS and thought about the Iranian pushing his girlfriend off the balcony. Why did love cause so much trouble?

"Can you drive us all the way into the city to the station?" Deenie asked.

"At your service."

"The last man we were with had some photos with him of a naked lady named Loretta."

"That's the trouble with hitchhiking. You never know who you'll get."

"That's why I'm glad you stopped. I was kind of worried when I fell asleep that he'd be all over my cousin here. I tried to stay awake, but ever since we lost our bus in the desert, it's been a strain. Then, plop. I was out. The next thing I know the guy's buying us cheeseburgers and handing us Wash 'n' Dri's. I felt like I was waking up on an airplane, and this fat guy was the steward."

"He was nice, Deenie," Carrie asserted. "He didn't try to show me the photos. The trouble was that he was in love with this woman who dumped him."

"That's too bad," Lois said.

"Are you married?" Deenie asked.

"Nope."

"Divorced?"

"Nope."

"Have a scientist boyfriend?"

"Nope."

"Deenie, maybe she doesn't think it's your business."

"Are you married, Deenie?" Lois asked.

"Nope."

"Engaged?"

"Sort of. Deenie's getting married today," Carrie teased.

Deenie gave her a fierce look and pounded her on the shoulder. "Who were you visiting this weekend?"

"A friend named Terri."

"Does he live in the desert?" Carrie asked.

"She lives in Overton Beach, on Lake Meade. It's a very beautiful area."

"Is she married?"

"Nope. Terri's a bachelor like me."

"We met this old lady on the bus, Reena Fishblatt, who got married to a seventy-year-old man. And get this, they had a baby."

"As long as she wasn't seventy that would work."

"Do you have any kids?"

"Terri has a daughter named Brigit. I see a lot of her."

"Have you and this Terri been friends for a long time?"

"Since grad school."

"How close are you?"

"Deenie, it's none of your business. Leave her alone."

"I visit her two or three weekends a month."

"Tell us about Africa," Carrie said.

"I was there nearly ten years. I lived in a cheap apartment with paper walls in what they called a big city. I didn't catch malaria. That's about it."

Carrie wondered why more people didn't tell good stories like Ray Dubar. "Did you visit Kenya?" she asked. Maybe if she put enough excitement in her voice, Lois would catch on. She watched the eyes behind her little silver granny glasses for signs of enthusiasm.

"Kenya's beautiful, but it's hard to describe beauty."

"Do you see things scientifically?"

"What do you mean?"

"Well, my dad's an art historian, so he sees lines and contours all the time. He points them out to me."

"I look at you girls and it's not the dirt on your shoes that interests me, if that's what you mean."

"My dad used to collect soil from every state he visited," Deenie said. "Once I found this grungy shoebox in the basement, and he told me about his dirt collection."

"I see two nice-looking people. I don't usually pick up hitch-hikers, but you two seemed different."

Carrie watched Lois's right hand lying relaxed on her lap. Her nails were nicely manicured.

"Different how?" Deenie finally asked.

"Well, first of all, you're girls. Mostly young men hitchhike. Second, you look intelligent."

"What looks intelligent about me?" Deenie asked.

"Oh, I don't know. Your eyes, how you hold yourself."

"Are you and Terri in love?"

"We're close."

"My old English teacher was a lesbian," Deenie offered non-chalantly. "She was real nice. She didn't look dykey at all except for her shoes."

"Her shoes looked dykey?" Lois laughed.

"Do you know any lesbians, Carrie?" Deenie asked.

"A woman who teaches with my mom is one. I didn't know at

first, but then Vera brought this woman named Mary to our barbecue. Do you know Peter, Paul and Mary? Well, this Mary had long blond hair just like that one. She was wearing a lumberjack shirt, jeans, and high laced boots. She even had a canteen. My mom likes Vera a lot. She came from New Zealand, and her specialty is Chaucer."

"Land of the kiwi," Lois commented.

"Aren't you worried that we'll be afraid to take a ride with you?" Deenie asked.

"No more than I'm worried to pick up strangers. So it's a stand-off."

"I heard that Eleanor Roosevelt was a lesbian," Carrie smiled.

"Could be," Lois said without much interest. "Do you girls want some soda? I have to use the facilities."

They approached a Redi-Gas in Whittier. Its orange, yellow, and avocado green, the unpopular colors of the spectrum, made Carrie feel nauseous. She hadn't realized how tired she felt until her eyes nearly closed watching Lois fill the tank with gas. She tried to concentrate on the wavy invisible lines of the gasoline fumes to stay awake.

"Quick," Deenie said, nudging Carrie alert. "Let's get out of here."

"Why?"

"She'll make a pass before too long. Didn't you hear what she was saying about how we looked?"

"Deenie, Ray didn't make a pass even though he called you honey, and she won't either. Do you think she makes passes at that Brigit?"

"That's different. She wants to keep on good terms with Terri. Don't you see? She's giving us a chance to escape, and if we don't take it, she'll think we're accepting her offer."

"How will she subdue both of us?"

"Maybe she has a friend waiting. They like to network, you know."

"Deenie, I think you're crazy. Lois won't hurt us, and besides, we have to be there by four, remember? We can't look for another ride."

Lois approached the car holding two cans of orange Nehi. "Better not drink it, Deenie. It's probably drugged," Carrie whispered.

"Here," Lois said. "I hope you like orange."

Deenie hesitated before drinking hers.

"To four o'clock," Carrie toasted.

Deenie bumped her can into Carrie's and took a big swig. "Who knows a song?" Deenie asked.

It was so funny to hear her cousin be pleasant, even out of fear, that Carrie began laughing.

"What's so funny?" Lois asked.

"I know a song," Carrie said. "My parents and I sing it when we travel."

"So sing it," Deenie said.

Carrie yodeled, reared her head back, pretended she was cracking a whip, and began:

> *Keep rollin', rollin', rollin'*
> *Though the streams are swollen.*
> *Keep those dogies rollin'*
> *Rawhide.*

Lois joined in:

> *Keep movin', movin', movin'*
> *Though they're disapprovin'.*
> *Keep those dogies movin'*
> *Rawhide.*

Carrie thought what a beautiful, sincere voice she had.

"I don't know this song," Deenie complained. "Why don't we sing something else?"

"Okay," Lois said. "You choose."

Deenie's voice soared to a region Carrie found hilarious. In a cracked falsetto, she began:

I'm a little teacup, short and stout.
Here is my handle,
Here is my spout.

They all laughed together, and Lois turned onto a freeway that said
WELCOME TO LOS ANGELES, TOM F. BRADLEY, MAYOR.

MAE HAD BEEN in bed all day, dozing and thinking and glancing
at the pile of magazines she never read but kept messily stacked on
a wicker table. One cover said that Princess Di was pregnant again,
and another claimed that Prince Charles was moving out of the
palace. Both Charles and Di, however, pictured separately, looked
unperturbed. She tried to make a few phone calls around lunchtime,
but nobody was in. Probably Sarah and Jeremy were hunched over
a sandwich somewhere enjoying the nervous intimacy of the day the
girls were scheduled to appear. She couldn't remember when she had
last eaten, but that wasn't important. Focusing her energy on Deenie
was. Nothing could go wrong at the bus station. Nothing could
interfere. Sitting up in her king-size bed, she touched the blue silk
collar of her pajamas and felt the tiny pulse in her neck. She stared
at a fingernail, then followed its course across the pillow as she wrote
Deenie's name in big, looping letters. It was funny to think that
penmanship did matter, at least on bed linen. She could see the outline
of the large swirls creased into the fabric but couldn't really read
them. Looking at the phone, she considered calling Sarah again but
decided not to try. What would she say to her sister?
   There were so many things Sarah didn't know. The way she
idealized their childhood, for instance. Didn't she remember how
unhappy Ivy had seemed for years at a time, how many crossword
puzzles she had done wearing the same beige cable-knit sweater?
Mae imagined their drab little picture window and their leafless
maple tree. Perpetually framed in late fall, her mother wasn't talk-

ative. Her life was a secret shared with the undistinguished house. She expressed it in shivers and complaints about the weather. Now and then her father would enter in his wire-rimmed glasses, plaid shirt, and flannel pants, and Ivy's narrow face would become animated. Sometimes they went out dancing, and the girls, wet hair pressed to their temples, all bathed and dressed for bed in flowered, quilted bathrobes, would watch their parents leave from the flight of stairs. For once life seemed charged with warmth and romantic connection. But Sarah was naive to think that any marriage is good for very long. All that can be good is what it produces, a perfect and beautiful child.

Deenie, you were so solid, Mae thought. *I used to hold your pink feet on top of the palms of my hands and make you dance. I'd sing you "Pony girl, pony girl, won't you be my pony girl?" until your bouncing became frenzied and I collapsed with laughter into the sound of your amazed squealing. You were so happy, Deen, that when things were bad between Tony and me, I used to touch you to confirm that I was real. He'd be away for weeks at a time, but I'd look at your tiny, curved fingernails gripping my thumb and feel you pull me back into life. You made me a genius; I'd see your smooth little face and have all the right words for you. Of course, it was easy then to call you silly names and beautiful ones too. Sometimes you'd smile at the sounds they made. I'm sure you were too little to understand what they all meant, but you had such quick, intelligent eyes that I was careful what I called you.*

When you were too big for songs, you still let me rock you. Silent on my lap in the dark bedroom, we'd sit in your rocker listening for owls, then hoot back through the shuttered window. "Hoot, hoot," you'd say when it got dark, then race me to that chair. When Daddy was away, we used to pretend that there was only one owl, a prince who'd been changed by an evil sorcerer. If he

landed on our windowsill and we told him we loved him for-
ever, we could break the spell and he'd never leave again.

You had your own perfume, Deen. Sometimes I
knew where it came from—Play-Doh, milk and cookies,
baby shampoo—but other times it was rich and mysteri-
ous like you'd gone to the Spice Islands on that big map
of the ancient world in Daddy's study. At breakfast I'd
watch you pick at your food, peeling frosting from sweet
rolls or licking salt delicately off your little palm. I called
you my own little doe, my own little anteater, Deenie.
You were all I needed. Even when Dad was away, I had
you; even when I knew he was with Anita and the rest
of me felt stony and hollow, I could look in your eyes
and feel warmed. Sometimes it scared me that I loved
you so much better than anyone else. Did Tony sense it?
Would Sarah or Ivy know how I selfishly measured what
I could give them against what I saved for you? I
sloughed their love off and hoarded the rest for you.
How could they understand at their distance what we
shared?

When you got older, you became busy with things;
you wanted to have friends and sleep at their houses and
tell them your secrets, and I was all alone. Sometimes I'd
imagine you were with me in the afternoons as I did
what I needed around the house. I'd hum songs for you
as I weeded the garden or dragged a wet rag listlessly
over our kitchen counter, which never seemed to get
clean. The rag made a sound like bodies slapping to-
gether in bed, and I tried to remember how it felt to
make love with someone who wanted me. I thought back
to the first summer Dad and I were together. With Sarah
breathing at my door and Mom and Dad in the front
room—right under everyone's nose in my little teenage
bedroom with the autograph hounds and chenille bed-
spread and terrible dimestore paintings of big-eyed
waifs—we'd make love with almost all our clothes on
and no sound allowed to echo.

Sometimes I'd drink a little to make it seem that I hadn't lost Tony or you. Not that you didn't need to lose me, Deen. You were smart. You knew that I wanted more than you could spare. I could feel you move away from both of us to protect yourself. You had your friends: Angela and her family, who were so normal and wholesome; and that other little girl from Taiwan, whose eyes were round as moons. It's not that I didn't understand why you needed them, Deen. It's just that I had no one else.

I started going to the bar at the Beverly Wilshire Hotel and met someone I didn't want to know at first. But he was kind and lonely too, and it was hard not to admit that I needed him. He sold medical supplies and was in town every other week. I started looking forward to his visits. Later, he became truer than you or Dad, Deen. He was insistent as a factory whistle or a date in history. Not that he pressed me or demanded things of me, but loving him, loving you, trying to love Dad, even after all that was wrong for years, I felt worn out. After Sam and I would meet at his hotel, all I wanted to do was sleep. In my dream we'd be lying on a floor in a room with no furniture. There would be the sound of buzzing from beyond the curtains like a swarm of honey bees was hovering just out of sight. Outside of the window there was a wrought-iron balcony and an ocean. The beach in my dream was always empty of children. I couldn't have seen Sam anymore if I had imagined that you knew. You couldn't be in the dream. So I met Sam for years, Deen, and dreamed you and Dad away from me. Oh, Sam and I eventually stopped seeing each other. Maybe he had someone else he liked better, but I didn't mind. I was more or less content for a while writing to Drew and drinking and feeling like I understood things pretty well.

Then one day I looked at you, and you seemed to be dying. You were all bones. I remember your baby ankles, sunk in cushions of flesh. Looking at your knobby joints, I'd never felt more frightened in my life. I went out in the garage and screamed until my throat hurt.

I panicked, Deen, and ran from your misery. I found Sam again. After all those years of dreaming him and losing him, Sam was undressing me again, his face swaying above me like a rain cloud. But it was you I wanted. I couldn't please anyone when all I could think of was you. I stopped seeing Sam, I stopped dreaming, I stopped thinking. Your name was like a marquee that never changed.

After Grandpa died and Dad bought the new car, he stayed home more and more, and we started to make love again. With all the problems that had driven us apart, we barely spoke. I don't know which one of us was more afraid to change the atmosphere that car provided. We both hated to admit that those ads mingling sex and chrome might be true, because this wasn't frivolous. This was life and death. We were re-creating you. I told Dad how I'd sit with you at night listening in the dark. He said he'd done that too. He'd made shadow puppets on the wall to make you laugh. I never told him about our owl, because you were the only myth we shared. We existed in the past tense only. Amnesia might have wiped out our whole family.

We drove off the freeway to that park where kids go to make out. Oh, I can't remember its name, but maybe you and Branch drive there sometimes in the evening when the fog comes in and sit on that hill. And I hope Branch loves you, truly I do. I want to tell him that it's okay for him to love you. I imagine him holding you and knowing how to make you well again. You told me he takes care of you, and I believe you. I have to believe there is someone you love enough.

It was a Tuesday night and the sun wasn't down yet. Tony was quiet and so was I. I was mostly thinking about you, Deen, and Grandpa, how I miss you both.

When we went back to the car at the end of the lot fac-
ing the ocean, we noticed a shiny white toy glider scoop-
ing in and out of the patches of salty, rolling fog. We
never saw who was operating it, but I pretended it was
you flying that glider, Deenie. I made love to your dad
right there and pretended we were a family.

SARAH DRESSED QUICKLY in what had become her Los Angeles uniform: Romanian gym shoes, Hong Kong jeans, and one of her Haitian blue blouses. Women in sweatshops all over the world had helped to complete her total look. She relaced her gym shoes, re-brushed her hair, and applied lipstick, careful to stay within her lip line. The rest of her face was pale, but she didn't care. As long as her lips could offer Carrie a pretense of calm authority, the rest of her would suffice.

They had two more hours to wait until the bus, delayed four times since they began calling the information number, was scheduled to arrive. Jeremy had gone down to the pool, and from the window, where she'd watched the woman doing breathless laps two days before, she saw him sliding through the water. Waiting for Carrie had turned her into a viewer—or was it a voyeur?—peering behind curtains at people. Maybe she'd get to the bus station and merely be able to watch. What did she do when she wanted to act? Brush her hair, train her face to look sane and motherly, call Scotty but reach Larry, who never had words beyond dull civility or hopeful vague premonitions of her success with Carrie.

She looked at the phone and thought of trying again. She pre-tended momentarily that this was a simpler day, thinking of her wedding photo, where she'd worn an austere, high-necked gown and baby's breath in her hair. The Red Guards might have cautiously approved of the tone of her wedding, given it was a bourgeois Amer-ican affair. Pomp and ceremony would have been obscene in the turmoil of that year, so they'd been married on a private beach by a bearded judge, who was officially low-key. He wearily consented to read whatever was placed in his hand. Exchanging lyrics by Walt Whitman, Sarah and Larry had spoken so softly that it had been a furtive occasion, even though a hundred of their friends and relatives were looking on.

It had been a year of cicadas. They chattered above the hush of their ceremony and found their way into the tent where the wedding brunch was served. Their uncrowned cake had to be defended from the hard-bodied insects as big as the yellow tea-rose boutonnières the groom and his ushers wore. With Nixon in the White House, protesters on the street, and bodies accumulating in Southeast Asia, it was duly ironic that a plague had descended upon their wedding cake.

Sarah tried to confuse time by taking herself back to that setting, where danger was impersonal and distant as weather. Ivy and Stanley had been fairly youthful when they'd waltzed together on the makeshift tent floor. Mae had been a young wife with shiny black curls and an elegant head full of plans for life when her husband returned from Vietnam.

Sarah had always liked her wedding photo, where they'd posed like an old-fashioned couple, faces expressionless with the sobriety of the occasion. Years later they still looked correct in it. The photo had become a survivor of their marriage. She imagined it years from now turning up in an antique shop, where someone would buy it as a period piece. She thought of sepia photos of couples in top hats and bustles, and wondered how many of their marriages had lasted.

Sighing at the grim turn of her thoughts, she looked back down at the pool, where Jeremy perched in the grayish air, dangling his feet in the calm water. Maybe she'd call home and talk to Scotty. If Larry answered, she'd simply hang up.

"Hello," Larry said.

"I'm going crazy with waiting, Larry, and decided to call."

"I've been thinking all day that I should have flown out there, Sarah. Carrie should see we're together."

"But we're not together."

"In welcoming her."

"Well, I'll stand in. I feel helpless too, and I'm so close. How's Scotty doing?"

"He's home for once. All his friends must have died."

"Scotty," Larry called, "it's Mom."

Sarah tried to trace her son's indifferent path to the phone.

"Hello?"

"Hi, Scott."

"What's new?"

"In about an hour I'll be leaving for the bus terminal. I'm very nervous." She paused. "And I miss you."

"Do you think Carrie will be there?"

"Why shouldn't she be, Scotty?"

"I keep thinking about that time we lost Joey. You said maybe we could find him, but I knew you were wrong. And I never understood how we'd be able to tell him apart from other canaries. He didn't do anything special."

"Not even sing," Sarah laughed. "Carrie will be easier to recognize than a canary. Did she tell you anything about Deenie's boyfriend?"

"He's tall and skinny. That's about it."

"Well, after I have Carrie, I'll call. She'll probably want to talk to you."

"Why?"

She could live without Scotty's candor. "Because you're her family, Scott."

"If I ran away, Mom, I'd change my route and disappear."

"Mae said that too, Scott, but Deenie wants to meet Branch more than she wants to escape. She'll take the risk."

"When you come back, Mom?" He hesitated. "When you come back, there'll be a lot of changes."

"I think so."

"I told Dad that, but he didn't believe me or something."

"He believes you, Scott, but he doesn't want to think about it all at once."

"Do you still love Dad?"

"I don't know, honey. I know I love you."

"Do you want to talk to Dad?"

"Not unless he wants to talk to me."

She heard him put down the phone. He must have been holding his hand over the receiver. Then she heard nothing.

Putting her head back on the hard foam pillow, Sarah looked at the stucco ceiling. She still wondered why she had said radishes that first night at grief therapy, when her real grief, she knew, was Larry. Things will improve, she had always told herself. Things are improving, she reported to Rachel and Mae with a self-conscious smile. But what was the evidence? That they lived and worked together, that they ate at the same table, that their children were growing. "I think we should rent a cottage this summer" and "I brought home that Romanian wine you like" were part of the proof. She gathered language and gestures like crumbs. After Carrie was born and she decided not to leave, her only alternatives had been to admit that she wasn't loved or insist on the comfort of her vagueness. Like her own slowest pupil, she had willed herself ignorant, displaying a false bravado when confronted by the facts. She'd kept a stiff upper lip for a decade and a half, burying herself in her work and her worries and her children's everyday crises. She'd watched Larry leave the house to meet women and known where he was going. *I have too much pride to stop him,* she'd thought before she realized she hadn't any. Then, humiliated, she'd turn her back on him for whole seasons. Winters and springs had passed this way and the earth had orbited around the sun fifteen or more times. And the doomsday clock had moved closer to midnight, then farther away, and the millennium had nearly ended while she had faced the wall, eyes closed. The rings of Saturn had been discovered to be made of dust and gases, while Sarah, silent and filled with a growing, inarticulate rage, had done nothing to alter a simple stumbling sentence of history.

Millions of women had more courage. They'd walked out of marriages with babies in their arms, at their breasts, or in their wombs, with no money and nowhere to go. She had taken ages to understand that it was time to wake up. She wished that Nora Sampson, Pipkin, and the others could see her again so she could tell them the truth. Finally.

. . .

"WHY ARE BUS STATIONS always in neighborhoods like this, Jeremy?"

"To remind travelers of their humble origins? Property's cheap? Bus stations attract humble people and change the neighborhood? All of the above?"

Sarah regarded the monumental, nondescript building. She wondered if it cost more to make architecture look distinguished. On the sidewalk in front of the entrance on Sixth, two men were stretched out. The sleeping one wore a brown ski cap, out of which unkempt gray curls bloomed. Sarah could tell the other was awake by how his body stirred, but couldn't see his face. His head and chest were hiding under a pillowcase or part of a dirty sheet. He was wearing houndstooth slacks and filthy red gym shoes with no socks. Over the lower half of his body was a yellowing plastic drape. Street people like these had become part of the urban landscape. You stepped over them as you would curbs or puddles. In Chicago, some wouldn't make it through the winter.

Trash blew around at her feet. As far as she could see, there were parking lots and greasy spoons and vagrants, two to a doorway. A bag lady pushing an overloaded shopping cart stuffed with Hefty bags clanked down the street. When a car honked at her, she responded by slowing her progress until the wheels of the cart barely whined along on the pavement. The day had continued to be gray. Wispy clouds high in the sky looked like roots or fingers. Somewhere under that dull sky Carrie's bus was approaching the terminal. Sarah said Carrie's name softly under her breath.

"What?" Jeremy asked.

"Just mumbling."

They walked into the station. As early as it was, many people seemed to be settling in for the night. One young woman with a dirty tie-dyed t-shirt, an ankle-length brown skirt, fuzzy blue socks, and heavy sandals had rolled out an army-surplus sleeping bag near a tall garbage can she was using as a backrest. Near her was an arrival board announcing another delay. The bus was now due at 6:17.

They sat in the same chairs they'd chosen the day before, next to an elderly Chinese man in a cheap mint-green sports shirt. His sinewy arms held a checkered cloth suitcase tied with twine. Sarah watched his eyes move under his lids in what must have been a dream, though his body didn't betray sleep. Maybe he was pretending to sleep. She knew that Chicago police located decoys like him in unlikely places. One of her semi-derelict students had written an essay about getting arrested that way. Seeing a sleeping drunk with ten dollars falling out of his pocket, Howard had made a move. The drunk woke up, placed handcuffs on him, and read him his rights. Nighttime el cars were filled with policemen disguised as muggers, real muggers, and Polish cleaning women. Sarah encountered them only by accident or chance.

Surrounded by them, Sarah wanted to distance herself. She could pretend a movie was being filmed in which extras and out-of-work actors had dressed for the bus-station scene. Denying them their reality, the most frightening moment of her life might become manageable. They could be her supportive chorus. Carrie would be serenaded off the bus into Sarah's embrace. Maybe drama was invented to get people through events like these. For the death of children, consult *King Lear*. For usurpation, see *Hamlet*. Certainly opera with its boundless, senseless spectacle pertained. She remembered seeing Verdi's *La Forza del Destino*. The star had the audacity to beat his breast and sing with a serious face, "If only I weren't an Inca, I could marry you." The nerve of art, to be so implausible when it was life that lately didn't seem real. If neither could be trusted, what then?

Suddenly the Chinese man shuddered deep within his body, said something incomprehensible, and blinked his eyes awake. Curling his hands protectively around the suitcase string, he cleared his throat. Sarah thought he might be preparing to speak to her and craned her neck to listen.

"Read," Jeremy commanded, placing his hand on her knee and giving her a section of his paper. "There's still an hour to go."

"Read? What's that? I feel like a sentry. Maybe I'll look around."

"Okay." He smiled. "Don't get lost."

Waiting near the newsstand was a skinny blond with a punk cut and one earring. He was in his late teens and would be handsome in a few years. Most things about him were still tentative. Would he fill in? Would the intelligence she saw in his eyes determine his future? She forced herself to look away before he noticed her staring. She heard him say "All right?" to a woman emerging from the ladies' room nearby. Could it be Deenie and Carrie already? Her heart jumped as she watched him hook his elbow around the waist of a slightly older, dark-haired woman with feline copper eyes and a silver-and-velvet bolero vest. As they walked away like two graceful wading birds, Sarah envied their calm. She combed the crowd for more possibilities. Maybe the boy reading *Car and Driver* next to the old woman in the lavender-checked housedress was Branch, but he was slack-jawed and uninterested in his surroundings. Branch would be at the edge of his seat just as she was.

Sarah bought two Cokes and was bringing them back to Jeremy when she saw Mae seated next to him.

"Hi." Mae waved coyly. She looked dazzling. She was wearing pegged magenta pants, a black turtleneck, a black blazer, and long black-and-magenta metal earrings that twisted like ribbons.

Sarah hugged her. "Where's the rest of the crew?"

"Tony and the Baron of Bulimia will be here soon. One wonders how people get attracted to their specialties," Mae said, pretending to make herself gag with her long index finger. "Anyway, I decided to come on my own."

"Are you nervous as Sarah?" Jeremy asked.

"Pretty nervous," she said almost gaily. Sarah could see that Mae was excited. "Oh, I talked to Mom, Sarah. She says you're avoiding her, which is probably wise. And she has all kinds of theories. I'd call her first one the appropriate-burial-partner plea."

"What's that?"

"She's already commuted your infidelity sentence. She thinks it's vital to be buried next to someone you love, and if Larry isn't the one, then Jeremy will do. Imagine sailing that one in divorce court:

" 'Your Honor, my client doesn't want to share the same ground with her husband.'

" 'You mean the property they hold in mutual trust?' the judge asks.

" 'No,' the attorney explains with exasperation, 'the burial plot, Your Honor.'

"The second theory's related to the first, and it's so perverse that I wrote Drew the second I was off the phone with her. I try to keep him amused, and this one is prime. Our mom, the world-class skeptic, claims that she communicates with Dad daily. She can conduct her private séances most anywhere, but she's most successful on express buses and in the Marshall Field's cafeteria smoking section. Poor Dad, still being hounded." Looking amused, she added, "She thinks he made this all happen." Mae blushed with satisfaction.

"What do you mean?" Sarah asked.

"She thinks Dad's haunting us. Ever since he died, things have gotten sinister, she says, and unpredictable. Let's see. There's you and Larry, you and Jeremy, me and Tony, me and the car, and, of course, Deenie and Carrie. She sees a chain of events, expressly designed to make her unhappy, all unraveling since Dad's death. Doesn't she know we've all been miserable for years? Doesn't she know how miserable she's been?" Mae laughed sarcastically.

"I never thought she was miserable." Sarah frowned.

"Don't you remember her crossword-puzzle phase? Her shivering phase?"

"Not really. I remember that they were a happy couple."

"To a small degree," Mae said, pinching air between her fingers.

"And why would Dad want to make us miserable? And how could he?"

"That's what she doesn't understand. She's trying to find out from him just how much control he has over the lives of mere mortals. And he was so uninvolved when he was our dad. Funny how he's changed character. And how does he do it, Sarah? Does he wave his ghostly arm or arch his invisible brow or what?"

Jeremy looked intrigued. "Did your dad name Carrie or Deenie?"

"He suggested Carrie's name be Carolyn. Where did Deenie come from again, Mae?"

Mae took an apricot out of her duffle purse and looked at it. "From Tony. Deenie's named after a man named Dean whom Tony knew in Vietnam. It escapes me why at the moment, but I think it had to do with his Saigon escapades. They were the best of friends, Tony and this man Dean. I would guess they visited whorehouses together. At the time Tony suggested it, Deenie sounded like a good idea. Androgyny was big then. Everyone was Britt or Brooke, and

Deenie was different. Did Sarah ever tell you who Mom named us after? Sarah Bernhardt and Mae West. Mom's a pioneering feminist in the name department."

"Why do you ask about the girls' names, Jeremy?"

"There's a story about naming that I know. The namer, in this case your father, has eternal power over the child he names."

"Beyond the grave?" Mae hummed a measure of the *Twilight Zone* introduction.

"But my mother's not very spiritual, Jeremy," Sarah said.

"She wouldn't have to be to feel her husband's presence. If the namer . . ."

Mae nudged Sarah. "Look! It's Branch."

Sarah was surprised at how soft and pale he appeared. She had expected someone all angles like Deenie, a praying mantis for her mating dance. "He looks angelic," Sarah said. "This is the boy who launched a Greyhound bus? Are you going to let him know you're here?"

"Not just now," Mae whispered.

"Why?"

"I want to see what he does."

"Well, he has forty-two minutes and counting."

"Your black eye's pretty splendid." Mae smiled, caressing her sister's cheek and grimacing for her. "Remember the one you got from me?"

"You hit me with a bat."

"You walked into my bat."

"My cheek hurt for days, and Mom kept shoveling French vanilla ice cream at me, as if that would help. I hate vanilla to this day."

"How can you hate little brown beans? By the way, Sarah, what are you going to tell Carrie?"

"I hadn't thought I'd have to tell her anything."

"You don't want her to think that Jeremy hit you. It would create a bad impression."

"That's true."

"Let's catch her first. Then we'll create what we need to keep her," Jeremy reassured them.

Branch had sat down near the arrival area, leaning forward and playing with a cigarette. "Is Branch his real name?"

"It's his real last name," Mae said.

"What's his first?"

"You know what? I don't know."

"HURRY UP," Carrie told Deenie, who was spooning melted orange sherbet out of a blue plastic cup. They were at Rick's Steak and Egger, the closest restaurant to the terminal. "Shouldn't we call the station again?"

"We just called ten minutes ago. The bus is arriving in seventeen minutes, and we're on it," Deenie said. "There's no use beating it there. Besides, if anyone's found out what we're doing, it's best to show up at the last second."

"What do you mean?"

"Don't you just suppose," she said licking the spoon delicately, "that your parents and mine might be a little interested in where we've gone?"

"I'm sure they are."

"Maybe someone's waiting for us. If we sweep in there, we can find Branch and get out as fast as possible. I don't want to stand there like a target."

"How do you know Branch will know the bus is late?"

"God, Carrie, how stupid can you be? He knows to check the time."

"So what do I do?"

"As soon as I see Branch, you run with me. We can run faster than old people."

"My dad's a pretty fast runner."

"Good for him."

"Deenie, I don't think I want to go to Costa Rica."

"You'll get in the car. We can always drop you at Disneyland."

The sullen counterman gave Deenie her check.

"More water, please."

The counterman whispered a remark to an elderly bus driver
eating toast and runny eggs. The bus driver stole a glance at Deenie,
laughed, and agreed. The counterman delivered a plastic pitcher of
water to Deenie, placed it in front of her, and stared out the window.
Deenie saw a piece of newspaper get caught on an updraft and sail
as high as the roof. She watched people entering and leaving the bus
terminal. She wished she saw Branch. If he could be intercepted, they
would be safe for sure. They'd walk to his car and sit and talk.
They'd kiss. They'd drive Carrie somewhere safe and take off forever.

"C'mon, Deenie. The bus is due in seven minutes. Sometimes
they're early, you know."

"That bus? That bus isn't likely to be early." Deenie hadn't
realized how much she hated the stupid silver bus and Adrian Fishblatt. She felt like spitting when she thought of him.

"What's the matter?" Carrie asked.

"What's the matter with what?"

"You look angry."

"I'd like to kill Adrian Fishblatt, that's all."

"Then why did you give him your coat?"

"Let's go," Deenie sighed, pushing Carrie ahead of her. "Don't
ask so many questions."

TEN MINUTES before the bus was due, Dr. Weber and Tony strode
through the main door like a well-dressed SWAT team. They didn't
notice Sarah, Mae, or Jeremy. Sarah watched them reading the arrival
board. Dr. Weber was dressed in the same outfit as the night before.
Tony had also dressed in a business suit.

"Shall we?" Sarah asked, standing to approach them in the
central area.

"No," Mae said, gripping Sarah's forearm and talking in a stage
whisper. "Leave them alone."

"Why?"

"They don't know I'm here."

"Why?"

"Just because." Mae's nervous fingers alternated between her long earring and her earlobe.

"Have they met Branch?"

"They weren't able to reach him."

"So we should keep our eyes on him."

"Right."

"Aren't you going to point him out to Tony and Dr. Weber?"

Ignoring Sarah's question, Mae seemed to be searching endlessly for something inside her handbag.

At six-fifteen Jeremy and Sarah and Dr. Weber and Tony converged on the arrival area. Sarah kept her eyes on Branch, who'd progressed from playing with a cigarette to resting his head back, eyes closed. She couldn't believe the casualness of youth. If she had been Deenie's boyfriend, she'd have lofted herself over the gate and pushed past agents into the unloading area.

"Are you ready?" Sarah asked Tony.

"This has been some ordeal. Mae can't stand it anymore. She's not even coming here."

Sarah looked furtively at Jeremy, who continued studying the ground. "Well," she said cautiously, "all this waiting is hard to bear. How many times has the bus been delayed? Four or five?"

Before Tony could answer, passengers were pouring past them. As she stood on tiptoe, trying to see Carrie's or Deenie's face behind those approaching her, Sarah felt her mouth go dry. An endless trail approached her: ungreeted sailors, women carrying heavy, old-fashioned luggage, men in sweaty shirts.

After the first swell, more travelers trickled out. A handsome black woman walked slowly, holding the hands of her two little daughters in identical puff-sleeved dresses. A pudgy man waddled in, carrying a cage and talking to something inside it. An elderly woman with swollen ankles plodded forward on a walker.

"Damn," Tony said. "Where the hell are they?"

If they weren't on this bus, Sarah knew they were lost for good. Her legs filled with so much panic that she couldn't keep still. Without looking at Jeremy or Tony, she rushed over to Branch, who appeared to be sleeping.

"Branch?" she said loudly. "Branch." When he didn't respond, she shook his shoulder. "Branch?" she repeated.

"What?" The surprised boy looked no older than Carrie.

"Are you Branch?"

"Who?" He squinted at her.

"There must be some mistake. Sorry."

Sarah turned to look at Mae for a clue. She was standing with a thin, long-legged man who was wearing an aviator's jacket. He had a pleasant face and shiny black hair that was shaved in the back but longer and stylish in front. They were confiding about something. First Mae looked very serious. She was touching his shoulder as she emphasized a point. Then she fumbled in her purse and, with a quick, nervous smile, handed the real Branch an envelope. Sarah continued to watch as Mae pointed nervously in Tony and Dr. Weber's direction.

Bewildered by Mae's flagrant subterfuge, Sarah cast a quick glance at Tony. He was talking rapidly to a baggage-handler and gesturing toward the empty bus.

When Sarah looked back at Mae, Branch was gone and Carrie had miraculously appeared. Sleepy and bedraggled, she stood shyly next to Mae.

"Mom?" Carrie asked as their distance from each other narrowed. First bewilderment filled her face, then relief. Sarah felt comforting tears in her eyes. There'd be no need to chase her. There was nothing to fear. It had happened like snow falling in the night.

"Hi, Carrie," Sarah said, taking her hand and holding it so tightly she could feel Carrie's fingers pulsing in her palm.

"I'm thirsty, Mom," Carrie said.

She thought of all those stories of children falling into dry wells and being rescued. How wonderfully mundane it must sound when the child asks for water. "Let's get you a drink, honey."

They were ordering lemonade and popcorn when Tony and Dr. Weber stormed back from the arrival gate.

"Where are they?" Tony demanded of Carrie.

"She doesn't know, Tony," Mae said calmly.

"What's going on, Mae?" Jeremy asked.

"Deenie and Branch are running away."

"And you're helping them?"

Mae's face wallowed in satisfaction, her smile as bright as neon. "And Tony's not."

"I don't get it," Sarah said. "Were you on the bus, Carrie?"

"We were most of the time, but we lost it in Nevada and hitched here."

"And you weren't planning to go with Deenie and Branch?"

"No way," Carrie said between long gulps of lemonade.

Sarah touched Carrie's hair and held it between her fingers.

Tony, who'd been listening with his face half-hidden in his palm, seemed to have gathered resolve. "You've got some nerve!" he shouted at the entire group. "You're accessories. To a kidnapping." Sweat was dripping off his desperate upper lip.

"They didn't know anything about it. I planned it myself, Tony," Mae lied.

"You damn . . ." he whispered. Cutting himself short, he appeared ready to move at her.

"Let's sit down and talk," Jeremy said.

"Fuck off." Tony looked for support to Dr. Weber, who seemed puzzled into silence.

"I can't believe you let it happen, Mae." Pleading with every nerve in his face, he seemed about to cry. "She needs our help! Why would you help Deenie get away from us?"

Mae's answer was silent contempt. She quickly kissed Sarah and Carrie and walked away.

"Where in the hell are you going, Mae?" Tony asked desperately.

"Home," she called without looking back. She headed for the station door, Tony trailing her. Even when she heard his footsteps approaching, she didn't speed up her casual retreat. Sarah and the rest of the group followed them like a dissonant quartet.

When Tony caught up to Mae, he grabbed her and held her wrist.

Without speaking, she lunged away from him, dropping her handbag, picked it up, and was out of the door.

"Let her go, Tony," Jeremy said, placing his hand on Tony's back.

Tony, head down like a charging bull, plowed into Jeremy's

side, but when Jeremy just stood there like a tree, solid and impersonal, Tony covered his eyes and slumped against a wall.

Jeremy cautiously moved away. "C'mon, Sarah," he said.

Looking exhausted, Tony was mopping his brow with a hankie and flexing his jaw muscles. "Mae will never have Deenie again." He looked from Sarah to Jeremy. Then his voice caught in a sob that frightened Sarah. "Let's get out of here, Frank." Dr. Weber followed him obediently out of the station.

"C'mon, Carrie," Sarah said gently, taking her hand again. "Let's go somewhere and talk."

MONDAY

CARRIE THINKS of walking through the door to Jeremy and Sarah's suite but hesitates: It's strange that your mother having a lover can give you better manners. She remembers the racket she and Scott would make on vacations, bickering over who got the cot, who the queen-size bed with the green, satiny strip on the blanket. Sometimes they fought over how to ration bath towels or bars of soap shaped like miniature tongues. None of this will happen again. Her life is divided into two neat halves like an apple on a plate. Childhood ended when she got on the bus. She doesn't know what to call the new phase of her life. Her mother's face still wants to please, but the bruise on her cheek is a warning that she might not be able to. Her eyes look more serious. Will her dad look different too? What's happened to them all?

Last night, when Sarah tried to explain the invisible process of coming apart, she said it was like glacial ice cracking at the bottom of the ocean. Although it's been cracking forever, nobody heard it until adequate instruments were invented to record the old noise. She made it sound like beautiful time-lapse photography on a *National Geographic* special, as though divorce were a physical science. Then Jeremy, inspired by her mom's vague explanation, digressed into geology for the rest of the dinner. Carrie watched her fettuccine carbonara steam up at her face while he told about Lake Agassiz, the glacial lake that existed before Lake Superior. What else? That another name for Saint Paul is Pig's Eye. That there are so many lakes in Minnesota that they've run out of names. One lake's called This Man, one is That Man, and a third is Other Man. That'll be the name she uses when she talks to Scotty about Jeremy, she thought, and covered a smile. That northern Minnesota's so bare in winter one legend has it that God created the land when he was just a baby, before he knew how to use colors very well. Then Jeremy poured them all half a glass of wine and smiled at her mother like she was beautiful.

When she tells them her travel stories about Ray Dubar and Lois the lesbian agronomist, she tries to sound like an adult. Sarah hugs her and Jeremy smiles. They don't understand that she's told them nothing. They pour more wine and toast her return. When she clanks her glass into her mother's, wine spills all over the tablecloth. She's frustrated with colors, impatient with the history of the world before people appeared on it. Her parents' marriage ending is more than a glacier cracking. The desert is more than a high white sun over orange-and-purple hills. Why does everyone accept inadequate descriptions?

They eat hard, powdery biscuits soaked in blueberries over which sweet cream has been drizzled. Deenie is the comic relief in Carrie's travelogue. Jeremy and Sarah like the part about her English teacher's dykey shoes. She doesn't tell them much about how she felt seeing the moonlit desert from the shoulder of the highway or writing the note she left for Sarah to find on her bed.

When she speaks to her dad on the phone, he uses simple, four-letter words, Anglo-Saxon words. *Love, good girl,* and *home,* he says. He could be talking to a dog. But his choky reticent voice contains feelings he can't pry open with words. An instrument needs to be invented to help them all along. She wonders what happened to her mother's eye, but she knows she can't ask her dad.

It's wonderful to lean back into a long bath until water plugs her ears and Carrie hears nothing around her. Ears submerged and eyes closed, she can concentrate. Why do people screw things up so badly? Look at her parents. Look at Mae and Tony. Maybe you should live alone and not keep track of events with television and radio or calendars. Take leap years, for instance. When the calendar requires an extra day, craziness enters people's lives. Her mom met Jeremy in a leap year. Her dad, she's pretty certain, punched her mom. She ran away. It isn't hard to understand the facts. Facts are as simple as bare light bulbs, as sentences she diagrams in English.

"Ready for breakfast?" Sarah asks, tapping on the door between their rooms.

"In a minute, Mom." Carrie is surprised that her mother acts so normal. Toweling herself dry quickly, she reaches for her underpants, hooks her bra in front and turns it around in one motion, and pulls on a denim dress with a low waist that gathers around her hips. She grabs a brush, drags it through her wet hair, and steps through the unlocked door between their rooms. A week ago she'd have barged in without thinking. Now she opens it with care.

Sarah motions for Carrie to join her on top of the made-up bed and puts her arm around Carrie's shoulder. Her mother smells of lilac soap. They sit in the same position, hands in their laps, heads back on the wall, their identical chins tilted toward the ceiling. Her mother's hair is wet too. The waves and curls are plastered onto her skull. There are no captions in family albums, because the caption for this photo, for instance, would have to read, *Mother and daughter reunited in Los Angeles after daughter runs away and parents' marriage ends.* And that would be only half of the caption.

"Where's Jeremy?"

"He went to a travel agent to get us return tickets. We thought we'd get a connecting flight to Minneapolis and stay over tonight."

"What for?"

"Jeremy wants to visit his grandmother. He hasn't seen her in two years. She's very old and not well."

"Is she an Indian?"

"Of course, honey."

"But isn't Dad waiting for us?"

"Sure he is."

"Then why aren't we going right home?"

Sarah hesitates. She looks like she's about to say something. Then she swallows and begins again. "I know we all need to talk. But we won't be talking like a family again because we aren't a family anymore in that sense. We're all going to have to figure it out, but before then I want to spend a little time with you. Just the two of us."

"And Jeremy."

"And Jeremy and his grandmother."

"What'll Dad think?"

"He's already expecting us tomorrow evening. We spoke earlier. I'm sure he misses you. Aside from that, Carrie, I'm not really concerned with what he thinks."

"What if I want to go home instead?"

"Then we'll take you home."

"What's Jeremy's grandmother like?"

"I've never met her."

"Where are Jeremy's parents?"

"His grandmother raised him."

"Why not his parents?"

"They weren't very stable."

"I don't have to live with Ivy, do I?"

"Are you worried about that?"

"Not really. Could Branch get arrested if Uncle Tony finds him?"

"Yes."

"Could Jeremy?"

"No, Carrie. I'm not a minor."

"Did Dad do that to your eye?"

"Yes."

"Because I ran away?"

"No, honey."

"Then why, Mom?" Carrie begins crying, but she's careful not to make much noise.

Sarah strokes her hair, hesitates, and begins slowly. Each word sounds separate from the next one, like she's not sure how they will fit together. "Your dad and I, we haven't been happy for many years, honey. But we've always loved you, and in some strange way I think we still love each other. We're not good for each other, though. I think we've both known that for a while."

Carrie sees Sarah look at her hands, her lap, her own unhappy, expectant eyes. "So I started going to those sessions on Thursdays. I was so sad about Grandpa. He was such a nice father, and such a good grandfather, and I missed him. While I was going there I met Jeremy, and we became friends.

"And later we began loving each other," she says quickly. "I tried to tell your dad, and he finally knew."

"And then he punched you?"

"And then we had a fight."

"Do you love Jeremy more than Dad?"

"I love you."

"But what about you and Dad?"

"We can't be together anymore."

Carrie looks for a long time at her mother, who doesn't appear to notice. She imagines their house empty of them. She can't remember not living in her sunny attic bedroom with its window bench and sky-blue-painted paneling. She'll miss their bathtub's lion's-claw legs and the funny old-fashioned doorjambs. She'll never see their back wall disappear under the ivy in summer or ride the tire swing that she barely fits into anymore.

Where will she live? Some of her friends live in apartments alone with their mothers. Jenny's mother's place has wrought-iron curlicues on the balcony and is called the Orleans. She's always thought Jenny's papery walls so thin and inadequate. You can hear her neighbor's toilet flush, doors bang, appliances buzz. You can hear other people's conversations. Of course, she'll have to take her new daybed and all her books wherever she goes. She's saving those books for her own children someday. Other friends have given their childish books away, but Carrie keeps everything. Where will she put it all?

A fluorescent light is humming in their hotel washroom. Maybe they're being X-rayed by an invisible machine. How will her mom's hand look, illuminated bone by bone, patting a spot on Carrie's head until it feels warm?

BRANCH IS SWEATING and chewing on a piece of plastic string. He looks like a cowboy, Deenie thinks, except for his scrawny chest, so poignant with its tiny pink nipples and patches of light brown hair. It's like a forest with lots of clearings. They're at the Harms Court in San Ysidro, a town made famous by the crazed gunman who shot up McDonald's. They've rented a toaster-shaped antique green trailer no bigger than a full-size car for two hundred and fifty dollars a month, furnished. They have a cigarette-singed maroon velveteen sofabed, one set of daisy-flowered sheets, two permanently stained off-white towels, a card table with a marbleized top, two brown director's chairs, a toilet, a sink, and a little kitchen without a working stove. If they want to heat something, they have to use the hibachi grill on the picnic table near the cold-water shower.

Branch is dipping iced oatmeal cookies into piña colada yogurt. Deenie watches him with concentration. "You'll have to wait here, Deen," she hears him saying. "Helen needs her things."

"Forget it!" Deenie grimaces in disgust.

"How can I forget it? She's paying for this."

"My mom gave you money too."

"We spent it on the security deposit. They think we'll haul our apartment away while they're asleep."

Deenie narrows her eyes. "Then Helen should do better. I wouldn't mind a stove. Or a shower. Or a phone. Did Helen ever have to shower outside?" She plops a peanut into her bottle of 7-Up and watches it foam over. "Besides, I don't want to stay here alone, Branch," she pleads, looking at the floor and thinking they'll have to buy a broom and Lysol and some paper towels.

Standing at the card table, she mixes lettuce, American cheese, and ranch dressing in a mustard-colored plastic bowl. She pours lots of Season-All onto it from a paper shaker. She wonders how she looks preparing food. Her mother always looked worried in the kitchen, like an emergency was imminent. She had timers and special forks for pasta and scientific instruments to stick into meat and piles of calico pot holders. She had an electric knife sharpener that made a noise like a soprano screaming. There was a fire extinguisher between the kitchen and the utility room and a whole row of hardcover cookbooks on the bread rack. But probably all you need is a big spoon and one of those spotted-enamel roasting pans, Deenie thinks.

"Lunch is ready," she says. "C'mon." A line of sweat drips from her armpit onto her hip. She wipes it off in a sweeping motion. The radio said it would be ninety-six degrees by noon, twelve minutes from now. She stands with arms akimbo. "I've slaved over this!" she says, pointing at the salad. Stamping her foot in mock irritation, she wipes more sweat from her forehead with her t-shirt tail.

Branch pulls back a director's chair, sits down, and pretends that he's rolling up long sleeves and tying on a cloth dinner napkin. "I think we need some entertainment to cheer us up," he says. "Let's go to the laundromat. It has a TV."

"Maybe we'll be on the news," Deenie smiles. "I hope they use my sophomore picture. My hair was hennaed in it." Crunching on a wedge of iceberg lettuce, she searches a pile of newspapers and maps they've removed from Branch's car. An article about infertility printed over the silhouette of an infant holds her interest for a minute. She studies the abstract pattern in the photo of a Petri dish containing an egg and sperm. Then she presses a quarter into her palm and stares at it.

"Who's on the quarter, Branch?"

"Mel Gibson?"

"Wrong."

"I hope it's a sports show," Branch says.

"In the middle of the afternoon in a laundromat?"

"Why not? Maybe they have cable."

"Who goes to a laundromat?"

"Women with ugly babies. Men with no underwear. And us."

"What should we cook for dinner?"

Branch takes a last bite of the salad, puts an oatmeal cookie between his jaws, and stands at the door.

Deenie grabs some underwear, a nightgown, and some socks off the floor and collects her 7-Up, a *People* with William Hurt's photo on the cover, and her purse.

"Let's buy a pie," she says.

"What for?"

"What's tomorrow?"

"Tuesday."

"What else?"

Branch looks like he's pulling the answer out of the air with his eyes. "Your birthday. Just think, if we stay here a year and a day, you'll be old enough to cross into Mexico."

"How about lemon meringue? It's my favorite. We used to have it all the time before my mom got interested in fancy cooking."

"Why did she get interested?"

"Because I stopped eating."

"Why did you stop eating?"

"Because she got interested."

"Better lock up," Branch says, slamming the door behind him

and checking the latch. "We don't want anyone to take our Conan glass or our jar of sugarless peanut butter."

"Maybe we should buy a little Christmas tree too. And decorations. It's almost December."

"How little?"

"Oh, as tall as this." She holds twelve inches of air between her palms.

"I'll call Helen. Maybe she can think of a plan."

"I thought it was hard to get into the United States, not out of it."

They drive in silence down a street with spindly palm trees and no other vegetation. Compared to the desert and mountains, the landscape here seems like an afterthought.

"The air's so hot you can't breathe," Branch says.

"I can breathe," Deenie says. "Watch." She inhales and exhales with exaggerated moans.

Branch reaches over and touches her at random. She watches his hand graze her nose, her neck, her left nipple, her pelvic bone. Now it rests on her thigh. She wraps her fingers around his thumb. They pass a line of stores. Knapp's Hardware and the Tasti-Cone have new royal-blue awnings piped in metallic silver. Both display HELP WANTED signs.

"Maybe we should get jobs," Deenie says.

"And we'll rent a little white house on a shady street. We'll put up shutters. And you'll be the prom queen. And I'll earn my swimming letter."

"I wonder what Carrie's doing."

"It's like a Disney cartoon, Deenie. She's purring on a pillow and eating ice cream and caviar. We're in the pound. We don't even have a real shower."

"It could be worse."

"I guess," Branch says. "Your dad could be visiting us."

They see a sign for the Soak and Suds. They choose a parking meter just down the street. Branch gets out of the car empty-handed. Deenie carries their meager wash in the crook of her arm.

"See?" Branch says. "They're showing sports."

Glancing up at the highlights of a San Ysidro High girls' bas-

ketball game, Deenie sees a squat Hispanic girl making a basket. She
buys a miniature package of Tide, throws the wash into a machine,
and fills the slot with quarters. "It's costing us a dime to wash each
sock," she says.

The sports segment of the news has ended. The ruddy weatherman wears an obvious toupee. A huge red arrow saying HOT sits
heavily on all of Southern California. The weatherman seems distracted reading the grim figures.

"Shit," Branch curses. "Maybe we can work in a meat locker."

Deenie looks around her. Three Mexican men are waiting for
one dryer-load to finish. A woman with a sobbing little boy is trying
to get an orange clown balloon to stand on cardboard feet.

"I'm going to find a phone and call Helen," Branch says.

Deenie feels panicky, but she knows it's silly to think he'll never
come back. He'll be back to tell her she'll have to wait in the crummy
trailer while he goes to Costa Rica alone. Then she'll use the same
phone to call her mom. Maybe Mae can stay with her till Branch
comes back, or take her to a Hyatt, where they'll order room service
for every meal and put it on American Express. She sees a silver
goblet of strawberries and whipped cream. If her dad answers, she'll
hang up.

A soap opera's replaced the news. A young couple in a noisy
supper club are arguing over a bunch of names. Deenie knows that
people their age would never eat at such a stuffy place. Maybe she
can get a job writing soaps. Hers would be authentic. Without any
particular provocation, the man clears the table with his forearm
and storms out of the scene. There is a close-up of the woman's upper
lip quivering. Then she takes a plate and hurls it unconvincingly in
his direction. Pulsing organ music accompanies the picture of the
wobbling plate that fills the screen before the Irish Spring commercial.

"Hey, mamacita," one of the men whispers as he passes her.

Deenie ignores him and goes to the window to look down the
street for Branch. She sees him sitting on his car hood, kicking his
legs rhythmically and reading *Interview*. When he comes back into
the laundromat, she'll call him Gene. He hates his first name more
than anything. "What did Helen say, Gene?" she'll ask. Then they'll
have a fight to clear the air.

• • •

SARAH LOOKS DOWN the snowy runway as their plane taxis in at Minneapolis–St. Paul International. She asks Jeremy how many names Minnesotans have for snow. Is airport snow, huge white globs highlighted by searchlights, one of the kinds?

"Now I've been to eighteen states," Carrie says beaming at her mother, sitting between her and Jeremy.

"And all on this trip," Sarah teases.

"And all in five days," Carrie adds.

"Where does your grandmother live, Jeremy?" Carrie asks.

"Does Franklin Avenue mean anything to you?"

"Nope."

"Mainly old people live there. And poor people. There are also lots of stores that sell surplus goods that come from the railway yards. Do you need a thousand light switches or forty pair of purple socks? You can probably find them on Franklin."

"Does she know we're coming?"

"She knows I'm coming."

"Not us?" Sarah asks surprised.

"Nope."

"Should we wait at a motel?"

"For God's sake, Sarah, I want her to meet you."

"Then why didn't you tell her?"

"Because you won't mean anything to her until she sees you."

When Sarah was little, Stanley would give her a nickel for candy. She could get to the nameless general store without crossing a street if she walked down an alley and through two gangways in neighbors' yards. The proprietor's wife wore cotton stockings the color of the liver sausage she sold. In all her visits, Sarah never encountered another customer as she placed her order: two cinnamon lips, a bull's-eye, a spearmint leaf, a pretzel stick, and a Sputnik gumball for dessert. She hasn't seen a blue sugared gumball since then. Nor has she seen a store like the one Betty lives above. In the window the owner's taped a yellowing picture of himself in a World War Two air force uniform. There are thirty-year-old signs advertising fresh potato salad, mittens, and kites that look as old as the photo.

They walk up a long staircase to Betty's apartment. The hall-way's naturally dark, but the late hour emphasizes its gloominess. Sarah lets Jeremy lead the silent procession to 2-F. She and Carrie will fade into the shadows and wait to be introduced.

The first time Sarah met Larry's mother in a suburb of Cleveland, they'd all sat around an oval dining table under a Miro poster while Larry's mother brought out exquisitely poached salmon crisscrossed with spring asparagus, each topped with a tiny pimento S. It was spring break of 1970. They had vowed to limit conversation to their studies and their future plans, but not talking about Vietnam was like sitting on your hands until they fell asleep.

Finally, Nixon's bombing of Cambodia became the topic of the afternoon, but Sarah held her tongue as the conversation heated up. At the moment that Larry was calling his mother a warmonger, Sarah was cutting pieces of the Black Forest torte in the kitchen and placing them on bird-of-paradise dessert plates. By the time she had brought them into the dining room, lunch was over. Larry was reading the newspaper, and his mother was silently clearing the table. For years they had laughed about that first meeting. *The Cleveland offensive*, Larry had come to call it. It was sad to think about the jokes they used to share, a line of sympathy that held the past together.

"Hi, Gram," Jeremy says. Sarah can't see her yet. She waits to hear her voice. Her relationship with Jeremy is a series of thresholds crossed with varying degrees of hesitation.

"Gram, this is Sarah Holm, and this is her daughter, Carrie." Jeremy includes both of them in an arm-spanning embrace.

Sarah faces a tiny woman whose face is thin and taut. Her hair is still black and cut short, and her eyes are round like Jeremy's. She's wearing a blue housedress with white tatting on the pocket and collar. She has white bobby socks under black toeless scuffs.

"Pleased to meet you," Sarah says, but the woman has already turned and walked into her apartment. Standing in her spare front

room, Sarah watches Carrie's eyes land on objects. There's an old
green couch with a black-and-red comforter thrown to one side.
There's a small kitchen table on which a portable television rests.
The beige carpeting with scalloped leaves is covered with transparent
dust in several areas. On the wall are ancient photos of a man in a
broad-brimmed hat and a dark suit standing on the porch of a log
house with a young woman whose slip is showing. She's smiling
almost undetectably and looking down at her t-strap high heels.

"Sit down." Betty motions by nodding her head toward the
couch. She reaches up to quickly stifle a yawn.

"It's late, Gram. We're sorry to keep you awake."

She disappears, then comes back with a brown plastic pitcher.
Placing it on her end table, she goes back twice more to gather four
plastic cups, some napkins, and a plate of butter cookies.

"Want some apple juice?"

"I'll have some," Carrie says.

When she makes no effort to serve it, Carrie gets up and pours
herself a glass. Beyond her, in the kitchen, Sarah can see what remains
of seasons of canning stacked in Mason jars on a small enamel chest
of drawers. There is a perfect row of green beans, some light, some
darker, under a row of thick, seedy tomato juice. Sarah knows Jeremy's grandmother hasn't lived in Red Lake for two winters. What
remains must be her least favorite foods.

"How are you feeling?" Jeremy asks.

"The same." Her lids, which slant downward, close for a second.
"I was sick in November."

"This is November," Jeremy says.

"Then it was October. I was real sick for a week."

"Did you see a doctor?"

"No."

"Gram doesn't believe in them," Jeremy explains.

"What was wrong?" Sarah asks.

"She has heart trouble. She has real bad times now and then."

"When you were little," she begins, "I had heart trouble too.
It's no different now. You worry now because I'm old. All those
years in Red Lake, I'd walk miles. I'd take care of the garden and
go fishing with Jim on the ice. My heart's been bad ever since I had

that flu." She waves the trouble away with her hand, pulls at her chin, and stares away from them.

"Want to sleep now, Gram?"

"Fine. You stay," she says.

"We will."

"There are covers in the closet. You two take the bedroom. Me and the girl can use the couch and the floor."

"We don't want to evict you, Gram."

"Are you sure you'll be all right out here?" Sarah asks.

Betty looks at them defiantly.

Jeremy shakes his head. "She never changes her mind, Sarah. You're wasting your breath."

"Me and the girl will be fine."

"Carrie, will you be all right with blankets on the floor?" Sarah asks.

"Sure," Carrie says meekly. "Where's the washroom?" she asks after Sarah kisses her good night.

Carrie tries to sleep. The small room is bathed in streetlight pink and seems to be rocking to the noise of Betty's deep, strained breathing. Now and then she grunts and snorts. Between breaths Carrie worries that she's died. Twice she's startled awake because Betty cries out. Once it sounds like *church row*. Another time it's a long string of syllables that come out like a gush of wind. Betty stirs then, rises slowly, wraps herself in a blanket, and walks to the bathroom. Carrie hears her move through the hallway, her hands making a dry, slapping sound on the walls.

"Go to sleep," she tells Carrie when she returns.

"Good night," Carrie says.

The air is dense with old cooking smells, and the hazy outlines of Betty's meager furniture populate the room. Carrie feels so alone. It's not like the fright that she used to feel after nightmares. It's something deeper that won't go away. She wants her mom to comfort her, but she's embarrassed to go into the next room, where Jeremy, a stranger, sleeps with his arm around Sarah. When she pictures her mother's peaceful face on his bare shoulder, she feels like she might smother. Carrie can hear his occasional snores. They must sound like musical riffs to her mother, who loves this man. She's probably dreaming about him right now.

It's so strange to be sleeping on a floor in Minneapolis next to an old lady, so strange to be unable to enter her own mother's room. Her mother doesn't love her father, she tells herself again and again. Still, she can see his face more clearly than anything else. She knows that he is waiting to take her back to their house, which is still her house for now. She'll sleep in her own bedroom tomorrow night, where she knows each shadow. Closing her eyes, she'll think about when they all were a family and her grandpa was still alive. He'd muss his funny shock of white hair, then chase her and Scotty around the backyard making monster sounds. He'd rub his beard on her cheek and tickle her until she was breathless. There used to be no Minneapolis, no Betty, no Jeremy. Why couldn't her dad be here right now? Why did he have to hit her mom?

In the dark, foreign room, it's hard for her to accept that anything's real. That she saw a desert. That she rode a Greyhound bus and almost kissed Adrian and hitchhiked with strangers. That her aunt helped Deenie run away, that her crazy cousin is somewhere in Mexico by now. She hears an occasional car accelerate at the light in front of Betty's apartment. Someone's car radio is so loud that she hears the slur of the first words of a song. Where are people rushing to at three in the morning? Probably to see their lovers. Probably all over people are listening to sad music and wondering what happened. She looks over to where Betty is lying. Her slow breathing means that she's fallen asleep again, face covered. She's so small under her blanket that Carrie has trouble believing she's there.

TUESDAY

CARRIE FEELS a hand on her shoulder. She's startled to see the back of her mother's head on a pillow next to her. Sometime during the night Sarah has slipped into the room and lain down beside her.

"Wake up," Betty's whispering to her. She's wearing the same dress with a man's gray, red, and white cardigan. She motions for Carrie to follow her into the kitchen.

"Before I was your age, I left school," Betty begins. She's seated herself at the kitchen table and is drinking a juice glass of buttermilk. "Want some?"

"No thanks." Carrie has always hated the trail buttermilk leaves in the glass. She joins her at the table.

"Before that I was at boarding school. The Sisters thought we didn't understand them so they talked real loud to us." Betty imitates them, making her voice rise in emphasis at the end of the sentence.

"Why would they think that?"

"Because some girls knew tribal languages."

"How about you?"

"I knew English. My father was Welsh, but he was born in Canada."

"How did you get your name?"

"Betty?"

"Jeremy said you had another name."

"My mother named me because she once lived by that river, Totogatic, but I never liked my name much. It sounded wrong in my ears." She seems distant for a moment, her eyes glistening with thinking.

"On warm days at school," she finally continues, "we used to ride down a hill in a hay cart, lots of us together. The cart would go real fast and land in a field. Sometimes girls would fall out, but we'd try not to get dirty because we had to wash our own clothes and iron them too. When I was fourteen, my mother wanted me home. My father wasn't around much, so she needed help. I was real good in school. I got some medals."

"In what?"

"Music and handwriting. I had real nice writing."

"What kind of music?"

"Whatever the Sisters taught. Mostly hymns."

"Did you miss school?"

"I was busy. I helped my mother. There were always little ones around. Her sisters left theirs with us, and Ma had a few when I was pretty old. I would have them watch me do my work. They'd sit all in a little clump like mushrooms. They were quiet things.

"One day I was helping Mom put up some blueberries, and one of the little boys named Leonard came screaming. He had burns on his mouth and tongue. Wouldn't you know he got into some lye? I ran all the way to the store with him—I was real fast then—and we got him a ride to the hospital. I had to stay with him three nights. He'd cry every time I tried to leave."

"That must have been terrible."

"The hospital was full of old people like me. A woman named Mary from Red Lake was there. She was so sick that her hair had turned white. When the little boy slept, I'd listen to Mary. Sometimes she'd ask me to brush her hair, but I'd only pretend to fix it because it was too tangled to comb through. She'd ask me how she looked and I'd say, 'Real pretty.'

"Mary remembered so many things. When she was small, the school burned down. She watched the flames and cried because the books were gone. She asked me to read to her sometimes, but the hospital didn't have much around for the sick people. A man down the hall was a barber. He'd brought some *Life* magazines from his shop, and sometimes I'd read her those.

"Once she told me about her uncle who lived to be 106."

Carrie likes how she said the age: 1-0-6. "Really? I don't know anyone older than eighty."

"When he died, they had a real nice funeral. They sang him a song that makes a path to heaven. When Ma died, I tried to remember that song, but mostly the men know those things."

"My grandfather died last winter." Carrie remembers his long, pleasant face. She remembers how he once let her smoke his pipe because she told him the tobacco smelled like apples. How he called her boys' names like Gus. He used to do a magic trick in which he poured milk from high in the air through a rolled napkin into a glass. "Now drink it," he'd demand in a corny accent. She can see him make a quarter appear from behind his ear. There seems to be a standard repertoire of grandfather tricks, but Stanley was more deft performing his, an actor playing to an audience of one.

"Here," Betty says, placing a photo in Carrie's hand. Carrie sees a little boy sitting on a crude, unpainted fence. A hut with a metal roof and a small pine tree are in the background.

"Is that Jeremy?"

"And that's my house. You could lie in bed and hear rain smacking the roof. I always thought it sounded pretty. Jeremy was a smart little one, but he had a real temper. Look at those eyes. His temper shows. Once, when he was angry at me, he threw his shoes in the lake. 'Go find those shoes,' I told him. Jeremy took some string and a pole and spent two days fishing for his shoes. Jim told him to use socks as bait," she chuckles.

"What was he angry about?"

"I don't remember anymore. While Jim made him save up for new ones, he had to wear his old shoes that hurt." She shakes her head. "Jeremy'd make me things at school and wrap them in newspaper and tie them with string. Then he'd give me them as presents."

"Where were his mom and dad?"

"His mom was all over. She was in Bemidji, Sioux City, and Duluth. She lived in Chicago too for a while with a nice man, a truck driver who used to come up here to buy timber and to sell beer."

"What about his dad?"

"His dad already had a wife in Firesteel, South Dakota. All his family was there. My daughter met him in Duluth when she was working as a waitress in a little coffee shop. My daughter was a pretty girl then." Betty gets up and pulls a cast-iron pan from the cupboard. "Want some breakfast?"

"Sure."

"I can fry bacon and make toast, but I'm out of eggs. I have coffee, tea, and juice."

"I'll have tea."

"Do you wear brassieres?"

"Sure."

"I need a new one. Can you buy me one today?"

"I can find a store. What size do you need?"

"Not too big. Like you, I guess."

"What color?" Carrie sees Betty frown. "I guess you want white."

"But don't tell Jeremy."

"Why?"

"He'll want to buy me more things. All I need is one brassiere. The one I got has pins in it." She tugs at her sweater and dress. Carrie sees the wrinkled skin on her neck, her taut shoulder, the pinned bra strap.

"Okay, I won't."

"Do you like tomato juice?"

"Sure."

"Take these." She reaches inside a cabinet filled with paper bags and several rows of canned goods and Mason jars. "It's seedless," she says, filling her arms with jars and handing three to Carrie.

"Thanks."

"What's your name again?"

"My name is Carrie."

"Carrie what?"

"Carrie Olivia Holm."

"That's a nice name."

"Thank you."

"Does your mom like Jeremy?" She cranes her neck and glances at Sarah asleep on the floor.

"I think so. Very much."

"What's her name again?"

"She's Sarah."

"That's from the Bible."

"Right." Carrie can smell the bacon searing on the stove. She watches Betty lean over the broiler, where the bread is toasting.

"How much do brassieres cost?"

"Seven or eight dollars, I guess."

"Does she want to marry him?"

"I don't know."

"Where's your father?"

"Home with my brother."

"What happened to your mother's eye?"

"My dad hit her," Carrie says quietly.

Betty places the plates on the table and takes one slice of bacon and piece of toast for herself. She gives Carrie a chipped white metal serving tray containing two more pieces of toast and four more strips of bacon. "Jam's there," she says pointing to a silver-hammered cup. "Sometimes people get real angry like that."

"They had a fight after I ran away. I keep thinking it happened because of me, but my mom says it didn't."

"Then I expect your mom is right."

"Don't you want more?"

"I don't eat much. You know, Jeremy used to run away."

"He did?"

"The first time I was just sick. I thought I'd never see him again. I took Jim to go look for him, and there he was in the bus station. He was curled up on a seat like a little snail. Jim picked him up and carried him to the car, and then I walloped him good."

"I bet he was glad to see you anyway."

"I expect he was."

Reaching into her dress pocket, she pulls out some wadded Kleenex and some folded money. She hands Carrie a ten-dollar bill. "It doesn't have to be a fancy brassiere. I'm an old lady."

"I like plain bras too," Carrie says.

"Do you like Marilyn Monroe?"

"I guess so."

"I think she was real pretty, but I felt sorry for her."

"Why?"

"She couldn't have children. She was a bleeder."

"My mom once had a miscarriage before my brother and I were born."

"I bet she was real happy when she had you."

"I guess."

"I bet Marilyn wore real fancy underclothes."

"I bet she did."

"WHERE'S CARRIE?" Sarah asks, alarmed. She wipes her eyes and sits cross-legged on the rug.

"She went to the dime store for me. I'm out of some things," Betty says.

"Did you all sleep well out here?" Jeremy asks.

"I have too many dreams," Betty says. "Last night I woke up three or four times. I dream about Ma all the time. I don't know why. I'm a little girl and Ma's working in the house. She's making bread or canning peas or frying potatoes. Sometimes I smell cooking in my dreams."

"I slept like a log," Jeremy says, stretching.

"Does Carrie know where the store is?"

"I told her."

Sarah watches Betty prepare bacon and toast and coffee for them. She clanks pots together on the stove and turns down the heat when the bacon sizzles louder than their speech.

Sarah wonders if Ivy will want to know Jeremy. She imagines them in Ivy's apartment, crowded with knickknacks, for Sunday brunch. Ivy will serve her banana bread and make an omelet after she shows them her view. Then she'll ask Jeremy what he does, but when he begins to tell her in his thorough, detailed way, she'll signal impatience by fumbling with her lighter. She'll become more animated only when she shows them Stanley's photos and tells Jeremy about the flowers she brings to Stanley's grave: irises, roses, and mums, in season.

It's strange that her mother has never seen the man she loves. She looks at Jeremy's face bent over a photo with Betty, and suddenly she feels panicked. Where will her children be during this breakfast idyll? Will they be in the next room watching the lake from Ivy's balcony? Will they be with her at all?

"Here," Betty says, and places Jeremy's photo in front of Sarah on the table.

Sarah studies his face, which is broad and serious. "Why do you look so mean?"

"I was a bad seed." Jeremy smiles, but his eyes look grave.

"He was mad at his ma, I'd guess." Betty looks at Sarah tentatively, then stands up and leans over her shoulder. "That was our house. When Jeremy came to me, he was a tiny boy who talked a lot but didn't move around much. My daughter must have made him sit still for hours. He was surprised that I let him run around outside. 'Go chase the chickens,' I'd tell him. A simple thing like that, and he'd look at me for the longest time."

"We didn't have chickens. I didn't know if you were serious."

"He had this one toy when his ma brought him, a little blue water gun. He slept with it under his pillow. When his birthday came, I got him some new things, and he never looked at his old toy again."

Sarah pours herself and Jeremy more weak coffee. Betty holds her hand over her cup, meets Sarah's eyes, and says, "You have a nice girl."

"Thank you," Sarah says, knowing that Betty means more. Sarah glances at Jeremy, whose face is beaming because Betty has said what he had hoped she would. Sarah is accepted into the family that Jeremy has always desired. He and Sarah and Carrie are now a family of their own. But Sarah knows it isn't that simple. Betty is staring at her cheek. And without the man who made the bruise, Carrie and Scotty wouldn't exist.

In the long silence that follows, Sarah watches Jeremy. Now and then he looks about to speak but seems to think better of it. When he does speak, he doesn't look up. "Gram saved me a lot of times."

Betty makes a low noise in her throat. She frowns and looks at Sarah. "You can have him now. He made me tired forever." Then she laughs drily. Her voice sounds like a stick combing sand.

• • •

BECAUSE OF SNOW drifting on runways, the plane has to circle O'Hare for two hours. Twice they fly toward Kokomo, and each time the resonant voice of the pilot confides their location and altitude. Sarah wonders what they're supposed to do with his news.

"She liked you," Jeremy says, waking from a nap. He stretches and pivots his long body toward Sarah.

"How could you tell, Jeremy?"

"She gabbed away."

"I thought she was pretty subdued."

"*Yes* and *no* is her usual repertoire. And I hadn't seen that photo of me in twenty-five years. She never showed it to Lurene."

"Lurene used to visit her?"

"Lurene lived at Red Lake for a while."

"Oh," Sarah says. "Did you live at Red Lake with her?"

"No, we lived on Marine Drive in a building with art-deco elevators. We had a Haitian doorman named Florian. We were up-scale Indians. When we visited, Gram wouldn't give Lurene the time of day."

"Why didn't you ever mention Lurene in grief therapy?"

Seeing Carrie's interested eyes, Jeremy decides not to ask Sarah the same question about Larry.

Sarah feels proud that she's Betty's choice. It dispels her envy that Jeremy had a life before she knew him. It's better that he and Lurene never lived in Red Lake, a place she's unable to know. Florian, whom she pictures wearing a red carnation boutonnière, is a sign she can interpret. Her feelings are neatly contained by Jeremy's irony. No secret Indian rituals were shared between the lovers on the lake before sunrise. Her talent for imagining herself excluded from things is another legacy of her marriage.

One thing is certain. She prefers Jeremy's reserve to Larry's manic sociability. She and Larry had been young and exuberant together, but after the children were born, Larry was restless. He'd lie in bed next to Sarah with his eyes open, imagining the world he was missing. Even when the children crowded into their bed and shared their pillows, even when their warm breath blew in his face, Larry seemed lonely. His sharp features would take on more color only when they were at parties or gatherings. And if Sarah wanted to leave early to watch the small O's of her sleeping children's mouths, he'd be just out of her reach at the edge of a conversation. On the way home, his energy would dissipate, and he'd become moody and silent.

Larry had been more than exuberant. He had been pathological, "addicted to affairs," in the popular language of psychology. Sarah imagines the austere face of Donna next to a plate of chocolate truffles or white lines of cocaine on a silver tray. She remembers how Pipkin described one of her daughters-in-law as "a leather addict." "A good dresser?" Nora had asked. "A reconstituted cow," Pipkin had replied.

"I bought your grandma a bra," Sarah hears Carrie telling Jeremy.

"Why?" Jeremy asks, amused.

"Because she wanted me to. She says you're too generous. And look." Carrie opens her duffel bag to reveal to them three bottles of tomato juice wrapped in a towel.

"She gave you juice from her private collection?"

"Sure. And she likes Marilyn Monroe."

"Did you give her truth serum?"

Carrie shrugs. "She just did all the talking."

"We'll be landing soon," Sarah says.

"God, I hate to fly," Carrie moans.

SARAH REMEMBERS her first plane ride to visit her grandmother in Miami over a Christmas vacation. While snow covered Chicago, she and Mae did headstands and played chicken with someone's skinny grandsons from Teaneck, New Jersey, in a giant, turquoise clam-shaped pool. During Ivy's naps and their grandmother's endless games of mah-jongg on the balcony, they sat in the kitchen sharing trays of frozen chocolate-covered rum balls, a delicacy so exotic it provoked slapstick eating gestures. "Kiss me," Sarah whispered, teeth painted with thick chocolate. Mae smeared an ardent chocolate kiss on Sarah's cheek, then, seeing her horrified expression, handed her a wet rag to erase it.

Her grandmother's partners were three widows who used their husbands' names. "This is Mrs. Gerald Fontana," her grandmother said, placing a heavily freckled arm on each woman's shoulder in turn. "This is Mrs. Arthur Dennis. This is Mrs. Langton Long."

Mae could hardly control herself during the introductions, but it was common for her to invent reasons for laughter. "We are Stanley Linden's daughters," Mae mocked in a voice thick with sweetness. She wrapped Sarah in a half nelson and grinned so long and intensely that the women were left speechless.

On the last day of the vacation, the girls had gotten manicures and new bouffant hairdos at the Powder Puff, a pink-and-chrome confection in the lobby of the retirement hotel. Seniors got 20 percent off on Tuesdays, so the Cuban receptionist, who doubled as the manicurist, was happy to accommodate last-minute paying customers. Sarah had noticed that her hairdresser, Margot, a pretty woman about their mother's age with a strawberry-blond flip and long, curly eyelashes made thick by mascara, had blue concentration-camp numbers tattooed on her forearm.

When they landed at Midway, they were greeted by Stanley, who couldn't stop smirking at something.

"What's so funny?" Mae asked.

"You two."

"What?" Mae insisted, poking Stanley in the ribs. She stood on tiptoe to grab his shirt collar and butt her face affectionately into his.

"You and your sister have the same hairdos."

"So?"

"You look like dressed-up midgets."

"Thanks," Mae said huffily. "C'mon, Sarah." They took each other's hands and ran ahead the length of the terminal.

All the way home Mae pretended to be offended. Not even the coincidence of seeing the Oscar Mayer Wiener Wagon with its real midget driver parked in front of their local Certified Foods made her drop the pretense of anger. That was the comfort families provided, a stage for practicing emotions. Feelings flowed as harmlessly as water from an old-fashioned spigot.

By the time Ed Sullivan came on and Topo Gigio did his silly mouse routine, everyone was reconciled. Sarah curled up on Stanley's lap, rubbing her palm on his stubbly chin, while Mae narrated every bizarre episode of their vacation. Mae said that Mrs. Langton Long resembled a cocker spaniel with a crewcut. Sarah can still hear Stanley's and Ivy's appreciative laughter.

Sarah hopes that Larry has thought to call the airport for their arrival time. Thinking of Larry in such a pedestrian way makes her apprehension grow. The man who has hit her will be at the airport; her husband will be at the airport: the equation balances. She can remember his fist coming at her face, the humiliation of falling stunned onto Carrie's rug. She can also picture Larry's compact, vulnerable body searching for her in bed, caressing her blindly, and nestling near her chin. She can see her breast in his hand, the same hand that struck her. A sickening swell of emotion pushes everything of this moment from her mind: Where was the Larry she met in French class, the Larry who'd gotten arrested with her the night Nixon invaded Cambodia? Where was the sturdy young father carrying Carrie and Scotty through the waist-deep snow of 1979? Where was his hand stirring the coffee he made every morning of their marriage?

What will happen when she sees him at the airport? What will they say? She has mentally rehearsed the hug she'll give Scotty as his shoulders squirm in protest. She can see Jeremy's tactful retreat from their family group as they walk in a tentative V toward the car. She can hear the tone of their conversation, full of restraint and exhaustion, like people outside a sickroom at midnight.

Sarah will be glad to see their Victorian frame house on Lakeview, the one she hesitates to call hers anymore. She'll miss the beautiful wood they stripped for five years, the secret safe in their bedroom wall that contains so little. She has learned its history, how it was built at the end of the last century, when their neighborhood was still suburban, and how, for ten years before the Depression, their parlor had provided the neighborhood's only music lessons.

The spinet piano that neither child touches anymore stands in the sun and dust of the parlor. Seven families have lived in this house. All, she imagines, have made music of one kind or another. Sometimes, when the kids were little, the four of them would plunk away at the keys. Larry had the best sense of musical burlesque, upstaging them all in complex variations on "Chopsticks." Some renditions were dirgelike. Others, played in a solemn minor key, sounded Oriental or Middle Eastern. They were a family laughing to music.

Tonight she'll tuck her children in with eagerness, but her proper kiss will acknowledge their status as teenagers. As they shrink away from her almost imperceptibly, she'll understand the conditions they impose upon her love.

In the morning she'll begin circling ads for small apartments near the lake. Jeremy will understand that it's safer to live alone while lawyers debate how to split up Carrie and Scotty, her only important worldly goods. But tonight she won't bother herself with legalities. Before she surreptitiously makes a bed on the couch downstairs, she'll take a bath and change into the familiar nightgown that even after washing has the intimate smell of her own skin. She hopes Larry won't approach her as she brushes her teeth or combs her hair before bed. She doesn't want to look into his face or be pressed in any way. Maybe she'll lock the bathroom door and stay in the tub until she hears him safely in bed. She imagines how he'll sprawl diagonally, tucking her extra pillow under his side and wrapping the sheets tightly around his bare chest.

Will she be able to fall asleep? In the soft grayish light of the front room, objects will take on a melancholy eminence: their spice-jar lamp and pewter vases, the Depression glass bowls on the mantel, the traditional school photographs of their children in their rich oak frames. If Larry forces the issue in the morning, they'll sit at the kitchen table, drinking strong coffee and talking. She'll tell him to imagine an empty museum. All the exhibits have been removed.

"An empty room?" Larry will ask.

"Yes."

"A mausoleum?"

"A museum."

"The past wiped clean?"

"Not at all." Sarah will look at her kitchen curtains, the French lace curtains with creamy spring flowers, and wonder if this is the proper ending that she'd anticipated, mature adults in a clean kitchen discussing historical necessity: the antiseptic denouement, the bloodless coup.

She holds her hand over her mouth to smother an impulse to cry, then pats her cheek. The bruise is in its sixth day of ripening, green surrendering to yellow.

THE PLANE MAKES an abrupt landing on the icy runway. Carrie grips Sarah's fingers bloodless and closes her eyes, making delicate violet veins appear under her lids. They were a deep purple when she was little; her mother likes to tell the story of how a woman asked if the infant in the stroller wore eye shadow.

Even though flying frightens her, it wouldn't be fair for the plane to crash when so much has already happened. The worry that her mom got hit because Carrie ran away makes her stomach clench. What will her dad want to do to her? She knows he won't hurt her, but maybe his eyes will cloud with anger, and he'll never talk to her again. She can't imagine her mother not living in the house, but of course she can't live in it with Jeremy. Not even if her dad moves out can Jeremy ever sleep in the bedroom. She used to run barefoot there on February mornings to snuggle with her parents in the big brass bed when they were new to the house. She looks at Jeremy and for a second considers hating him. But her mother is smiling and talking softly to him, and Jeremy is touching Sarah's long freckled fingers.

Carrie finds Larry and Scotty before they see her. Scotty is standing at the wall of windows facing the arrival area and looking into the sky. It figures, Carrie decides, that he wouldn't know how important this moment is. She sees her dad's serious neck craning to locate them, and movement inside his pockets, where his hands must be fidgeting.

"There's Dad," Sarah says to Carrie in such a disarmingly simple way that tears come to Carrie's eyes. She didn't want to cry, and now she is.

"Hi, Larry," Sarah says, subdued. She tilts her head to the side, anticipating his reply.

Carrie watches his face tense. She can see him wondering if he should embrace Sarah, then placing stiff arms at his side and saying a flat, strained hello.

Larry steps forward slowly and takes hold of both Carrie's hands.

Carrie avoids his face, afraid her mother will leave her sight. She follows Sarah's movement to the windows, where she's found Scotty. She watches her tousling Scotty's hair and encircling his waist.

When Carrie turns back, Larry is still staring at her. His cheeks are pale and his mouth is sad. She has his full attention, but words won't come.

"Carrie," he says, taking her head and pressing it against his chest.

She feels the rough wool of his ragg sweater. She hears his heart pounding.

"I'm so glad," he whispers in a choky voice.

He's pressing her tightly, awkwardly, against the tight drum of his heart, but she can't adjust her head to resist his love.

ABOUT THE AUTHOR

MAXINE CHERNOFF is the author of five books of poems and a volume of short stories, BOP. She lives in Chicago with her husband, writer Paul Hoover, and their three children. She co-edits *New American Writing*.